M000008165

DALTON

and

GRACE

Whimsical Short Stories of Life in Charleston

BILL AND ANN STEVENS

Copyright © 2021 William Stevens and Ann Stevens

All rights reserved.

No part of this publication in print or in electronic format may be reproduced, stored in a retrieval system, or transmitted in any form or by any means, electronic, mechanical, photocopying, recording, or otherwise, without the prior written permission of the publisher.

This is a work of fiction. Names, characters, organizations, places, events, and incidents are either the products of the authors' imagination or are used fictitiously. Any resemblance to actual persons, living or dead, or actual events is purely coincidental.

Distribution and Design by Bublish, Inc.

Cover Art by Laurie Meyer

Cover Photography by Mary Wessner Photography

ISBN: 9781647043773 (paperback)
ISBN: 9781647043780 (hardcover)
ISBN: 9781647043766 (eBook)

For
Jon, Susan, Brooke, and Kara
Geoff, Suzanne, Charlie, and Ashleigh
Matt, Maggie, Ellie, Nora, Luke, and Mary
Jane, Eric, Cole, and Sam

CONTENTS

INTRODUCTION

Since 2004, we have had the pleasure of contributing stories to our local weekly newspaper, *The Daniel Island News*. Stories were published under the byline *Dalton's Drollery* by the author Dalton Williams. The byline also includes his silhouette. Read "The Makeover" for the story behind this silhouette. While we have each contributed in both roles, Bill has been the primary author and Ann, red pen in hand, the masterful editor.

We used the somewhat southern-sounding pen names Dalton and Grace Williams for the main characters in our stories. Dalton's name came from Dalton Street where we lived and Bill's given name. The name of Dalton's lovely wife, Grace, comes from the derivation of Ann as "full of grace." The use of pen names provided a little more latitude with our storylines, and as Dalton says, "may have kept the house from being egged."

Dalton and Grace have recently retired and moved to the Charleston, South Carolina neighborhood of Daniel Island. Of medium build, Dalton's hair has traces of gray, but his spirit and outlook on life are still youthful. He is well-meaning and kind-hearted but often has his plans go awry. He enjoys golf and is partial to a Maker's Mark Perfect Manhattan. Most of all he discovers, over and over, how fortunate he is to be married to his lovely wife, Grace. Is Dalton modeled after Bill? That is a state secret.

Grace is the wise and practical one who guides Dalton through problems of his own creation, sometimes with a subtle suggestion, sometime with a pat on the arm. Trim with dark brown eyes and medium-length hair, she smiles with her eyes and heart as well as her lips. Always the gracious hostess, she is kind and cheerful, although occasionally becomes exasperated with Dalton. Is Grace a lot like Ann? You bet! Ann edits all the stories.

Aunt Toogie arrived in 2005. A witty counterpoint to Dalton, she is barely five feet tall, has a bouncy silver bob, and is sassy and acerbic. She usually sides with Grace on issues between Dalton and Grace but will, at times, join Dalton on one of his silly escapades. Despite her age, Toogie behaves as someone much younger. She does or says the things we all might like to do on occasion. The character is named after a real person: Bill's Aunt Bertha, nicknamed Toogie. Where that nickname came from is lost, but she was, in real life, a lot like the Aunt Toogie you will meet here. Later on, we presented Toogie's dapper, refined, old-line Charlestonian gentleman caller, Brevard. Other family members, real and made up, pop up periodically.

Our intent from the beginning has been to write humor. As a counterpoint to news too often filled with turmoil, economic ups and downs, and political and social unrest, we have tried to present a pleasant distraction that brings a smile, chuckle, or laugh. On some occasions, we were sentimental. While we have poked fun at a few people of note, we have tried to avoid controversial topics and to stay above "bathroom humor." You can be the judge.

Dalton's Drollery column won two humor column awards from the South Carolina Press Association. As we segue into our stories and characters, Dalton is honored to receive these awards. His lovely wife, Grace, is glad he has something else besides golf to talk about with the kids yet wonders if too many sentences ending with a preposition kept him from garnering more awards. His Aunt Toogie grumbles, "If South Carolina was going to give him anything, it should have been hard time, or at least community service!"

This book is a collection of some of the stories written over sixteen years. A few have been edited to make them more contemporary. For some others, we have noted when they were written to set a context for the content. We have enjoyed writing them and producing this book and hope you will enjoy reading it.

Bill and Ann Stevens
Daniel Island, South Carolina
2021

DALTON
AND GRACE

THE RESOLUTION

My LOVELY WIFE, GRACE, HAD finished putting away the holiday decorations and vacuumed the last of the pine needles. She then reorganized the cupboards, set up her new calendar, and updated the address book. For her, this marks the true end of the old year and the start of a new one. Still energized, she was now circling the kitchen island like a panther ready to pounce. I began to circle away from her advance.

"I've decided upon a New Year's resolution for us," she announced.

I could have said her next words before she did, but I refrained.

"This year, we are going to eat only healthy foods that are good for us," Grace proclaimed.

It was the same declaration she makes every early January. I could see it coming in the days following Christmas. As family members departed, so did some of my other dear friends: Ben & Jerry, Harry & David, Russell Stover, and Fannie Farmer. It was as if they packed up, just like the children and grandchildren, and drove off to wherever they live for the rest of the year. My sweet buddies were to be replaced by a grotesque group of new arrivals to the Williams' household: The "Winter Squash Family." This misshapen mix—Acorn, Butternut, Banana, Turban, Hubbard, and their dullard relatives, Zucchini, Pumpkin, and Eggplant—just lie around like slugs in the fridge until Grace beckons them. Then, they show up in countless mealtime concoctions. The Tournament of Roses Parade in Pasadena on January 1st is followed by the Parade of Pumpkins in our kitchen throughout the entire month of January. They are baked and broiled, mashed and minced. Grace hides them in casseroles, pureed sauces, and pasta dishes. I swear, once last year, she hid them in my oatmeal.

These dishes are simultaneously served with a sermon about the benefits of winter squash: "It is chock-full of vitamins, beta-carotene, antioxidants, and fiber." I want to respond: "There is fiber in mulch, but I don't eat mulch," but I know better.

"These are good for you," Grace will declare. "Plus, they are yummy."

I've often theorized that there must be some kind of law or rule that "good for you" and "yummy" are at two ends of a spectrum, inversely related. But, as I do each year, I will eat the winter squash and say, "Yep, this is yummy."

"So, what is your New Year's resolution?" the panther asked from across the kitchen island.

"You're not supposed to tell, or it won't come true," I replied.

"That's when you blow out birthday candles, you ninny," Grace answered, adding, "Dr. Phil says the first step to improvement is acknowledgment."

"You mean, according to Dr. Phil, if I tell my resolution, it will improve my odds of accomplishment?"

"That's what he says, and Dr. Phil tells it like it is."

"Then my New Year's resolution is to make a hole-in-one."

"Dalton, you are impossible, and so is your chance of making a hole-in-one."

"Okay," I replied, thinking quickly. "My New Year's resolution is not to eat winter squash."

"Giving up something is what people do at Lent, but as a sacrifice!" Grace shot back. "I suggest you think of a better New Year's resolution—one with a higher purpose." After a pause, she continued, "I think I'll bake us an acorn squash for dinner, with a touch of butter and brown sugar. It's good for you and yummy. You'll see."

Grace's "You'll see," like her "We'll see," served notice that the conversation was over.

Later that evening, I considered a resolution with a higher purpose. Then it hit me like a ton of tubers—my new New Year's resolution. I'm going to shred some carrots, acorn squash, and sweet potatoes, then mix in some Metamucil and add it to Grace's bourbon pecan pie recipe. That way, I think I can make a dish that is both truly good for you (Metamucil is full of fiber, after all) and yummy. Maybe I could even get on Dr. Phil.

Lost in Publix

I FEEL NORMA DESMOND'S PAIN. YOU may recall the aging movie actress in *Sunset Boulevard*. Like Norma, I used to consider myself "big," a captain of industry—making global strategic decisions and mobilizing thousands of fellow workers. Then came retirement. I descended the corporate ladder to assume a new role—administrative assistant to my lovely wife, Grace. I'm not lamenting being back on the bottom rung in this latest chapter of life. Grace has run the home ship superbly and deserves the skipper's seat. It's just the sobering reality in the adage of old dogs and new tricks.

I recently accompanied Grace on a run to Publix supermarket. As usual, I found myself following her around the store. I concluded this was part of the training for my new job, akin to the centuries-old practice in which guild apprentices, before embarking on a trade or craft, first observed the great masters of their day. Still, I felt prepared to take it to the next level. I suggested we could complete our chores more quickly if we each fetched items from the grocery list. Grace brought the shopping cart to a halt, looked at the list and then at me, and finally replied, "Okay, I'll let you try one item."

"I can do more than one," I proudly boasted.

"No. We'll start with one," the master reaffirmed, perusing the list. "How about bananas?"

As I made a step toward the produce aisle, Grace grabbed my arm like a coach with a player poised to enter the game. "Remember, get four. Now, if they come more to a bunch, just break off four." Gazing intently into my eyes, she held up four fingers and asked, "Okay? Got it?"

"Got it," I reassured her, holding up the same number of digits. "Be right back."

Finding the bananas was no problem, nor was culling four good ones from a tropical six-pack. I hurried back to the place I had left Grace only to find she was no longer there. This presented a new obstacle—finding her among the corridors that crisscross the length and breadth of the store. This called for stealth and speed. I walked briskly along an aisle running perpendicular to the long aisles, peering down each. I caught a glimpse of her moving in the same direction at the other end of baby products and medicines. I trotted a few steps and turned sharply into the laundry supplies and bath products aisle. I didn't see a shopping cart exiting the aisle until it was too late. The collision knocked some of the cart's contents—Old El Paso taco and tortilla shells—onto the floor.

"I'm sorry," I apologized, reaching down to retrieve the jettisoned items.

The cart driver, a young woman, inspected the mess. "I hope they aren't broken."

"Let me get you replacements," I offered.

"That's okay. I can get another box," she replied, soothing a toddler in the cart seat who had begun to whimper.

"No, no," I pleaded. "It was my fault. I'll get them for you. What aisle are they on?"

"I think on the one with soups and pasta, or maybe coffee and condiments. That way," she pointed while offering the kid some gummy worms.

"Make sure the taco shells say 'Stand 'N Stuff,'" she said, adding, "while you're there, could you also get me another can of refried beans?"

"Got it," I responded and headed off feeling proud to be trusted to secure more than one item.

As I turned down the cake mix aisle, I saw Grace again, still at the far end but now headed in the opposite direction. I made a mental note. Reconnaissance relies on good intelligence. Fortunately, there was one box of Old El Paso taco shells. I swapped the box of broken shells for it, made my way back to the young mother, placed the provisions gingerly in her cart, and offered one more apology.

"Oh, that's okay. It's just that Trey here loves his tacos," she smiled, nodding toward her little boy, who pulled a gummy worm from his mouth and held it out for me to see or maybe even taste.

I declined the sticky treat and walked briskly in the direction I had last seen Grace. Passing each aisle, I looked for her while also keeping a safe distance from any exiting carts. At paper products, I saw Grace again, now doubling back in her original direction. I turned and jogged that way, noting I was gaining on her with each aisle we passed. It was a bit like playing the board game Clue when you know the culprit and weapon (e.g., Colonel Mustard and the lead pipe), and you are racing to reach the crime room before your opponents. I sprinted ahead and dashed down the next aisle hoping to intercept Grace. Midway, I met the Old El Paso mother and child. She saw me coming, pulled her cart sharply to the side, and bent over it with her arms sprawled out to guard the kid and contents.

"Thanks," I gasped as I sped past. At the end of the aisle, I came face-to-face with Grace.

"Where have you been? I've been looking all over for you," she inquired.

"Getting these bananas," I replied, holding up my right hand and then my left. Unfortunately, both were empty. I must have set the damn bananas down when I picked up the taco shells and refried beans.

"Be right back," I declared and then paused. "Don't move," I pleaded, holding both palms out. "Stay right here," I begged as I trotted toward the taco shells.

"Bananas are the other way, Magellan," Grace called after me.

"I know. You'll see," I shot back over my shoulder. I located the bananas nestled among the salsa and picante display. I hurried back toward Grace.

She had ignored my request and meandered toward the bottled water shelves.

"Yes, we have four bananas," I sang, offering my trophy as I caught up to her.

"Oh, those are too ripe," Grace declared.

My heart sank. My reach for more responsibility wasn't going well.

"Always get them yellow-green but not too green. Never all-yellow. They over-ripen so quickly. Think chartreuse," she explained. "And be sure to put them in this," Grace continued, holding out a small plastic bag that she, like a magician, made appear from nowhere.

I trudged back to the banana bar and surveyed for chartreuse, wishing I had paid more attention in art appreciation class. I located four that looked the appropriate hue and stuffed them into the plastic bag. Sensing Grace was on the move again, I surveyed the aisles anew, locating her in frozen foods.

"Here you go," I stated, handing her the bag of yellow-green bananas.

"Let's see, four bananas in fifteen minutes," Grace said slowly, looking at her watch. "At this rate, we should be out of here by next Tuesday."

"I can do better," I pleaded. "Give me another assignment."

"Do you think you can find the yogurt?" Grace asked.

"Find it?" I gasped. "I've passed the dairy aisle four times getting the bananas. Why didn't you—?"

"One item at a time," the master interrupted, holding up a single finger. "Now, if you want to be useful, get six yogurts. But don't get any strawberry. Be sure to check the expiration date."

"Okay, okay, got it," I replied, making my way to the dairy aisle. I picked out six yogurts (two each of cherry, blueberry, and harvest peach) and carried them back to Grace's cart.

"Where's the bag?" she asked inspecting the pile of yogurt containers cupped in my hands.

"Bag?"

"Yes! I always put them in a bag to keep them together."

"What kind of bag?"

"Like this one," Grace replied, holding up the bag of bananas.

"Sheesh! Where are the bags?" I sighed.

"Right next to the bananas, dear," Grace smiled. "Just past the dairy case."

As we loaded our purchases into the car, I figured I had flunked my initial apprenticeship test. I was caught off guard when Grace smiled and said, "Thanks for your help, Norman."

"Norma? You mean like Norma Desmond?"

"No, I said, 'Thanks for your help, Norman,' as in Norman Thayer in *On Golden Pond*."

"Oh, you're welcome," I said softly.

"How about a mocha?" Grace suggested. "I'll treat."

"Sure."

"Plus," Grace added, "this isn't the only treat I have for you today."

"Really?" I replied, eager to hear what else she had in mind.

"I got you something special for dinner."

"What?"

"Mexican fare," Grace smiled. "Publix had a special today on Old El Paso, and I got the last box of taco shells!"

Can You Hear Me Now?

"WHAT ARE YOU DOING?" MY lovely wife, Grace, asked.

"Taking out the trash," I replied.

"Didn't you hear me?"

"Hear you what?"

"Hear me say not to take out the trash until I looked through the fridge first," Grace said rather emphatically.

"When did you say that?" I inquired with a little smugness, oblivious to the trap I was stepping into.

"Two minutes ago," Grace answered as the trap closed.

I gave her my best "deer in the headlights" imitation. After a short pause, she declared, "Dalton Williams, you should have your hearing checked."

I am. Grace and I are having our annual physical examinations soon. One of the procedures is a hearing test. First, let me say that medical check-ups and wellness programs are good things to do. At the same time, this upcoming diagnosis may settle a debate that has gone on for years in the Williams household. Namely, whose hearing is better—mine or Grace's?

Our conversations are punctuated with smatterings of "What?" and "Huh?" The things we sometimes think the other said range from the comical to the bizarre. I accuse Grace of not hearing me at times, to which she rejoinders that I mumble. She remarks (I'll admit a little too often) that I didn't pick up on something she just said. I rebut this by saying she may have thought she said it, but she really didn't, and I don't have a hearing problem. Grace trumps the move by announcing she agrees I don't have a hearing problem; I have a listening problem.

All this reminds me of the story about a husband who was beginning to believe his wife's hearing was failing. To test his theory, he entered the kitchen when she had her back turned, stirring a pot on the stove.

"Darling, can you hear me?" he asked from across the room.

No reply.

He stepped halfway into the room and asked again, "Darling, can you hear me?"

Again, no response.

Finally, he stood right behind her and asked once more.

She turned and replied, "For the third time, yes!"

We made a small wager on the outcome of our hearing test. Grace predicted confidently she would prevail since, as she says, "I don't make bets unless I think I can win." I wanted to achieve the better score because whoever did so would gain important aural bragging rights. I began practicing. Serious, rigorous practice. For example, I sat in the living room and listened to the grandfather clock in the front foyer. It makes a slight *click* as it advances each second. After much training, I could sit in the next room and still hear all nine hundred clicks in the fifteen-minute interval between the Westminster chimes. I practiced deciphering hard-to-hear sounds. I am proud to report I can now distinguish the different sounds of *snap, crackle*, and *pop* in a bowl of Rice Krispies. They are unique to the highly trained ear.

As the exam day approached, I began my final tune-up exercise. I turned on the upstairs bathroom radio, then stood in an adjacent room and listened intently. I could make out what the talk show host was saying. I next turned the volume down and tried it again. Over and over, I lowered the volume and then stood silently in the next room, eyes closed, concentrating on nothing but the sound of the radio. I could decipher the faint banter. I was truly stretching the limits of the auditory range. I felt like Demosthenes with his pebbles, a legend in the making. I was in the zone. I was ready!

"Dalton, are you up there?" Grace called from downstairs.

"Yes, dear," I cooed.

"Well, come on down. Lunch is ready—and turn off that radio. I can hardly hear myself think!"

I was dumbstruck.

"Plus, I think your UPS package is here. You can pick it up when you come down."

"UPS...is...here?" I sputtered.

"Yes. Didn't you hear the truck pull up just now?" Grace inquired.

I hadn't heard the truck. I hadn't even seen the bus that had just run over me.

"Don't forget to turn off the radio," Grace chimed in.

It was like somebody boxed me on the ears. I was numb. I staggered downstairs. All I could sense was a buzzing sound. Finally, I heard Grace's voice, "Dalton, I said, do you want mustard on your jam sandwich?"

"Mustard on a jam sandwich?"

"No, dear," Grace replied. "I said do you want mustard on your *ham* sandwich?"

She drew out the word "ham" slowly and loudly.

I nodded affirmatively.

Over lunch, Grace inquired, "You know that wager we made on the hearing test?"

I looked up.

"The bet's off," she added.

I held my palms up and shrugged.

"Well, I've been thinking...," Grace continued. "Hearing and hearing tests are serious topics. It isn't something we should bet on. I hope both of us, and anyone who may take the test, does well."

After a pause, she added, "What do you think?"

I pondered my reply. While I would surely lose if I insisted we keep the bet going, I had already won something much bigger being married to Grace. I smiled and answered, "I hear you, sweetheart."

The Time Trick

I'VE NEVER UNDERSTOOD DAYLIGHT SAVINGS. Oh, I know what happens with the hour-change in time. I just don't understand *why*! I read somewhere that the idea was proposed by Ben Franklin to save candles in winter and by some Englishman who wanted to play golf longer in summer. I also seem to recall it has something to do with milk cows in Indiana, although I've yet to see any breed of cow—Hoosier, Guernsey, or other—wearing a watch. I do remember Jimmy Carter, dressed in his cardigan while sitting by the White House fireplace, urging us to give daylight savings a try during the 1970s' energy crisis. So, once again, the time for the "fall back" bookend of daylight savings time was nigh. My lovely wife, Grace, wasn't jazzed by the whole thing, which she sees as a precursor to winter. I, on the other hand, just hate changing the time on all our clocks.

Advancing the time one hour at the "spring forward" change isn't so bad but moving the clocks back an hour is a bummer. It is especially difficult with digital clocks. Mine don't have "back" buttons. So, one has to advance the time twenty-three hours, then check the a.m./p.m. setting, and then the day of the week *and* the date to ensure both are still correct. I get tired just thinking about it. And, boy, do we have a lot of digital clocks—on the stove, the coffee maker, outdoor lights, sprinklers, radios, alarm clocks, and, well…you get the picture. I began doing finger exercises a week in advance of this autumnal drill.

As T-day neared, I contemplated my attack on the monumental task ahead.

"Have you started changing the clocks?" Grace inquired.

"I'm fixing to get ready to do it."

"Well, time's a-wasting," Grace answered a tad more earnestly.

I poured some Maker's Mark over ice and sat down to ponder the problem. Bourbon has magical powers to facilitate pondering. Sure enough, a few sips produced the desired epiphany. There *was* a way to change all the digital clocks at once! Eureka! I felt like Archimedes in the bathtub. As we turned in for bed last Saturday night, Grace asked, "You didn't change the clocks, did you, dear?"

I answered swimmingly, "Not yet, but I will…and before dawn."

"What the heck does that mean?"

"You'll see," I chuckled as Grace turned off the light.

My alarm went off at 12:55 a.m., and I sprung from bed ready to work my magic.

"What in heaven's name are you doing?" Grace inquired, turning on the light.

"Changing the clocks," I replied, rubbing my hands together.

"At this hour? Are you nuts?"

"They scoffed at Ben Franklin, too," I answered.

"Go fly a kite," Grace shot back as she turned off the light and rolled over.

I hustled downstairs—time waits for no one, you know—turning on lights as I made my way toward the utility room. I reached the electrical box at 12:59—one minute until the witching hour. Checking my watch, I began counting down the seconds until 1 a.m. A few seconds before one o'clock, I tripped the master switch, and the house plunged into darkness. A few seconds later, I threw the switch again, and the lights came back on. Just as planned, the digital clocks automatically reset themselves to 12:00 a.m. The flashing time was a beautiful sight.

"Grace! Grace!" I hollered, running up the stairs two at a time. "Look at this!"

When I reached the bedroom, Grace was sitting up in bed with her arms folded.

"I just changed all the clocks," I gasped. "All at once."

"I want to change my 'Are you nuts?' to you *are* nuts!" she declared.

"No, no, I'm not nuts. Look at the clock. See what time it is?"

"It is after one o'clock in the morning," Grace said slowly and emphatically.

"Right, but look at the clock. It says 12:02. Isn't that neat?" I squealed.

Grace just stared at me.

Feeling like a professor at MIT, I explained how the clocks had all reset themselves to 12 a.m. when the power was shut off and then turned back on again at 1 a.m. Continuing the lecture and holding my arms up, simulating the hands of a large clock, I espoused about how, at 2 a.m., when the time "fell back" one hour, the real time would be perfectly aligned with the digital clock time. Grace swiveled her right wrist in a circular manner. "Wind it up, Einstein," she proclaimed, pulling the blanket over her head.

I, however, was too excited to go back to bed. I went downstairs to the kitchen, fixed a celebratory Maker's nightcap, and settled in to watch the digital clock on the stove. I imagined this must have been how Edison felt when the first electric light blazed forth. I imagined my picture on the cover of *Popular Science* or even as *Time*'s Person of the Year.... "The Man Who Tricked Time."

It was somewhere around 1:40 a.m. when everything went black again. The folks at Dominion Energy would later explain that a car ran into a pole near a power station in North Charleston. The driver, I read later, was charged with having an open bottle of Maker's Mark in his car and was also charged for the damage done to the electrical apparatus. The pole he managed to hit held a transformer box, which, when knocked out of commission, tripped some other gizmo that, in turn, triggered the blackout. The next day, Dominion proclaimed proudly that power was restored in a matter of minutes. Matter of minutes? *Matter of minutes*?! Sitting in the pitch-dark kitchen, those minutes were an agonizing eternity. After a few flutters, the lights flickered on. As I feared, the damage felt like a category-five storm. All the digital clocks had, once again, reset themselves to 12:00 a.m.

I sat stunned. There was no way to recover. The time-trick only worked at 1 a.m. I would now have to reset the clocks by hand in the old manual manner, one by one. Sadly, I trudged upstairs and flopped into bed.

Grace rolled over in the dark. "How's my big, bad, Ben Franklin?"

"It didn't work," I sighed.

"Poor Richard," she soothed, patting my arm. "I'll help you set the clocks tomorrow."

In the solitude of the early morning darkness, I mused for a while. Maybe, just maybe, there could be another way to change those darn clocks all at the same time. Finally, I decided to sleep on it. After all, that Saturday night was the one night of the year when I had an extra hour to do just that.

THE BIG GAME

THIS WAS AN EPIC CONFRONTATION as two worthy combatants vied for the ultimate prize. The game was high drama, a tactical tussle for only the swift, the agile, and the fearless. In the end, one side basked in the glow of a goal achieved and the bragging rights that go with it. For the other side, there was only the quiet pain of what might have been and of having come so close to the brass ring. Super Bowl? No, I'm talking about the contest each evening in the Williams' household for control of the thermostat! My lovely wife, Grace, likes the temperature set at a level she calls "comfy." I find her preferred setting a tad above the comfy level—frankly, closer to "parboil." On the other hand, I tend to like things on the cooler side, sort of in the "brisk and invigorating" range. Grace, of course, describes my preference as "meat locker."

The tug of war usually begins each night around dinnertime.

"Do you think it is cold in here?" Grace queried.

This was the start of the pre-game psychological sparring.

"Ooh, I've got a chill," she piled on.

I countered quickly with, "Remember that heat rises. I'll bet the upstairs is warm and toasty—just the way you like it," knowing that the big brawl would be over the second-story bedroom thermostat. I gave up points in the kitchen to keep her out of the end zone upstairs.

"We'll see," countered Grace, letting the clock run down to kick off.

After supper, I found a way to slip past her defense in the kitchen and ran a quick down and out for the bedroom thermostat. Changing the mode setting to "cool," the thermostat responded with a faint *click* followed by a gentle breeze of mountain air. Having scored on my first possession, the strategy for tonight's game was now to control the ball and the clock. I set up my defense in the den to read, ever mindful of Grace's moves. A little later, she joined me and asked if I want to play cards. Grace hadn't suggested playing cards, especially gin rummy, in years. After a few hands, I announced that I was going to get some ice cream, partly to combat the swelter downstairs. Grace followed me to the refrigerator. Then it hit me: She was playing an aggressive man-to-man defense. I should have picked up her defensive alignment sooner. She must have scored on the upstairs thermostat when I wasn't watching.

I wandered upstairs to change for bed. Grace shadowed me like an all-pro defensive back on a wide receiver. Passing the thermostat, I glanced at the dial. It was set on "heat." The opposition had scored, and a blast of Saharan torridity began to fill the room. Fortunately, I could huddle in my locker-room closet and design a new strategy. As the second half began, I tried to establish the running game. Grace stuffed it. I tried to throw under the coverage. Grace swatted it down. She was on top of her game tonight, and she knew it.

"Forget about touching that thermostat!" she trash-talked.

After several more three and outs, I checked the clock. Only a few minutes were left. Time for the trick play I had been saving for just this moment. I strolled downstairs and turned on the television—loud enough to register upstairs but not loud enough to be understood, a maneuver carefully rehearsed. Then I meandered back upstairs where Grace had fallen back into a prevent defense, guarding the thermostat.

"What are you watching?" Grace inquired.

"Oh, some celebrity thing," I replied coyly. "This Hugh Jack-somebody guy is modeling swimsuits or something…."

"Hugh Jackman?" she asked, going for the fake.

"Yeah, I think that was it."

"Did I set the coffee?" Grace mused to no one in particular, getting out of bed. She headed downstairs, having bit on "the old Hugh Jackman play." I hooked and headed downfield to the thermostat and reset it to cool.

We were inside the two-minute warning as Grace returned upstairs.

"Are you sure it was Hugh Jackman?" she asked. "All I could find was some talking heads arguing politics."

"That's interesting," I answered to continue the distraction. There were only a few ticks of the clock left before Grace turned off the light—the official end of the game. She pulled back the covers and reached for the lamp. *Click.*

In the still quiet of the dark room, my senses were heightened. Did I hear one click—the light being turned off? Or did I also hear a second, faint click timed almost perfectly with the louder click? It would take an extraordinary effort to reach the light and the thermostat at the same time, but then Grace had been working with a personal trainer. Still, the timing would have to be perfect—practiced for hours.

"Goodnight, honey," Grace said sweetly as she snuggled under her blanket and heating pad. Then she added, "Comfy?"

It is then that I knew. Even before the Santa Ana winds begin to blow anew, I knew. She had pulled off a Hail Mary on the last play of the game. The clutch players rise to the occasion when the chips are on the line.

Grace was now savoring her well-earned victory warmth. I kicked off the covers. My mind was plotting Xs and Os for tomorrow's match. Would she go for the "George Clooney on Ellen rerun play?"

In the darkness, my worthy opponent said softly, "Don't even think about it!"

The truly great ones are always a play ahead of the game.

Ladies, Start Your Engines

"L ET'S GO TO THE OPERA!" my lovely wife, Grace, suggested as she studied a brochure for the Spoleto Festival. This is a declaration she makes each year as Spoleto approaches. She enjoys scheduling a plethora of performances for us to attend. I knew I was cornered and couldn't object to the opera.

"Sure," I replied but added a quid pro quo: "How about we also go to a NASCAR race?"

"We'll see," Grace sighed.

Based on this lack of enthusiasm, I figured that women don't do NASCAR.

The following Saturday, however, I discovered how wrong that assumption was. No, I wasn't at Daytona. I was at one of our local warehouse club stores. Grace had sent me on a mission to buy bottled water. I thought water was sort of free, from the tap, but Grace wanted me to get several hefty cases. She expounds on the advantages of hydration, and these bottles are a necessity for car rides and walks.

I arrived at the warehouse store in the wee hours of Saturday morning. The place overpowers me. It is huge. The carts are enormous. The sizes of the items they sell are gargantuan. For example, last fall, Grace wanted shaved almonds for a dessert she was baking. I bought a fifty-pound bag. We ended up mulching the trees with the excess. The squirrels loved it. I retrieved a cart from a rack in the parking lot. The back wheels wobbled, just as they did on most of the other carts. I made my way toward the store to find a long line of ladies-in-waiting with their carts two abreast, facing the front door. Most wore sneakers and colorful sweatshirts. Some were doing stretching exercises or deep knee bends. Their carts were decorated with signs, stickers, and numbers. I took my place at the end of the line.

One woman was pushing her cart vigorously back and forth in a zigzag fashion. The lady in line in front of me noticed how intently I was observing the spectacle.

"Heats up the tires," she explained.

"Excuse me?" I replied.

"Makes 'em handle better in the corners. Name's Dale," she offered, extending her hand. "You must be Duke," she added, pointing to my sweatshirt.

Before I could respond, she inquired, "You new here?"

"I guess so," I answered sheepishly.

"Hey, girls, we got us a rookie here at the back of the grid," hollered Dale.

Soon the swarm of shoppers surrounded me and my shopping cart with comments and questions coming faster than I could respond.

"Them factory tires?"

"Where's your decals?"

"You need a restrictor plate with them wobbly wheels?"

Finally, I asked, "You girls come here often?" pulling up a line I recalled from a very different time and place.

"Every Saturday!" a hefty, elderly lady with blue hair chortled. Her cart was at the front of the line on the left. I sensed that she was regarded with some degree of respect and fear by the other women. Dale introduced me to Blue Hair and the other regulars.

As we waited for the store to open, the flock engaged in animated conversation about the sale items, the layout of the store, and strategies to secure their stuff in the least amount of time. I began to realize this was no ordinary shopping errand. In a few minutes, a store employee began to raise the big metal door. Women tightened their grips on their cart handles. Shoes shuffled nervously back and forth; no one spoke. Out of the corner of my eye, I noticed one lady cross herself. Finally, the door was lifted high enough for a person and cart to slip underneath. Blue Hair was off like a shot. The pack followed fast, speeding straight for the cosmetics section.

"Hurry up or you'll be a lap down," Dale called over her shoulder. I took off in rapid pursuit. I reached cosmetics and picked up a twenty-four-pack of dental floss and a plastic tub of ten thousand Q-Tips. The crowd was already headed to canned goods. I dashed behind them, adding a twenty-pound jar of olives, a gallon of peanut butter, and a 256-ounce box of cornflakes to my cart. I was feeling the rush of the shopping frenzy.

Blue Hair passed me and headed back to the front of the store. Her husband was positioned at the checkout line. Blue Hair pulled alongside him, gave him her full cart, grabbed the empty cart he was holding, took a slug of his Mountain Dew, and was off again. The whole exchange lasted six seconds.

"Quite a pitstop, huh?" mused Dale.

"Pardon me?"

"She's the best at splash 'n go."

Blue Hair then led the crowd down a wide aisle toward frozen foods and beverages. I hustled to catch up. I pulled up closely behind a lady in a turquoise and orange sweatshirt. I have since learned that this is called "drafting." As we approached a stand where a store employee was handing out samples of pigs-in-a-blanket, I pulled out and passed.

"Nice slingshot!" yelled Dale as I headed for the bottled waters. I took on three cases (the maximum allowed per customer), grabbed a deep-fried pork rind from another sample stand, and headed for prepared foods. I was moving up. If I could make up time here, I might catch the Blue Hair special. I quickly snatched up a bag of one hundred dinner rolls, a side of beef, and a cheesecake the size of our patio table. I then tore off back down the main aisle toward the checkout line.

I was gaining on Blue Hair and believe I could have caught her...until the last turn. At the end of the aisle, she cut sharply around the corner. I followed, but my cartwheels wobbled. I skidded, then veered to the right, and crashed into a rack of phone cards. My cart flipped over several times before spilling its contents. I first thought it was a clumsy blunder. I now realize that while I assumed I could follow the groove, my cart was too loose to hold the line. My tires wouldn't bite, and I probably hit some marbles above the groove and ended up with a Darlington stripe and a bruised ego.

The entire field passed by me as I reloaded my purchases into the cart. I checked out and slowly made the way to my car. Dale was waiting.

"Tough break, Duke," she offered.

"Yeah, I thought I had her for a while there."

"She was running a rail," Dale smiled. "And she hung you out to dry. You'll learn though," Dale added, patting me on the back. "You did well."

"Yeah—for a guy!" cackled Blue Hair, leaning out the window of her pick-up truck. With that, she smoked her tires and sped off.

When I got home, Grace asked, "Find the bottled water okay?"

"Yeah, no problem."

"Was the store crowded?"

"No, not really," I calmly replied.

I didn't try to regale her with a replay of my cart-racing experience. I don't think she likes that stuff. But I did have some explaining to do about those other purchases.

So, we will go to the opera in May. It is *Romeo and Juliet*. We will watch the Montagues and the Capulets duke it out. But secretly, I can't wait to duke it out with Blue Hair next Saturday at the warehouse club. This time, I'll come prepared. Perhaps I'll purchase my own custom cart and adjust the jacking screws for weight distribution. I might even add a spoiler. I know it would handle great and I'd be dialed in. That would keep the fat lady from singing. I'll just have to drink a lot of bottled water between now and then to justify my return visit to the warehouse store.

HIDE AND SEEK

"Honey, do you know where my glasses are at?" I inquired as I foraged through kitchen cupboards and drawers.

"Never end a sentence with a preposition," my lovely wife, Grace, replied.

"But I don't know where they could have gone to."

"I rest my case," answered Grace. "By the way, here's your case," she added, handing me my glasses from underneath the newspaper.

"How did you find them?" I asked.

"It's a special knack women have," she smiled. "You wouldn't understand."

It is a secret gift. We were recently at a warehouse club store. Grace assigned me to get one item—an over-the-counter medication. After scouring the pharmacy aisle, I returned to tell her that they did not have the product.

"Follow me," she announced and set off toward the pharmacy section. As Grace walked, she began to omit a small noise: *beep, beep, beep*. As she entered the pharmacy aisle, the *beeps* became closer together, higher-pitched, and louder. Other shoppers pulled their carts to the side as if an ambulance were approaching.

"Here you go," Grace proclaimed, standing next to a three-row display of the desired item. Other women shoppers nodded their approval. I inspected my shoes so as to not make eye contact with them. On the way home, I suggested that maybe, just perhaps, a store employee could have set up that display during the time between my search and Grace's discovery.

"Beep, beep, beep," Grace laughed.

I do appreciate Grace's skill at recovering lost articles. She takes great delight in finding something that I cannot. "Close your eyes and put out your hand," she will say, which I know means she has located a stray. This will then be followed by, "Now, what do I get?"

Another of her favorite techniques is to hum or sing from "Amazing Grace," "…I once was lost, but now am found…" She does this with great gusto, putting accents on the "lost" and the "found" parts.

I have occasionally accused Grace of moving or hiding objects…not to shift the blame, mind you, but because she has. One warm evening, I suggested we go out for ice cream.

"How about some at home?" Grace responded, pulling a pint of Haagen-Dazs coffee ice cream from the freezer.

"Where did that come from?" I inquired with astonishment, knowing that I had rummaged through the freezer for ice cream several times that week.

"Oh, I put it under the frozen baby lima beans," Grace replied. "I figured you'd never look there."

She is also adept—no, make that masterful—at finding stuff you don't want her to find.

"When did you go to Starbucks?" she asked with a slight edge of sharpness.

"What? Starbucks? When?" I replied feebly as my mind raced, *How does she know I went to Starbucks on the way home from the drug store?* I had even stashed the evidence, an empty venti Frappuccino cup, inside a trash bag and then put another trash bag on top of it.

"Plus, you're pulling your nose," she declared.

"What does that…have to do with…?" I stammered.

"Dalton Williams, you always pull your nose when you are trying to pull something. You might want to watch that, and your prepositions, too," she stated with an air of finality.

She is amazing, that Grace. Her talent gives me an idea. She could lead the FBI to Jimmy Hoffa and D. B. Cooper and very likely find Amelia Earhart and Bigfoot. While solving these mysteries may take her away for a few days, I can manage things at home. During that time, I promise not to go to Starbucks for a giant Frappuccino. Besides, if I did, she'd know.

The Fine Art of Crafts

M Y LOVELY WIFE, GRACE, COOED, "Honey, let's go to the holiday arts and crafts show at the coliseum."

My reaction was probably akin to what Grace would have felt if I asked, *Hey sweetheart, what say we take in a NASCAR race next weekend?* But having already played golf a couple (okay, three) times during the week, I mumbled, "Okay."

Grace even dangled an escape option. "I know this may not be your cup of tea," she offered. "Don't go if you don't want to. I just want to stop in and look around a little."

"No, I want to go," I countered, knowing this was the MC (matrimonially correct) response.

So, off to the show we went. The parking lot was jammed with cars, trucks, and busses. I thought it might be folks camping out early for the Steep Canyon Rangers concert scheduled at the same location later that evening. Consequently, we had to park at the far end of the lot. As we walked toward the entrance door, a creature laden with bags of purchases approached. It swayed like a pack mule under the weight.

"Oh, that poor woman," Grace announced. "Give her a hand, Dalton."

I hustled toward the beast of burden. "Here, let me help you."

"I sure do 'preciate this," she wheezed, transferring the entire load to me. "I should be parked somewhere around this area," she muttered as she marched forward, lifting her head occasionally to look left and right. "My car is sort of silverish."

As we navigated up and down the aisles seeking her car (which turned out to be a blue van), she and Grace chatted about the arts and craft show.

"Be sure to try the eggnog fudge and the jalapeno peanuts," she declared. "They are de-lish-us!"

"Oh, here are a couple dollar-off coupons for admission," she added, handing Grace some folded newspaper clippings. "Enjoy the show."

Once we entered the convention hall, Grace restated her earlier offer. "If you don't want to follow me around, grab a snack at the food court, and I'll meet you back at this door in an hour."

Before I could formulate the appropriate MC reply, Grace disappeared into the throng, leaving me with an hour to kill. Down the main aisle, I strolled. The place was a sea of sensory stimulation. Displays of colorful crafts cascaded in every direction. Energized shoppers on all sides perused and touched the wares as they chattered about their acquisitions.

"Where did you get the cute stuffed elf? It is just precious!"

"Next row over. By the booth with the beer-can windchimes. You can't miss it!"

Crowds mingled and munched at tables offering samplings of relishes, jellies, candies, soups, teas, and coffees. A pungent aroma hung in the air—I first thought it might be the aforementioned jalapeno nuts, but it turned out to be chili cheddar chips.

Soon, I arrived at an intersection of two wide aisles. Each corner featured a demonstration of household goods. The presenters had microphone head-sets, much like those worn by airline pilots, to project their presentation. I paused and then heard, "Hey, you." I looked toward one of the pilots who held what looked like a mop in one hand and beckoned me to come closer with the other. I stepped into the void. Five minutes later, I was the proud owner of a household cleaning apparatus that would have made George Jetson envious.

Actually, two mops because the buy-one-and-get-half-off-on-the-second-one offer was too good to refuse. The pilot in the opposite corner booth swiftly surpassed that discount with a three-for-one deal on a nifty, lint-removing gizmo for the clothes dryer.

Down another aisle, I found a metal "Frosty Root Beer" sign with a thermometer. My Uncle Bill had an identical one in his workshop, but mine would be an artful addition to the den. A steal at thirty dollars. Buoyed by these bargains, I traversed the great hall. One booth sold rubber gloves with small studs that can peel a potato by just rubbing it in your hands. Knowing Grace would love it, I snapped one up. As the time to meet her neared, I trudged toward the agreed-upon exit lugging my panoply of purchases. Grace was standing by the door holding a solitary plant: a Christmas cactus. The paucity of her purchases suggested she must not have found the same fascinating booths I had.

She looked up, saw me, and gaped. I don't use the word "gaped" lightly. It was the gapiest of gapes.

"Good heavens!" she gasped. "What did you buy?"

"Some great stuff," I beamed, handing her one of the Jetson mops.

She stared at it, then at me, and gaped a small gape, much less gapey than the first gape.

"It rotates 360 degrees," I boasted. "And picks up peanut shells."

"Peanut shells? What peanut shells?"

"*Voila!*" I retorted, holding up a bag of deep-fried peanuts. "I ordered a case to be sent to the house," I continued. "We could use them as hostess gifts, stocking stuffers, or eat them ourselves. They are de-lish-us!"

Grace put her hand to her forehead and looked toward her shoes. "Deep-fried peanuts as hostess gifts. Give me strength," she whispered and added without looking up, "And you bought two of these mops?"

"You bet!" I shot back. "Got a 50-percent discount on the second. But wait till you see this!" I continued. "This dryer filter brush prevents lint from forming and catching on fire."

Grace looked up, sans gape, and fixed me with a stare. "I've been drying clothes for quite some time, and I've never had a dryer fire!"

"There was a lady in Illinois who said the same thing," I replied. "But one day, her—"

"Stop!" Grace declared loudly, holding up her hand. After a pause, she said slowly and softly, "What else did you buy?"

"Some of it is a surprise."

"Oh, I'm surprised, all right! Trust me, I'm very surprised!"

Grace stood, arms folded, without changing expression as I removed the contents of my shopping bags one by one for her to reconnoiter. Chow Chow—quart-jar size. The potato-peeling gloves. Applewood-smoked beef jerky. Door chimes that play "Wind Beneath My Wings." Chocolate-walnut soap. A belt buckle with an LCD screen that scrolls messages just like the sign at Times Square. A piece of driftwood carved in the shape of a ferret, and a small woodworking tool.

Grace muttered, "What's that?"

"It's neat," I answered. "If you are in the woods with no matches, you scrape a branch or twig against this side to make wood shavings. And...," I continued, rotating the apparatus, "on the other side, you rub the flint to create a spark igniting the wood shavings. Presto. There's your fire."

Grace said nothing, held her hand over her eyes, and squeezed her palm, massaging her temples a few times.

"What do you think?" I queried, breaking the silence.

"What do I think? I think we are not going into any woods, nor are we going to start a fire even if we were there. I also think I will never bring you to another arts and crafts show," she sighed slowly.

"I liked it. I really did," I piped up. "I even had our tickets stamped for free admission tomorrow."

Grace put her hand on my arm.

"Tell you what," she smiled. "We'll do that right after we go to a NASCAR race."

Fit to be Fried

HERE'S HOPING THAT YOU HAD a happy Thanksgiving. The Williams clan collected, as they do each year, at our house to see one another, to talk about family members who didn't come, and to savor the festive fare prepared by my lovely wife, Grace. These times together are memorable milestones in a family's history. This year's gathering was made a little more memorable than most by the introduction of a new (to us, at least) technology in Thanksgiving turkeydom: the fried turkey.

Some weeks ago, I suggested that we try this new turkey technique. Grace replied, "We'll see."

"We'll see" are two innocent-sounding words that Grace uses a lot in place of "no (fill in the word of your choice) way," or in this case, in place of "Are you crazy? You'll burn the house down!" Still, I took her "We'll see" as an approximate approval (big mistake) and bought a turkey fryer, the chrome and brass model—guys love chrome and brass. When I confessed what I had done, Grace reluctantly agreed to let me fry the turkey for this year's banquet.

It was then that I noticed two other words printed on the package: "assembly required." Those are two words that strike fear into the hearts of most men, MIT grads excluded. Six hours and two trips to Lowe's for tools later, I got the darn thing assembled. Grace suggested that we give it a trial run to ensure that things would run smoothly on the big day. I countered that they didn't need to do a trial run of the Macy's Thanksgiving Day Parade. Grace closed the discussion by reminding me that they didn't do a trial run of the Hindenburg either, and as far as she was concerned, it was my parade.

On Thursday morning, my turkey fryer and I were ready to go. The fryer sat by the garage (Grace wouldn't allow it closer to the house), glistening in the sun. I donned my "Boss of the Sauce" apron, then patted the turkey fryer and gave it a pep talk. "This is it, girl." Men seem to always address exotic machinery in the feminine gender. I filled her with peanut oil and turned her on to the recommended temperature.

At the appointed time, relatives began to descend on the household. Kids played in the yard and raced throughout the house. The ladies assembled around the kitchen island with last-minute preparations. The men encircled the turkey fryer, looking intently at the new contraption. I imagined that this was how it might have been a hundred years ago when another small group of pioneers gathered on a hilltop in Kitty Hawk.

"Think she'll fly, Dalton?" asked my brother Mark.

"Better point her into the wind," added brother-in-law Tom.

It was nearing time for the inaugural fry. After fetching the turkey from the kitchen, I noticed that the fryer temperature was now far beyond the point at which I had set it. Cousin Ronnie saw me looking at the dial and spoke up.

"Turned her up for you, Dalton. Can't fry nothing less you get it good and hot!"

Cousin Ronnie had worked a spell in the fast-food business; so, I figured he knew frying. You have to respect experience.

I gently lowered the turkey into the vat. It sank below the surface, bobbed back up, then turned its neck into the wind and began to fry. The group around the fryer exploded into applause. This moment of excitement was followed by each of us standing there, hands in our pockets, watching the turkey bubble. We weren't sure what we were watching for, but if and when it did happen, we'd see it. The conversation turned to weather and then stalled. Slowly, the pioneers peeled off to watch football until no one was watching the turkey.

They say a watched pot never boils. I guess the corollary could then be that a pot not watched *will* boil. I'm here to tell you otherwise. Actually, it doesn't boil. There is another term for what happens next: flash point! I looked it up. It is the lowest temperature at which the vapors of a volatile oil will ignite. It is also the point at which all holy hell breaks loose!

"Dalton, your bird's on far!" yelled Ronnie. There wasn't time to tell him that it was actually on "fire," although "far" was not an inappropriate word either. The flames shot up about eight feet and were broiling the bougainvillea.

"Get a blanket," someone suggested.

"Not a good one!" cried Grace from the back door where the ladies had congregated to watch the conflagration.

"Douse it with water!" yelled Ronnie. Before anyone could stop him, Ronnie had the hose on the fire. Ronnie apparently hadn't done too well in high school physics (nor had I, based on my lack of knowledge of flash points). The addition of water to the brew caused an eruption that I can still see if I close my eyes—which is what I did then, too. When I opened them, the flames were higher than the garage and beginning to envelop lawn furniture.

I don't know who called the fire department. It was probably Grace; she always knows the right thing to do. The firemen arrived with a hook and ladder, a pumper, and an EMS van. The kids and the men were quite impressed—all that chrome and brass. The firemen took charge immediately and hit the blaze with a sea of thick, pink foam. The fryer was buried under a pile of the stuff. As the smoke began to clear and the foam pile evaporated, Ronnie began to hum Jim Morrison's "Light My Fire." When a young fireman shot him a stare, Ronnie stopped. Then the fireman turned to me with a look of disdain as if he were thinking, *Didn't pay attention in physics class, did you?*

I peered into the scorched cauldron. The turkey was nowhere to be seen, probably sunk to the bottom like the *H.L. Hunley* submarine.

"There she is," hollered one of the firemen. The turkey had breached like *Moby Dick*. The fire captain, who looked and talked a lot like Gregory Peck, harpooned it with a grappling hook. In all the excitement, I didn't notice whether or not he had a wooden leg.

After the firemen departed, the men gathered around to offer condolences and cheer me up.

"Sorry it didn't work out, Dalton," offered my brother-in-law Tom.

"You gotta be a professional to drive one of them babies," added Ronnie.

I, on the other hand, envisioned a vegetarian Thanksgiving and everyone trying to be nice and saying it was okay that way. So, you can imagine my surprise when I found the table set with a roasted turkey and a honey-baked ham.

Grace told everyone, "Dalton insisted on a backup plan in case of rain."

It was a fib, but one for which I was thankful. Grace is amazing.

After the blessing, Travis, Ronnie's boy, declared, "This is the best Thanksgiving ever. Next year, can we fry a turkey again?"

Before I could reply, Grace smiled and said, "We'll see."

AUNT
TOOGIE

GRACE'S VALENTINE SURPRISE

"**K**EEP WEDNESDAY AFTERNOON OPEN," MY lovely wife, Grace, declared as she reviewed her weekly calendar.

Looking up from the morning paper, I replied, "Why?"

"We are taking Toogie out for lunch on Valentine's Day."

My Aunt Toogie had recently moved in with us. How that unfolded is a longer story.

I'd taken Grace to the NASCAR race at Darlington last Mother's Day. Boy, was she surprised! I even overheard her tell a friend, "Can you believe he took me there, of all places?" Women seem to love big surprises. On our way home from the track, we visited my Aunt Toogie. She still lived in the rambling family house in a small North Carolina town where she and her sister and brothers grew up. Her husband, my Uncle Harold, had died a few years before. Although it was apparent she could use some help in a number of areas, she hung on fiercely to the independent part of "independent living."

So, it came as much of a surprise as Carolina winning the SEC in football when Toogie telephoned late last fall saying she had concluded the house was, indeed, becoming more than she could handle. She talked to Grace for a long time and revealed her growing concern for tending the house, yard, and even herself. It was a tearful call on Grace's end and, I suspect, on Toogie's as well. When the call ended, Grace sat for a moment and then mused, "I don't know whether to feel glad or sad." She went on to explain she was relieved Toogie had reached out for assistance but also sad to see her leave a place filled with so many happy memories.

Thus began a process of looking for a new home for Toogie. She and Grace inspected many options and locations. None seemed to quite measure up to their standards and high expectations while properly balancing available care, fine dining, and a cheery atmosphere. So, it wasn't a total surprise when Grace declared, "Dalton, let's invite Toogie to stay with us."

"Are you sure that's a good idea?" I asked.

"I know we can care for her better than the places we have visited so far. Think of it as a transition as she finds her way to her next residence."

"But you know how she is…," I continued. When Grace didn't answer, I described how Toogie always had a compulsion to say whatever was on her mind whenever the thought struck to whomever was in earshot.

Grace smiled and replied, "Sounds like the two of you will get along swimmingly." And with that, it was done.

"So, where are we going on Valentine's?" I asked.

"It's a surprise. You'll see," Grace responded. "A romantic setting."

I was about to opine that the words "romantic" and "Toogie" didn't fit in the same sentence but held back knowing it could generate "the look."

On Valentine's Day, we piled into the car. Grace drove, and I sat in the back seat. Toogie rode shotgun as we headed west on the Mark Clark Expressway. We exited onto Highway 61 heading toward Summerville. To my surprise, Grace slowed the car and turned into the entrance of the Middleton Place plantation.

After parking the car, Grace instructed me, "Help Toogie with her door, dear, while I fetch something from the trunk."

I opened Toogie's door and said, "I've heard the restaurant here is quite good."

"So have I, but we're not eating there," Grace replied, lifting her head from the trunk. Continuing her ascent, Grace held up a wicker basket. "We're having a picnic!" she beamed.

"Oh, my," Toogie whispered.

Grace closed the car trunk, handed me the basket, and took Toogie's arm. "This way," she said as she led us toward the grassy, terraced hillside overlooking the Butterfly Lakes and the Ashley River.

Grace spread out a blanket and laid the place settings. The gentle breeze did not disturb the plates or napkins, and we felt comfortable sitting in the sunshine. Grace pulled three old-fashioned, glass bottles of Coca-Cola from the hamper and handed one to Toogie.

"Will you look at that?" I exclaimed, studying my bottle. "I haven't seen one of those in years. Where did you find it?"

"Online," Grace answered, handing me a "church key" to open the bottles.

Toogie looked at the bottle, placed one hand to her throat, and said softly, "Oh, my."

Grace continued to unpack the picnic hamper. She identified each item as it was removed from the basket and placed on the blanket. "We have apples. Saltine crackers. A jar of peanut butter. Vienna sausages. And for dessert, a Hershey's chocolate bar."

I looked down at the feast before us and thought, *This is one sorry excuse for a Valentine's Day lunch.* When I looked up, I noticed tears beginning to trickle down Toogie's cheeks. I reckoned she was equally disappointed with the paltry provisions. She reached for Grace's hand and wept, "I must have told you the story."

"Yes, dear," Grace replied, reaching to hug Toogie. "Some years ago."

While they both dabbed their eyes and sniffled, I finally asked, "Okay, what story?"

Toogie pulled a handkerchief from her purse, wiped her eyes again, and took a deep breath. "Well," she began, looking out beyond the river, "it was on this very hillside…your late Uncle Harold proposed to me, back in…" She looked toward Grace.

"Sixty years ago today," Grace said softly.

Toogie nodded, dabbed her cheeks, and resumed. "We drove to Charleston for the day. Harold had taken off from work. I think it was a

Friday. The weather was much like today, unseasonably warm and sunny. Anyway, Harold said, 'Let's stop and have a picnic. There's something I want to talk over with you.' So, we found a roadside market…and we bought…"

Toogie looked down, and her shoulders began to shake. Grace squeezed her hand. Toogie inhaled deeply.

She continued. "We didn't have much money. And so, we bought… Coca-Cola, apples, saltine crackers, peanut butter, Vienna sausages, and a Hershey's bar." She faintly gestured toward each item on the blanket as she spoke, recalling the similar snacks from years ago.

"Although the plantation was closed, we found an open gate and made our way to this spot. Just like today, the camellias were in full bloom. It was a beautiful setting for a Valentine's Day meal and a marriage proposal."

Toogie looked out over the river and then back to the picnic setting. She closed her eyes and smiled.

She wiped a tear with her napkin, opened her eyes, and chuckled, "Your Uncle Harold loved his Vienna sausages. Personally, I couldn't stand them, then or now. But I loved Harold…then and now…and I said 'Yes' when he asked me to marry him. I still miss him so."

"It's a wonderful story," Grace exclaimed. "Thank you for sharing it."

Toogie pull her shoulders back. "Well, just look at me. I've been blubbering away. Lunch is waiting. Let's eat. Pass me the peanut butter. And Dalton, keep your mitts off that chocolate bar until we finish the other fare."

We ate in silence for quite some time.

"How do you like lunch, sweetheart?" Grace finally asked me.

"Good grub," I mumbled through a dry mouthful of peanut butter and soda crackers.

Grace gave me a glance that I immediately interpreted as a possible beginning of "the look." I quickly sputtered, "I mean great. It's great. A culinary delight!"

"And romantic?" Grace inquired.

"Yes, dear. Romantic. Very romantic."

Grace smiled. Toogie smiled.

As we sat in the warm Valentine's Day sun, we reflected on a lifetime of memories and polished off every morsel of the memorable, romantic repast…. Well, maybe not all the Vienna sausages.

THE MAKEOVER

[In 2006, Dalton did, indeed, get a new silhouette
for the banner in his columns]

"DALTON, YOU COULD USE A new look," my lovely wife, Grace, proclaimed.

"Huh?" I responded, looking up from the Sunday comics.

"It's a makeover, like on *Oprah*," Aunt Toogie barked. "Although, in your case, I'd say it is more *Extreme Makeover* or *Mission Impossible*.

"Consider it an image update," Grace explained. "You know, starting fresh for the new year." Then she put her hand on her hips. "Dalton, are you listening?"

I put my pen down and looked up again. I had been working the "Find Six Differences puzzle" in the comics. "Yeah, I'm listening. I was just looking for the final clue. I always have trouble finding the last one."

"Did you get the clown's tie?" Toogie piped up. "It has stripes in one picture and not in the other."

I looked down and muttered, "Oh, yeah," and then looked back toward Grace.

"I don't know why that silly puzzle intrigues you every week," Grace declared.

"It exercises the old gray matter," I retorted. "Here, let me read you the Slylock Fox mystery."

"Never mind," Grace interrupted. "There is a reason that section is called 'Comics for Kids.' Sometimes I wonder if you will ever grow up!"

Grace didn't see Toogie stick the tip of her tongue out at me. I was about to return the gesture when Grace continued. "Anyway, I've been thinking you need a new silhouette for your column."

"What's wrong with the current one?" I asked.

"It just doesn't look enough like you," Grace offered.

"It looks like a kid's," Toogie chimed in.

"What's wrong with that?"

"You're old!" she shot back.

"I know you are, but what am I?"

"Both of you stop, please!" Grace interjected, trying to calm things down. "I just think a new silhouette would reflect your distinguished countenance."

"Translation: Old!" Toogie repeated, wiggling two fingers on each hand a la quotation marks.

"In fact, I've made an appointment to have it done the day after tomorrow," Grace announced in the special way she has for concluding a discussion.

On the appointed day and hour, Grace herded us into the car. Imagine my surprise when she parked in front of a children's clothing store. You know, the place where all you hear is "cute," "precious," and "adorable."

"Say it isn't here," I moaned.

"Yes, it is," Grace declared. "A noted silhouette artist is here only today. Your appointment is in ten minutes."

"Don't be afraid. Mommy and Granny will go with you," Toogie chuckled from the back seat.

Entering the store, I gazed around rapidly, hoping not to recognize anyone. All the other patrons were young mothers with little children, dressed in finery, in tow. Not one of the kids was taller than my waist. As I approached the desk, one of the salesclerks offered her assistance. I explained we had the 2:15 silhouette timeslot. The clerk then stood on her tiptoes and peered out and over the counter, looking for someone younger and shorter.

"Is it your grandson or granddaughter?" she asked.

"No, it's…ah…me," I whispered.

The corners of her mouth turned up. She tried to make it a smile, but I know it was a smirk.

A few minutes later, the artist called out, "Next child."

I stepped forward. He gave me an up-and-down look, accompanied by a faint smile, and waved me toward a chair with legs no more than a foot high. The chair was pink and had the words "Hello Kitty" painted in white on the backrest. My knees touched my ears once I finally settled in the seat.

"Don't worry," the artist said. "I can omit the knees."

I gave him my best faint smile in return. Grace smiled as if a proud parent. Standing next to Grace, Toogie stuck out her tongue. I was about to return that gesture when a small face appeared at my eye level, blocking my view of Toogie. The face belonged to the previous occupant of the chair, a little boy around three years old. Pointing toward me, he turned to his mother, "What's him doing?"

I was about to provide him a tutorial on pronouns when his mother reached out and grabbed his arm. "He…he," she stammered pulling the kid to her side. I could tell she was grasping for a politically correct explanation. Finally, she blurted out, "He has his turn now, honey," and tugged the toddler down an aisle and out of view.

After what seemed like an eternity but was probably only a minute or two, the artist announced, "There you go," and handed the finished silhouette to Grace.

She declared, "I like it. It is a great resemblance, dear."

"Still not old enough, but closer," Toogie scoffed after her inspection.

I managed to make it upright from the chair, told the artist "Thanks" in my deepest voice, accompanied by a firm, manly handshake, and headed straight for the car. Grace and Toogie paid for the silhouette and met me in the parking lot.

"Well, do you like it?" Grace inquired on the way home.

Several responses jumped instantly to mind. Yet, after a pause, I replied, "Yes, dear."

"Right answer," Grace replied. "When we get home, I'll make you a drink before dinner."

"How about hot cocoa," Toogie giggled from the back seat, "with baby marshmallows?"

I turned and stuck out my tongue.

"I see what you two are doing," Grace announced. Then she patted my knee. "Now behave yourself and I'll fix you a Perfect Manhattan."

Later, sipping the cocktail by the fireplace and soothing the emotional scars of the afternoon, I gazed at the new silhouette. Even though I liked the younger, boyish-looking version, I concluded it would be okay to use the new one, especially if Grace favored it. Did it really look like me? Time flies by in a blink, doesn't it? Do you always imagine yourself younger than others see you? Is it true we define middle age as our own age plus ten years? I pondered these thoughts and the mysteries of life, aging, and mortality as the bourbon warmed my inner fire.

Toogie entered with a glass of her own favorite brew and announced, "Well, young man, it sounds as if you have been a really good boy today."

I glanced up from my musing.

"Grace says to get your coat. We're going to a topless place for dinner."

"Really? She said that?" I asked incredulously.

"Heard it with my own ears," Toogie replied emphatically.

I stood up, nearly spilling my cocktail, and walked into the kitchen, Toogie on my heels.

"We're going to a topless place?" I blurted out.

"Oh, good heavens," Grace sighed. "You know very well we're going to a tapas restaurant."

I pointed toward Toogie, who turned away as if she were never a part of the conversation.

"I wish you would act your age," Grace scolded. "It's not too late to grow up, you know!" she added, walking toward the hall closet to get her coat.

I looked again at Toogie. She just shrugged.

"I could have used some help there. Don't you have something to say?"

Toogie put her forefinger on her chin, looked skyward, and gave me a smirky smile. "Okay. Keep your mitts off the comics and let me have first crack at the Sunday puzzles."

THE MOOCH MARCH

"**W**HAT'S THE MESS ON THE dining room table?" I asked my lovely wife, Grace, as I strolled into the kitchen for a wake-up mug of java.

"A cheery good morning to you, sweetheart," Grace replied. "The mess you referenced is Aunt Toogie's project, so be careful what you say."

"Project? Like a hobby or arts and crafts?"

"Not exactly, dear. She is planning a trip to Florida."

"Florida? How soon does she leave, and is she coming back?"

"Dalton, that's not nice," Grace scoffed. "You know very well she can't go alone. So, we are driving her."

"We, as in you and me?" I moaned. "Driving Toogie to Florida? Say it ain't so!"

"Shush," Grace whispered. "I hear her on the stairs."

Toogie ambled into the kitchen, poured a cup of coffee, mumbled something, and trudged toward the dining room.

"Good morning, dear," Grace called after her. "How's the mooch march plan?"

"Almost finished," Toogie hollered back. "I just need to map out the final leg back to Charleston."

"Mooch march?" I whispered, leaning toward Grace.

"Yes, that's what she calls it," Grace answered. "The mooch march."

As I sipped my coffee, Grace explained that many of Toogie's friends have relocated or now spend the winter months in Florida. These include former neighbors and girlfriends from her school and workdays. As winter arrives, they all correspond and arrange to meet in Florida.

"All of them descending on the same place at the same time," I mused. "Sounds like the buzzards arriving in Hinckley, Ohio, on the Ides of March each year."

Grace shot me a smirk. "Not quite the analogy I would use," she lectured. "Think more of the swallows returning to San Juan Capistrano."

Continuing her commentary, Grace described how Toogie, armed with a red Sharpie pen, marks the location on a Florida road map for each person she wishes to visit on her swing through the Sunshine State. Then, using a ruler—no MapQuest or computer for Toogie—she ciphers (that's what she calls it, honestly) the distance from one destination to another. Next, following a guideline of driving no more than a certain number of miles per day (She claims long spells in the car give her "the vapors," to which I always tell her to "Just sit tight. You'll get over it"), she plots whom to see and in what order. She then marks the planned route of attack on the roadmap with a yellow highlighter. Finally, she corresponds with these friends to confirm the arrangements to visit on specified days.

"I think I understand," I stated, pouring a second cup of coffee. "But what does all that have to do with whatever you called it?"

"Well," Grace replied, "she stays only a couple of days with each person."

"Kind of like that quote by Mark Twain about guests and fish smelling after three days?" I quipped.

"Not quite the quote I would use," Grace retorted. "Plus, it was Benjamin Franklin."

"But the name... What does she call it?" I asked again.

"As I was trying to explain before you interrupted," Grace concluded, "Toogie stays a day or so to mooch—her term, not mine—off one friend, then marches down the road to mooch off another friend, and so on, all around Florida. Sometimes she even picks up or joins other moochers she knows for a leg of her trek. Consequently, the name is most apropos—the mooch march!"

I moseyed into the dining room and observed papers spread everywhere. Several earlier versions of the travel plan littered the floor. Beside a map on the table lay pencils and markers, an empty coffee cup, a wad of candy bar wrappers, and a ruler. Toogie feverishly punched keys on a small calculator. The scene reminded me of an old movie where Meyer Lansky was busy burning the midnight oil to balance Al Capone's books. I peered over Toogie's shoulder. The map, awash in red and yellow ink and crammed with cryptic notations, looked like the product of some pie-eyed pirate.

Toogie stopped ciphering and looked up.

"Darn, you made me lose my place," she barked.

"So, how goes the invasion plan, Ike?" I queried.

I was unprepared for the recitation that ensued. Toogie proceeded to take me through the trip, day by day, stop by stop, the mileage between each location with the estimated times of departure and arrival, whom she would see where and the length of each stay. All this was sprinkled with an unsolicited narrative about every host we were about to visit, such as, "She used to be a Hargrove, but after her husband, Pete—that's what everyone called him, although his real name was Deaneen—died, she married one of the Ratcliffe twins. I think it was Kenny from over in Aberdeen...," and, "You may remember her family. They operated the Pure station out on the highway before the interstate was built. She probably would have sold it by now anyway, what with her lumbago and all."

As Toogie droned on, I felt as if I knew these folks intimately. Midway through the monologue, I motioned for Grace to pour me a third cup of coffee. Just listening to the itinerary was exhausting.

"Why don't we take a break one night and stay someplace nice?" I interjected as Toogie neared the conclusion of the travelogue. Sensing my comment may have hurt her feelings, I added, "No offense intended."

"Some taken," Toogie snorted but then added, "What do you think, Grace?"

"I realize how hard you have worked on your mooch-march planning, dear," Grace soothed. "But I guess we could take Dalton's suggestion under advisement."

"That's good," Toogie smiled. "We'll take it under advisement."

A few days later, while I packed clothes for the trip, Grace said, "Don't forget to bring a sport coat and tie, dear."

"Why do I need them?"

"For our stay at The Breakers hotel in Palm Beach," she smiled.

"We're going to The Breakers? I thought we were march mooching, or whatever Toogie calls it, from one of her friend's homes to the next victim."

"It is her annual mooch march," Grace corrected. "We think a short sojourn at The Breakers is in order. Remember, you were the one who insisted we stay someplace nice."

"I only suggested it. You said you would take it under advisement."

"Well, we concluded it was sound advice," Grace announced with a sniff.

"I guess one night at a hotel would break up the trip," I offered.

Grace smiled. "It will be a nice break, and we're booked for four nights. Oceanview rooms."

"Four nights? Two rooms on the ocean at The Breakers hotel this time of year! Say it ain't so! What's that going to cost? Five hundred a night per room?"

Grace pointed a forefinger toward the ceiling without looking up from folding a silk scarf.

"Six hundred?" I asked.

Again, she motioned toward the ceiling with her forefinger as she continued to arrange her clothing.

Finally, I asked, "What about old Ben Franklin's adage about stuff spoiling after three days?"

Grace stopped packing, put her hands on her hips, and turned to face me. "Dalton, we will not spoil at The Breakers, Ben Franklin never stayed there, and we are going only because it was your idea."

I sat down on the bed. My head was spinning. Snared in a trap of my own making! I ciphered the total cost of two rooms for four nights at a multi-star hotel during high season.

"I don't feel well," I moaned, holding my head in my hands.

"Are you all right?" Grace responded.

"I just feel a little light," I sighed.

"There, there," she cooed. "Where do you feel light? In the head?"

"No, in my wallet!"

"It's probably the vapors," she announced, resuming her packing. "Just sit tight. You'll get over it."

REFILLS

"S HE IS NOT BRINGING HER fast-food drink cups!" I declared.
"Then you talk to her," my lovely wife, Grace, replied. "I've tried
and she won't listen to me."

"It's crazy," I added, "as well as illegal."

Grace gave me a wry smile. "Well, she is from your side of the family."

We were mobilizing for our annual winter pilgrimage to Florida, although the fairly nice weather here in Charleston had me questioning the need for the trip. My Aunt Toogie, on the other hand, had been planning for the journey ever since she received a Christmas card from a friend who had relocated to Boca Raton. Not wanting to disappoint Toogie, Grace leaped into a full project management role. She was issuing instructions like a football coach in a two-minute drill. "Did you stop the papers? Don't forget to check all your prescriptions. Water the house plants. Somebody wind the grandfather clock. Remember to bring envelopes and stamps for any notes to write or bills to pay."

The house had been cleaned following the departure of our last holiday guests, Grace's sister, Laura, and her daughter, Betsy. Since Grace had prepared so many meals throughout the holidays, I waived the "Williams Family DNA rule," which specifies one cleans the bathroom after his or her direct family members depart. This reasonable protocol has served us well—if your DNA matches the tub and other fixtures, you clean it. I stepped up to clean the rooms where Laura and Betsy stayed while Grace helped Toogie pack her clothes. I am sure Grace appreciated this effort, which made it all the more perplexing when she didn't jump to my side of the cup conflict.

Toogie has an extensive collection of empty drink containers from various fast-food outlets—all the usual suspects: McDonald's, Wendy's, Burger King, KFC, Taco Bell, Panera, Zaxby's, and more. She uses them for refills—endless *free* refills, mind you. She subscribes to the theory that the right to a free refill attaches to the cup. As long as one possesses the cup, one is entitled to a free refill. I, on the other hand, believe the right to a free refill ends when one departs the establishment. She and I have had this discussion numerous times with nary a budge on either side. Toogie sees nothing wrong with going back to the restaurant, empty cup in hand, weeks after her initial purchase and bellying up once more to the soda or iced tea dispenser. She will also refill at different outlets of the same chain—even in different states! I argue to no avail how this is wrong and could get her busted. I imagine the authorities hauling her away in a perp walk like some corporate crook or Mafia don.

So, I girded myself for a renewal of the refills debate. I staked out a seat on a kitchen barstool so I would, similar to a court judge, be positioned slightly higher than Toogie when she was seated at the kitchen table.

"I think I have everything for the trip once you help me find my Sudoku puzzle book," Toogie announced as she plopped down at the table.

"We'll find the puzzle book, but you need to leave the refill cups here," I announced. "It's just not right."

"Oh, yeah? Who says?" snapped Toogie. "And, by the way, who died and made you Elvis?"

This launched another war of words.

"You can't go into a restaurant and get a refill just because you have one of their cups."

"It says free refills, doesn't it?"

"But only while you are in there."

"I will be in there."

"No, I mean while you are in there only once."

"I will be in there only once."

"No, no. I mean you have to go in, pay for a drink, and then get free refills while you stay there. You can't come back later or go to another location and score a refill."

"It doesn't say that."

"Well, they mean it."

"If they meant it, you'd think they would say so, now, wouldn't you?"

"They mean it. One day, you'll see."

"Oh, yeah? Says who?" Toogie barked again, bringing the contest full circle to another tie.

This intervention proved no more productive than prior confrontations. Once, Grace suggested an educational approach. I searched the library for Reinhold Niebuhr's *Moral Man and Immoral Society*, only to discover the library copy had been stolen or never returned. At this point, I am ready to throw in the towel and let providence, or the long arm of the law, take care of Toogie.

I imagine the three of us—Clyde Barrow driving, Bonnie Parker riding shotgun, and Ma Barrow with her bevy of beverage beakers in the back seat—hightailing down I-95 to Florida. We pull the black roadster off the main road and roll up, headlights off, to a dimly lit hamburger joint.

Clyde peers through a hole in an old edition of *The Daniel Island News*. "Coast is clear," he whispers out of the side of his mouth.

"I'm going in. Watch my backside," Ma Barrow says softly, opening a back door and stepping on the running board.

"Gotcha covered," answers Bonnie, flicking a cigarette ash out the window as she curls her other hand around the handle of a Tommy gun.

With that, Ma Barrow sashays into the establishment, calmly helps herself to one more in a long trail of refills, and nonchalantly moseys back to the getaway car. Tires squeal, lights flash on, and we speed back to the expressway. We are desperados on the run, disguised as snowbirds, cleverly blending into the early bird buffets of South Florida.

THE LICENSE PLATE GAME

THE ELDERLY GENT SHUFFLED SLOWLY along the salad bar island, lifting each vegetable with plastic tongs for closer inspection. He then deposited the item either onto his plate or back to a salad topping crock—although frequently not into the one from whence it had come. While a few diners grumbled as the line to the salad bar began to back up like rush-hour traffic, I savored the leisurely pace because we were dining at four-fifteen in the afternoon!

My lovely wife, Grace, and I had once again driven Aunt Toogie to Florida—God's waiting room—for her annual mooch march. Toogie visits (the mooch) for a day or two with a series of friends as she traverses (the march) down one coast and back up the other of the Sunshine State. Keeping with one of her travel traditions, Toogie insisted we begin the license plate game as soon as we pulled out of the driveway. The contest consists of trying to spot the license plates from each of the fifty states and the District of Columbia before we return home. Armed with a small map of the United

States, Toogie insists upon riding shotgun so she can readily view the traffic ahead of us.

By the time we crossed the Don Holt Bridge, she had checked off four quick hits—South Carolina, North Carolina, Georgia, and Florida. Near the airport exit, she began to holler, "Pull over! Pull over!" pointing toward the far-right lane.

"That goes to the airport," I explained. "We want to continue on 526."

"Thank you, Magellan," Toogie barked. "I just wanted to get a gander at the license plate on that SUV. It has got to be from a western state."

I checked the traffic around me, signaled, and then motored behind the silver SUV.

"Montana!" Toogie whooped, marking the discovery on her map. "This is going to be a good trip."

After navigating back into the proper lane, I inquired, "So, how did you know it was from a far-away state?"

"It was sort of blue, white, and silver," Toogie proffered. "So, it had to be Nevada, Kansas, or Montana."

I let her comment percolate for a moment and then retorted, "How can you remember that sort of trivia but forget when it is your turn to buy dinner?"

Toogie continued her trance-like attention to the surrounding vehicles. When she didn't respond, I chipped in, "And how can you see those tiny license plates at seventy miles an hour and yet not find your glasses around the house?"

Toogie answered only, "Oklahoma!" as we passed a tractor-trailer.

Grace leaned forward from the back seat and said to Toogie, "That's the spirit, girl. Just ignore him. He gets irritable when someone else sets the agenda. It must be a first-born thing."

Toogie remained in the zone, map in hand, scanning the landscape, occasionally craning her neck to draw a bead on a passing car or truck.

Following the adage "if you can't beat 'em, join 'em," I succumbed to the siren call of the license plate game. Soon, I was shouting out new discoveries such as "*There's Maine…!*" as Toogie educated me about the color differences of the licenses, such as the shades of green among Vermont (dark), New Hampshire (pale), Tennessee (paler still), and the multiplicity of colorful plates from Florida. "*That's the manatee plate. There's the panther.*" Around

Daytona, I asked her which state was the "holy grail," the hardest license to find.

Toogie pondered a moment. "Maybe Hawaii and Alaska, for obvious reasons, but I'd say North Dakota," she mused. "Not a lot of people there, or maybe they don't travel much."

We also repeated other routines along the mooch march such as drinking brightly colored cocktails, telling people, who looked fair at best, that they hadn't changed a bit and looked great (and who, assuredly, did the same with us), and discussing the weather (particularly snowfall and wind chill) in northern cities we once called home. Most of all, we dived face-first into the numero-uno snowbird ritual—chewing the fat about the restaurants we visited during the day and the day before that as well as debating where we would dine the following day, all sandwiched around actual acts of eating. A three-ring circus act of gluttony.

One more example was this current early-bird dinner at an establishment that featured "Bottomless Margaritas from 3-5 p.m."

The senior citizen who created the logjam finally exited the salad bar and shuffled his way back to a table. I followed behind him, joining Grace and Toogie at a nearby booth. For some reason, I studied the old-timer.

"Honey," Grace whispered. "You're staring."

"I am trying to place him. He looks so familiar," I whispered back.

"I don't believe he is a former neighbor," Grace offered in a hushed voice. "Maybe someone from work?"

Toogie looked up from her grouper platter. "It's you," she declared.

"Say what?" I answered.

Putting her fork down, Toogie continued, "It's you in a bunch of years from now. See the way he looks down to poke at his dinner and the way he combs his hair?"

Her comment hit me like a ton of hush puppies. She was right. Like an old episode of *The Twilight Zone*, the scene before me was surreal. Could it be that the man twenty feet away was really me twenty years away?

Our server broke the trance. "Would y'all like some more tea?" she cooed.

"See that older guy over there?" I gestured. "Put his dinner on my bill."

"Oh, you mean Mr. Delaney," the waitress replied.

"You know him?"

"Sure, he comes here often during the winter months. Drives all the way to Florida by himself. From up north. I think, North Dakota."

Toogie's head shot up as her fork clinked the plate.

"Did you say North Dakota?" she sputtered through a mouthful of potato wedges.

In an instant, Toogie scooped up her iced tea and sauntered over to Mr. Delaney's table. I watched as the two of them conversed and smiled. After a few minutes, Toogie rose, patted the fellow on the shoulder, and made her way back to our table as Mr. Delaney smiled in return and waved to us.

"Name's Frank," Toogie announced. "Frank Delaney. Lives in Fargo."

When neither Grace nor I replied, Toogie continued. "Hello! Fargo, North Dakota. Drives a white pick-up. It's parked in the back lot, second row. Oh, and I told him I was buying his dinner."

"Does that mean you are picking up our check?" I queried.

"Not now," Toogie shot back. "I've got to hustle out back to spy that North Dakota license plate. You have to actually see it in order to count it, you know." Rising, she added, "You get the bill, Dalton. I'll get one down the road."

"The quest for the holy grail," I sighed as Toogie headed for the door.

After applying fresh lipstick and recapping the tube, Grace observed, "She did say North Dakota was the hardest plate to find."

"Who's talking about licenses?" I muttered. "I'm talking about Toogie springing for dinner!"

SIMPLIFY

"WHERE'S THE CHOW-CHOW?" I ASKED my lovely wife, Grace. "I can't hear you when your head is in the refrigerator."

"Where's the chow-chow?" I repeated. "You know, the relish I like."

"Oh, Aunt Toogie gave it a toss when she cleaned the fridge."

"She threw out my chow-chow?"

"Yes, dear."

"She cleaned the fridge?"

"I just said so, dear."

"Why?"

Grace explained how Toogie had been on a "straightening up and cleaning out" binge for the past few weeks. I poked my head left and right to peer beyond the mayonnaise and horseradish, hoping a small, multi-colored jar might magically appear.

"She thinned and organized her closet," Grace continued. "She is helping me do the same with mine, and she's fixin' to tackle your desk next."

"Don't let her mess up my desk!" I shot back, extracting my head from the fridge.

"It's a mess already," Grace retorted. "Toogie's only going to get rid of stuff you don't need anymore, like those dated travel brochures and faded golf scorecards."

A final peek behind the hamburger dill pickle jar produced no chow-chow. Grace reminded me of the definition of insanity—trying the same approach over and over, expecting a different result. I concluded my quest and closed the fridge door. "How did she get started on this neatness kick anyway?"

"She said a man told her to simplify," Grace replied, "and she is focused on following his advice."

"Sounds like Dr. Phil."

"She met him at the mall."

"She met Dr. Phil at the mall?"

"No, silly," Grace scoffed. "She said she met a man at the mall who told her to simplify. Ever since then, she's been busy tidying and organizing."

"Do you think this is a good thing?"

"It's a fine idea," Grace laughed. "She'll have this house shipshape in no time."

More seriously, Grace surmised my concern. She, too, was a little suspicious about the stranger Toogie reported meeting at the mall. Grace replayed questioning Toogie about this yet trying at the same time not to alarm her. Grace and I speculated. Could he have been an author promoting a new self-help guide, a street preacher, a harmless prankster...? We also didn't discount the possibility this could be a scam artist preying on an older woman.

"I wonder if he ever mentions financial matters," I mused, beginning to feel a little like Hercule Poirot.

"Toogie only commented about his advice to simplify. That's why she has been making all those trips to Goodwill and taking many of her old books to the resale shop."

"Perhaps we should look at her checkbook or watch her credit cards," I offered.

"I've considered that, but I don't want her to think we are nosey or don't trust her. I wish I knew what to do," Grace sighed.

"Let me have a word with her," I reassured Grace, reaching to twist my imaginary Poirot mustache.

That evening over dinner, I subtly introduced the subject of the peculiar persona. "Grace tells me you've met a man at the mall."

"Oh, Mr. Rodriquez," Toogie piped up.

"I...see...," I purred in my most sleuth-ish tone.

"He was in your Uncle Mike's band."

"Band?"

"The jazz band," Toogie clarified. She peered over the table, "Say, do we have any of that chow-chow?"

"We're out, honey," Grace answered without looking up.

"That's okay," Toogie responded, not looking up either. "It wasn't as good as my homemade."

"Uncle...? Jazz...? Band...?" I stammered.

"You remember, dear," Grace spoke up. "Toogie's brother—your Uncle Mike—played in a Dixieland jazz band. They wore such colorful outfits. They were very talented." She nodded toward Toogie.

"Yeah, the band," Toogie agreed. "He was wearing his band clothes."

"Who was wearing band clothes?" I pleaded, trying to keep up with whatever direction this conversation was headed.

"Mr. Rodriquez," Toogie clarified. "I told him my brother used to be in his band."

I cocked an eye at Grace.

"That's when he first suggested I simplify," Toogie concluded, setting down her fork.

"There's been more than one time?"

"Heavens, yes," Toogie smiled. "Each time I go to the mall, we talk, and he reminds me to simplify."

"So, this Mr. Rodriquez...he must be around your age?"

"Oh, no. I'd guess he is around thirty-five," Toogie replied. "Real cute, and fit, too. He's a hottie!"

I looked at Grace, who just shrugged.

After Toogie retired for the night, Mr. Rodriquez was the main event of an extended discussion.

"The whole thing sounds pretty fishy if you ask me," I declared.

"I just hope she isn't being tricked," Grace sympathized.

We finally agreed we would accompany her to the mall the next day to check out "Mr. Simplify."

I attempted to plant the hook during breakfast. "I'm going to the mall to look at some new fishing gear. What do you say we all go?"

"Nah," Toogie barked. "You kids go. I'll stay here and work on the pantry."

I arched my eyebrows at Grace, trying to signal "your line." Catching the cue, she suggested, "Oh, let's all go. It will be fun. I can help you with the pantry when we get home. Besides, I want to show you the fabric I'm considering for the guest room window treatments."

"I don't know," Toogie sighed. Suddenly, her expression lit up. "Hey, maybe we will see Mr. Rodriquez."

I gave Grace my best Basil Rathbone wink.

My pulse quickened as we entered the mall. I had been rehearsing what I'd say to this stranger when we turned onto the main aisle.

"There he is," Toogie announced.

I scanned the horizon, noting a watch repair kiosk, a Marine Corps recruiting desk, and a coffee island. "Where?" I whispered.

Toogie pointed to the recruiting desk. "There!"

Just then, a marine looked up, smiled, waved, and stood.

"Hello, again," he called toward Toogie, rounding the desk to approach us.

"This is my nephew, Dalton, and his wife, Grace," Toogie offered as he neared us.

"Master Sergeant Hector Rodriquez," the marine reported, extending a firm handshake. "It's an honor to meet you both."

My eyes darted between Rodriquez and Toogie.

"I enjoy talking with your aunt. She tells me her brother was also a member of the corps, although she calls it a band," he grinned. Then he patted Toogie's hand and said proudly, "Semper Fi."

Grace and I rapidly exchanged knowing glances…the blue trousers with a red stripe, the darker blue jacket with red piping and brass buttons, the white hat, and the Marine Corps' motto: Semper Fi… My glances then moved from his square jaw to his shined shoes as my feelings alternated between relief and embarrassment.

Toogie beamed at him like a teenager with a rock star. "I've been following your suggestion."

Grace quickly jumped in before anyone else could speak. "You are kind to talk with her, and she enjoys coming to visit you here."

"My pleasure, ma'am," he smiled. "If you'll excuse me a moment," he requested, motioning toward a young man looking at brochures. "I believe I may have a customer, but please stop by anytime." Then he touched his hand to the brim of his hat, nodded to Toogie, and said once more, "Semper Fi."

Driving home, Toogie broke the silence. "Mr. Rodriquez is nice, isn't he?"

"Yes, he is very friendly and so polite," Grace answered softly.

"Now, don't go telling the other ladies in my bridge club about him," Toogie stated emphatically. "I found him first, and he's my friend."

"We'll keep this whole thing a secret," Grace assured. "Right, Sherlock?" she inquired, giving me a Cheshire Cat grin.

"Dalton," Grace added, "I have been thinking you could use some of Mr. Rodriquez's advice and simplify. Maybe you could start with the garage."

After a pause, she added, "When you do, I'll buy more chow-chow."

So, I'll clean the garage. I plan to hide a secret supply of chow-chow in the garage fridge right behind the beer. More importantly, I pledge to offer a grateful prayer of thanks for Master Sergeant Rodriquez and all the members of his band.

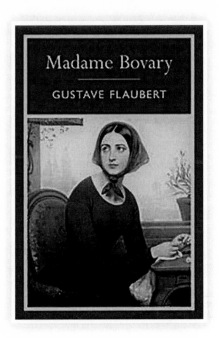

Madame Bovary

GUSTAVE FLAUBERT

Summer Reading

"DALTON, PUT THAT DOWN," MY lovely wife, Grace, murmured. "What?"

"Please," she continued a little louder through clenched teeth. "People may see you."

Grace was alternating side glances between me and the magazine I was reading in the supermarket checkout line. My favorite part of grocery shopping with Grace is reading the tabloids. While she unloads the shopping cart's contents onto the conveyor belt, I peruse periodicals such as the *National Enquirer* and *Globe*. These publications are part of a unique media genre featuring stories and tidbits found in no other place.

"Look," I announced. "Here is a story about a baby born with a wooden leg."

"Shush," Grace said in a stage whisper. "People can hear you!"

I put the magazine back on the rack, which was haphazardly arranged, a sure sign I was not the first person to grab a gander at these gazettes.

On the way home, Grace remarked, "Well, that was certainly fascinating."

"I know," I replied. "I guess one of the parents must have had a wooden leg."

After a pause, Grace sighed, "Give me strength."

"I didn't get to read the whole article. You made me put the mag—"

"Stop!" Grace declared. "I don't want to hear any more about the baby with the wooden leg."

Neither of us spoke for the remainder of the drive home.

Aunt Toogie was sitting at the kitchen table reading *People* magazine as we entered with our purchases.

"Shiloh Nouvel," she muttered. "What are those Hollywood-types thinking when they pick a name like that for a kid? Sounds more like a pinot noir or some new brand of disinfectant."

"I think it's an interesting name," Grace offered, ever the diplomat.

"Speaking of interesting," I interjected, "guess what I read at the supermarket?"

"What?" Toogie shot back.

"Oh, please, not again!" Grace moaned.

"No, it's not about the baby born with the wooden leg."

"Baby with a wooden leg?" Toogie asked, raising her eyebrows. "Tell me more."

"Don't encourage him," Grace pleaded.

Once calm was restored, I continued, "Anyway, a lady in British Columbia harvested a zucchini that looks just like Little Richard."

Grace just stared at me.

"You know, Little Richard," I explained. "He sang oldies like 'Tutti Frutti' and 'Good Golly, Miss Molly.'"

"I know who Little Richard is," Grace declared, hands on her hips.

"Don't forget 'Long Tall Sally,'" Toogie chimed in.

"That's it!" Grace declared. "You two need some encouragement to elevate your interests and topics of conversation. Perhaps I could suggest some more mind-expanding reading material. I know, let me find my summer reading lists."

The next day, we all sat down at the same kitchen table. Grace laid out several pieces of paper. I recognized some as items she had used during her teaching career.

"I have gathered several sources of books for us to consider. This is a list of classic books," Grace explained, "a roster of recommended biographies and history, and finally, *The New York Times* tables of current best-selling fiction and nonfiction."

Toogie and I stared at the lists.

"For starters, we might consider a light, current best seller, such as *Beach Road* or *Marley & Me*, or focus on the works of a local author such as Sue Monk Kidd or Dorothea Benton Frank. I think *Full of Grace* has a nice title, don't you?"

Toogie and I continued to stare at the lists.

"Or we could tackle a book from a reading list of these selected classics," Grace continued, handing me one of the pieces of paper.

"Do we read the same book?" I asked.

"Sure. That way, we can discuss it and compare our perspectives."

"Sounds like school," Toogie snorted.

"Think of it as summer camp or a sabbatical," Grace countered. "Good books stimulate the mind and renew the soul. Any one of these is surely more thought-provoking than the frivolous nonsense you have been reading."

"Okay, Toogie," I announced, holding the numbered list of recommended books. "Let's dive into deep water by choosing our first book from the classics. You decide. Pick a number from one to one hundred."

"Eighty-one."

"Why did you pick that number?"

"Never ask a woman that question," Toogie quipped.

"What book will we read?" Grace inquired.

"*Madame Bovary* by a guy named Gustave Flaubert," I declared.

"Oh, I've been thinking about rereading that one," Grace cooed.

Toogie and I just stared at each other.

I am presently about halfway through the book. It was a slow start at first, with all the peculiar names and writing style, but I'm picking up steam now—and so is Madame Bovary, to say the least. Emma (Madame) Bovary has dumped her physician husband, Charles, for this lawyer guy, Leon Dupuis. She then jilted Leon for another fellow, a rich dude named Rodolphe (unless it is a misspelling) Boulanger. The story is sort of *Desperate Housewives*, circa 1850.

One afternoon I declared, "I'm going to run a few errands," putting *Madame Bovary* aside.

Surprisingly, Aunt Toogie piped up, "I'll go with you, Dalton. Let me help," putting her copy on the coffee table.

"Hurry back," Grace responded. "We need to finish our books so we can share our thoughts."

Once we were in the car, Toogie asked, "You're going to Publix, right?"

"Yep."

"Good. I need a fix, too."

I immediately surmised her intent. We entered the store and both made a beeline to the checkout lane. She bought *Us* magazine, and I purchased the *National Examiner*. We took our goods to Blondie's Bagels and read them cover to cover over lattes and a cinnamon raisin bagel.

"Did you know Bono named his kid Elijah Bob Patricius Guggi Q?" Toogie scoffed. "Whatever happened to good old names like Bob, Jim, and Tom?"

"Look at this!" I exclaimed. "Elvis is alive and running a dry cleaner in northwest Oklahoma."

"I love this break, but we better get back before Grace becomes suspicious," Toogie advised.

We tossed our trash, bought some fresh vegetables at the farmers' market as our reason for being out in the first place, and drove home.

I am now sitting, again, with *Madame Bovary*. I'll just skim the rest of it. I think I've figured out this frolic through France. In the end, I'm pretty sure things will work out for Emma. What I really want to know is the full story about the remains of two space aliens and their aircraft, secretly hidden by the government in a hangar at Area 51 in the Nevada desert!

Toogie's Tag Sale

"WHY IS MY OLD BASEBALL mitt stacked in that pile of junk on the back porch?" I asked my lovely wife, Grace.

"It's not junk," she replied. "Aunt Toogie is collecting some household items for her garage sale."

"She's having a yard sale?"

"Garage sale, yard sale, whatever. The sale is on Saturday."

"Slow down here," I pleaded. "Toogie's having a garage sale, yard sale, or whatever at our house this Saturday?"

"Bingo!" Grace beamed as she prepared her homemade gazpacho.

I launched into a diatribe about how The Neighborhood Association, the ARB, or somebody needs to be consulted before one just goes and does something like this.

"Then I'd recommend you get involved to help her," Grace suggested. "Now, what were you saying about your old baseball glove?"

In contemplating the image of my eighty-year-old aunt running a flea market bazaar on the front lawn, I had momentarily forgotten about my ball mitt.

"Yeah," I sputtered. "It's mine, and I'm keeping it."

"Sort of like *Catcher in the Rye*?" Grace offered.

"No," I answered. "It's not a catcher's mitt. It's a fielder's glove."

"Whatever," Grace said softly after a pause. "I just wondered about your sudden interest in a battered piece of sports equipment because you never use it."

"Plus, it's an antique," I added.

"What's an antique?" Toogie barked as she shuffled into the kitchen and the conversation.

"Dalton was suggesting his old baseball glove might be an antique," Grace clarified.

"Bull-pucky!" Toogie scoffed. "It's no antique, but I'd say it qualifies as certifiable junk."

"There you have it, Dalton. Right from the expert," Grace smiled. "You were right when you said it was a junk pile."

"Expert...? Expert...in what?" I stammered.

Grace described how Toogie's cleaning, sorting, and simplifying phase had progressed into an interest in antiques and collectibles.

"There are big bucks in old and rare stuff," Toogie exclaimed.

"You ought to know. You're an antique yourself," I quipped.

"Dalton, that's not nice, and it's not correct either," Grace said while Toogie glared. She explained that, generally, items need to be at least one hundred years old to qualify as "antique," and there are other guidelines for specific items. For example, automobiles are considered antique at twenty-five years.

"This teak knife chest is an antique," Grace illustrated, pointing to one of a few family heirlooms Toogie brought from her former house.

"My Grandpa Leo made it," Toogie added proudly. "The antique catalog values one like it at well over a thousand dollars!"

"Toogie is considering selling these antiques to a dealer on King Street," Grace continued, "and she plans to sell the remaining items here this Saturday."

"I bet I make at least five hundred big ones," Toogie boasted. "I just wish I could find the rest of my teak collection. I swear I had more at one time, but I don't recall where I stored it."

Grace prolonged the antiquities lecture, noting that other terms, such as "vintage" and "classic" had unique meanings as well.

"So, would I be classic or vintage?" I inquired, preening just a tad.

"I'd say you are older than dirt," Toogie snorted.

Before I could retort to getting dissed by an eighty-year-old, Grace came to the rescue.

"Classic means timeless or enduring," she clarified. "A good example is the style of the original Corvette or Thunderbird. Vintage means old-fashioned, or from a particular year, like wine, or it can describe a unique characteristic such as fashion in the style of, say, Edith Head."

"So," she continued, "I'd say you are both classic and vintage, at least to me, dear."

"If you ask me, I'd say fogey or fossil fit him better," Toogie chimed in before I could thank Grace for the kind compliment.

"Dalton has offered to help with your garage sale," Grace announced to Toogie. I looked at Grace, wanting to say, *No, I didn't*, but I couldn't decline following her nice words. So, I just nodded in Toogie's direction.

"It's a tag sale, not a garage sale," Toogie declared.

"Whatever," Grace smiled. "But you can't sell the baseball glove. Dalton wants it. It has special memories, sort of a *Catcher in the Rye* thing."

Before I could correct her again about the fielder's glove, Toogie chirped, "Oh, I loved that book. Was that by Pierre Salinger?"

"Whatever," Grace sighed with exasperation. "After lunch, Dalton will check the attic for those missing teak pieces."

As Grace diced more vegetables for the gazpacho, I asked Toogie why she had this newfound interest in antiques, collectibles, and making money.

"To buy gasoline," she proclaimed. "Prices are going up so fast. We need to save around here and conserve our resources."

I nodded vigorously. "Now that's the first sensible thing you've said in a long while."

"Thank you, Methuselah," Toogie shot back.

We both began talking at once. I described how my last fill-up cost over forty dollars. Toogie recalled how her parents burned old furniture for warmth when times were tough. After we each finished, Grace looked up from the soup she was seasoning.

"That may explain the shortage of antiques on your side of the family, but I'd also like you two to consider this."

She pulled a calculator from the kitchen desk drawer. "Now, there are four quarts in a gallon, four cups in a quart, and eight ounces in a cup, right?"

Toogie and I nodded.

"That makes [punching of buttons] 128 ounces in a gallon. So, gasoline is selling at approximately two cents an ounce. The bottled water you drink, Toogie, looks like [more punching of buttons] it costs at least five cents an ounce. Dalton, your Grande Mocha from Starbucks [still more punching of buttons] works out to more than twenty cents an ounce."

Toogie and I just stared. Finally, I managed a weak, "So…?"

"I am concerned about gasoline prices. Don't get me wrong," Grace declared. "But if you want to easily save some money, you could start by drinking water from the tap and brewed coffee right here at home. Now, let's sit down together and try some of this homemade gazpacho. It's delicious, good for you, and much less expensive than driving to a restaurant and dining out."

The gazpacho was yummy. As I savored the blend of tang and spice, I thought about Grace's advice. There is wisdom in drinking and eating more at home. It promotes quality family time, saves gasoline money, and helps our country be a little less dependent on foreign oil. Grace is a smart cookie. I'll bet Grace could concoct a compelling case that it would be better to donate all of Toogie's stuff to a charity rather than to sit in the hot sun all day doing her tag sale. Then I could play golf on Saturday! I'll get Grace on it now.

Say What?

SETTING: WE FIND DALTON, HIS lovely wife, Grace, and his aunt, Toogie, sitting at the Williams' household kitchen table. The following is their verbatim conversation.

Grace: Look at this article in the newspaper. It says some researchers at the University of Maryland School of Medicine think there is biological evidence that women are more talkative than men. They reference a study claiming the average woman speaks about twenty thousand words a day while a man says around seven thousand words a day.

Toogie: How do they know that? Did somebody follow people around counting how many words they say?

Grace: It's crazy, and I, for one, don't believe it. Dalton, do you think women talk more than men?

Dalton: Maybe.

Grace: Oh, you wouldn't know. Plus, you can't hear. The article says women have a higher level of some protein…let's see here…called FOXP2…that they term the "language protein." Ever hear of FOXP2?

Dalton: Nope.

Grace: They studied four- and five-year-old children and found the girls had thirty percent more of this protein.

Toogie: And did the little girls talk more? Ever been in a daycare facility? All the kids are jabbering—the boys and the girls—most of the time.

Grace: Right. I don't remember Jane talking more than Matt when they were little. Matt may have started talking at an earlier age. Honey, remember how Matt would say, "Me do" for some activity he wanted to manage? And he was, what, maybe eighteen months old?

Dalton: Yep.

Grace: Anyway, Matt talked earlier than his sister, but he didn't talk more or less than she did at the same age. I drove carpool with those kids for years, and I don't think Jane said more than Matt, maybe even less. Although, when I had several of Jane's friends in the car, the girls probably did talk more—you know, feeding off one another.

Toogie: A group of girls can get chatty. My knitting group is that way at times. But I do remember my dad yelling at my friends and me once when we had a pajama party—I think today they call them sleepovers—at our house. We girls were up telling stories and giggling after midnight. Dad came downstairs in his nightshirt and told us to go to sleep or he'd take the other girls home and take me to the woodshed. Well, I'll tell you, we were quiet as church mice after that.

Grace: I had a similar experience with my dad. I was the cheerleader captain, and the other cheerleaders came to our house after a basketball game.

We just ate popcorn and drank sodas, but I guess we made too much noise. Dalton, did you ever have a pajama party or sleepover as a child?

Dalton: Nah.

Grace: So, this story reports that girls start off with better language skills than boys. I'll grant you that, but I don't think it is just at the onset. I'd say women have superior language skills overall compared to men, certainly when it comes to grammar.

Toogie: Remember the plumber we had a while ago, the one who talked about the backflow valve?

Grace (giggling): Yes, the one who had his pants so low you could see the top of his boxers?

Toogie (giggling, too): Yes, yes! Thank goodness it stopped there. Anyway, remember him saying, "They was a man over in Goose Creek whose backflow didn't work?"

Grace: Verb tense, subject-verb agreement... Don't they teach this stuff anymore? Don't get me started on pronouns. Every time I hear "me and him" did something, or "me and him" are going somewhere, I want to scream.

Toogie: It's like fingers on a blackboard.

Grace: While I'll admit that I hear some faulty grammar from women, but it seems to be more prevalent in men. That's just my opinion. Dalton, do any of the guys you play golf with use bad grammar?

Dalton: Some.

Toogie: My late husband, Harold, was a man of few words. He was a farmer and so spent a lot of time alone in the fields. I took care of the house.

Grace: There you go. You took care of the house and had to deal with the milkman, the postman, the neighbors who called, the preacher if he dropped by...

Toogie: I did that and more. Helped the vet with birthing calves, too. Harold didn't have the stomach for that.

Grace: Those things took conversation. Talking to the milkman, the postman, and the veterinarian. Why, that could add up to that...that... thirteen-thousand-word difference right there. (Grace sips her coffee.) Well, I'm glad we put that silly study to rest. (After a pause) Were you surprised that *Argo* won the best picture Oscar over *Lincoln*?

Toogie: Nothing coming out of Hollywood surprises me anymore. I think the whole scene is as political as it is artistic.

Grace: I was truly surprised by the best director award. I know Ang Lee is a talented director, but I thought Steven Spielberg would win. Have you seen *Life of Pi*?

Toogie: No, I started reading the book and put it down. I understand the visuals in the movie are spectacular.

Grace: They won Oscars for it. Let's go see it. Dalton, I know it may not be your cup of tea, but would you go see *Life of Pi* with Toogie and me?

Dalton: Okay.

Grace (rubbing her hands): Well, that was a nice chat we all just had. Now, what's on tap for everyone today?

WHO KNEW?

"BAG? I DON'T SEE ANY bag," I announced while peering all around the vacuum cleaner.

"Look inside the canister," my lovely wife, Grace, offered.

"There's a bag in there?"

"Yes, dear. Where did you think all the dirt went?"

Rubbing my chin, I mused, "I guess I never gave it much thought... So, how do you open this thing to get at the bag?"

"Give me strength," Grace sighed. "Better yet, would you please just get me a fresh ice pack and a glass of ginger ale—no ice?"

Grace is recuperating from an appendectomy (what the heck an appendix is, why we have one, and why it sometimes needs to be removed is an enigma even the sage Grace can't fully explain). She is feeling better each day thanks to the support of generous Daniel Island friends and some questionable assistance from the dysfunctional duo of yours truly and my Aunt Toogie. Grace's friends lavished her with cards, flowers, gifts, and enough delicious food to feed us through the hurricane season. Toogie not only advised Grace to "milk this for as long as possible," but also announced she would be in charge of protecting and allocating the many dishes that arrived at our doorstep, taking a particular fancy to a coconut cake baked by Grace's friend Gail. After every lunch or dinner, Toogie would inquire, "How about a little bite of a sweet?" The occasions when Grace demurred did not deter Toogie from helping herself to yet another slice of coconut cake or some other alluring confection.

Toogie and I took on the daily routines Grace generally handled such as the marketing, food serving and clean up, house cleaning, and laundering. We soon came to learn about other activities that we, heretofore, had no idea Grace managed or that needed attention. For example, early one morning, a gentleman arrived at the front door and explained he was here to tune the piano. Toogie gave him a good perusal but did not invite him past the threshold. I suspected he might be a cat burglar casing the joint. A quick check with Grace, convalescing in bed, cleared the stranger for entry.

"Certainly, you remember Mr. Miller," Grace declared.

"I had no idea Grace had a piano tuner!" Toogie remarked as she and I took a break from clearing the breakfast dishes.

"Who knew?" I added, blowing on a steaming cup of reheated coffee.

As Toogie and I struggled to keep up with the chores, Grace provided definitive coaching from her bedside command post. For example, "When you buy oatmeal, be sure to get Quaker Oats, and buy the one that says 'old fashioned.' The label is blue on top and red on the bottom. It is my favorite for both cooking a hot cereal and for baking cookies. Don't get the oatmeal labeled 'quick—one minute.' That one is red on top and blue on the bottom."

"I didn't know there were so many varieties of oatmeal," I remarked to Toogie as we searched the grocery store shelves for the proper product.

"Who knew?" Toogie replied, finally finding the elusive blue-over-red brand.

The most intricate and complex of all tasks, however, is laundry. The best analogy I can provide is that laundry is a lot like baseball. At first blush, baseball looks rather simple—hit the ball, run the bases. Yet, as we know, baseball has a myriad of intricate rules—fair and foul, strikes and balls, force out, hit by a pitch, sacrifice fly, and more. Laundry is just as complex!

Oh, it looks easy. Put the clothes in the washer, then into the dryer. But not so fast, Mr. Clean!

Washing

Rule 1 (Sorting): Be sure the clothes are sorted into three piles—whites, lights, and darks. Once you think you have that mastered, it turns out the "three piles" principle is modified by Rule 1A: Red is neither a "white, light, or dark" but is, in fact, an exclusive fourth color category. Witness Grace calling from the bedroom, "You didn't put the red kitchen towels in with the darks, did you?"

"Who knows this stuff?" I moaned to Toogie. "Where is it written?"

Toogie just tapped her forehead. "Right here," she replied, reaching over to snatch an ecru tee-shirt out of my "white" pile. This subtle reprimand prompted me to seek Grace's counsel on a few items close to the dividing line.

"I have a few items of laundry here that are questionable on the light-versus-dark scale. I'll hold them up, and you tell me whether they are light or dark."

"Oh, good heavens," Grace wailed, pulling back the blanket. "I'll do it. Give me the basket."

Shooting me a disdainful glance, Toogie coaxed Grace back to bed with an offer to fetch a piece of coconut cake.

"Watch closely," Toogie huffed, peering at me over the laundry basket. She reached in and took out two items. "This is light," she declared, shaking the garment in her left hand. "And this is dark!" she sputtered, waving another one in her right hand.

I wanted to tell her that the blouse she identified as "light" was, very possibly, a borderline "dark," but I refrained and trudged back to the laundry room and set about dividing the dirty laundry, attempting to combine Toogie's tutelage with the wisdom of Solomon. Sorting laundry may sound simple, but it's no piece of coconut cake! Try the following test. Consider these shades of green: lime, emerald, pear, asparagus, loden, chartreuse, hunter, olive, shamrock, jade, celadon, moss, tea, Persian, myrtle, and Charleston. Now *you* correctly sort those babies between "light" and "dark!"

Rule 2 (Pilling): Some garments need to be turned inside out before washing to avoid "pilling" (whatever the heck pilling is). This is not a further modification of Rules 1 and 1A (and, consequently, does not necessitate more than the aforementioned three or four "piles") but can be accomplished as the presorted clothes are put into the washer. Identifying the clothes needing to be turned inside out is still a mystery to me. Unfortunately, they are not labeled "Warning: Men, turn this garment inside out before washing!" That would be too easy. One must learn these secrets through trial and error. Who knew?

Rule 3 (Detergent): Oops! I screwed up already! Rule 2 above is actually Rule 3. The correct Rule 2 is: Always put the soap in the washer before the clothes. That is "always" as in "*always*," not "sometimes" or "when I remember." Otherwise, soap residue on "darks" is a telltale sign that may cause the "umpire" to charge you with an error.

Rule 4 (Settings): Set the dials for everything from load size to water temperature to type of fabric. Perhaps only my friend Bob, a former airline pilot, could fathom the complexity of such a control panel. If a setting is not properly activated, the machine responds with a loud, beeping alarm.

"Don't forget to set the type of spin cycle," Grace will holler, somehow deciphering which setting is out of whack just by the pitch of the beep.

Who knew?

Drying

It would seem that drying should not be as difficult as washing. Au contraire.

Rule 1 (Air Dry): Some items, while soaking wet, do not go into the dryer at all, even though they would be dry within minutes. These items (lingerie, delicate fabrics, jeans) are hung on hangers, rods, or door and cabinet knobs and every other protruding object all over the laundry room (which soon takes on the look of a Marrakech bazaar) where they will then hang for hours to dry. Much like Rule 2 of washing, the clothes have no visible tags or markings indicating whether they should be directed to the dryer or toward the closest doorknob. Devoid of this knowledge, apparently clandestinely passed from generation to generation of experienced dryer masters, the novice is left to fend for himself.

Rule 2 (Loading): While all the towels in a bathroom can be washed in one large load, they must be separated into two smaller loads for drying for them to "fluff up." This is the "infield fly rule" of laundry. Why one load to wash and two loads to dry? I can't describe it. Which explains why I overlooked it and put all the wet towels into the dryer.

"You didn't put those towels in all at once, did you?" a voice behind me asked softly.

I turned to face Grace.

"Why are you up...here?" I stammered. "You need your rest."

"I need to move around a bit," she replied, opening the dryer door and removing a mound of towels. "You and Toogie have worked so hard. I'll finish this. Why don't you take a rest?"

Like a baseball manager removing a rookie pitcher from the game, the message was clear: Take a shower, kid. Better luck next time.

I trudged downstairs to the kitchen. Toogie was seated at the table working on a crossword puzzle.

"I think I'll have a glass of iced tea and a piece of coconut cake," I sighed.

"Cake's gone," Toogie barked without looking up from her work.

"Gone?" I answered.

"Yep, yesterday. Every last crumb."

I slumped into a chair across from Toogie, closed my eyes, imagined the taste of that coconut cake, and thought, *Who knew?*

I'll Drink to That

A BLOG POST (DALTON IS TECH-SAVVY) at *townandcountrymag.com* reports an amazing and inviting scientific finding: Drinking three glasses of champagne every day may help prevent the onset of dementia and Alzheimer's. Professor Jeremy Spencer (tip of the glass to this guy!) and a team at Reading University (a property in Monopoly, I think) carried out experiments on rats. The good professor described the results as "dramatic."

This news could not come to the Williams' household at a better time. Here are two reasons why. First, we are rapidly approaching the holiday party season when my lovely wife, Grace, reminds me not to "overserve" myself. Now I can comfortably assure her that those extra glasses of bubbly are my contribution to medical research. Second, Professor Spencer's breakthrough holds out the hope that champagne may one day replace "you know what" as the de rigueur superfood. Yes, say it with me...kale.

The first time, several years ago, that Grace plopped some kale on a plate in our household, I stared at the pile of greenish-purple plant life and quipped, "Is this food for humans or rabbits?"

"Nobody likes a smart aleck," she replied. "Try it. It's good for you."

I have come to learn that "It's good for you" also translates to "It doesn't taste good," and bitter kale fits this axiom perfectly. I poked with my fork at the strange leaves. They looked vaguely familiar. Where had I seen them? Then it hit me. Years before, I saw this in a supermarket produce department. It was the stuff used to separate fruits and vegetables from one another. Now the store uses a green plastic divider that looks a lot like what was now sitting on my plate. "Aha!" I declared, holding a kale leaf up on the end of my fork.

"Do you have something to share with the table?" Grace stated. "And don't play with your food!"

I sputtered out my recollection of kale's former use as a display item rather than a food source.

"Whatever," Grace retorted, dismissing my observation. "Kale has oodles of vitamins. So, eat up."

"You know," my Aunt Toogie piped up, "Dalton's right. My brother, Orville, worked at Piggly Wiggly, and they used kale, or some kind of cabbage, to display produce."

While Toogie normally sides with Grace in family discussions, I sensed she was with me on this one based on her expression following a first taste of kale. Seizing that advantage, I pressed on, offering a proposition that, when plastic display material was introduced, farmers and grocers conspired to do a brand makeover on an otherwise excess byproduct. The result was the new trendy superfood, kale!

"It's possible," Toogie interjected. "Orville said they used to just throw it away when it went bad. Nobody ate it."

"How would they know if it was bad?" I shot back. "It's already purple."

"Maybe by the odor after—"

"Enough!" Grace interrupted. "Everyone knows that dark-colored foods are nutritious and high in antioxidants." When neither Toogie nor I responded, Grace added, "Such as blueberries and these leafy greens."

"How about licorice?" I asked. "It's dark."

Before Grace could reply, Toogie giggled, "Remember Chuckles, the candy with five flavored gummy chews? I used to love the licorice one."

"You are in great shape for your age," I proclaimed. "So, Grace must be correct about dark foods. By the way, the licorice Chuckle was on the far right, wasn't it?"

"Nah, it was in the middle," Toogie barked.

"Bet you it was on the right."

"What's the bet?"

"Loser has to eat the winner's kale?" I suggested.

"You are going down," Toogie boasted, reaching for her cell phone. "Let me Google Chuckles."

A moment later, she exclaimed, "Yeah, baby!" and thrust the phone at me. The screen displayed a photo of Chuckles with licorice smack in the middle of a line of five colored treats.

"Here you go, health boy!" she chortled, sliding her plate of unfinished kale toward me.

"Laugh if you will," Grace sighed. "If you want to learn something useful, Google the vitamin contents of kale."

A short time later, Toogie reported, "Score one for Grace. Looks like kale is high in vitamins A, C, and K. Especially K. One serving of kale has nearly 700 percent of your daily recommended amount of vitamin K."

Toogie peered at my plate and added, "Or around 1,400 percent for a double-dose like Dalton has."

Grace smiled. Toogie grinned. Finally, I asked, "Excuse me, but doesn't vitamin K help with blood clotting?"

"Yep," Toogie answered.

"I'm no doctor," I continued, "but it strikes me that if one ate a serving or two of kale every day, eventually their blood would have a consistency somewhere between strawberry preserves and spackle."

"That does it!" Grace declared, setting down her silverware. "I'm just trying to serve healthy meals here. So, I'll make you a wager. You find a food as healthy as kale, and I'll serve it."

Which brings us back to the present and my newfound hero, Professor Jeremy Spencer. He and his team conducting their study on the salutary benefits of champagne "now hope to move on to trials involving pensioners."

Sign me up! Heck, move the entire experiment to Daniel Island! It's full of retirees. I'll bet a bunch of them would be glad to guzzle champagne for the good of medical research. We will welcome Professor Spencer and his colleagues with open arms, hoisted flutes, and nary a leaf of kale.

A Wii Bit More or Less

PRESENTING A BELT TO ME, my lovely wife, Grace, declared, "Now, see if it fits."

Threading the gift through the belt loops of my trousers, I sucked in my stomach and prayed it would gird my girth. This wasn't any off-the-rack belt, mind you. It was a needlepoint creation in a monogrammed golf motif design painstakingly made by Grace. She had been working on this belt at her "stitch and (you-know-what)" group gatherings off and on for several years. Unfortunately, during that span, I had been gaining waistline faster than Grace had been needlepointing. Fastening the buckle prong into the last opening on the far end of the belt, I proclaimed, "A perfect fit!"

Grace circled me, inspecting the belt. Occasionally, she would tug on the belt or my britches.

"Not an inch to spare," she mused. "Good thing I stitched the entire length of the pattern."

"I'll lose some weight," I offered.

Rather than calling me out for a pledge unfulfilled in the past, Grace replied encouragingly, "You can do most anything if you put your mind to it, dear."

Folding her arms and standing back, she added, "Pretty darn fine job of petit point if I do say so myself."

"Yep," I answered.

"Do you like it?"

"Sure do."

"Right answer," Grace smiled.

My Aunt Toogie ambled into the kitchen to join us.

"How do you like Dalton's new belt?" Grace inquired.

Toogie peered at me as I executed a pirouette to provide a 360-degree view.

"I'd say," Toogie grumbled, "too little belt…or too much Dalton!"

"Grace made it," I chimed in, hoping to steer Toogie away from a comment that could hurt Grace's feelings.

"I know that," Toogie barked. "She's been working on it for years. Exquisite work."

Grace smiled as Toogie added, "But on Dalton, it's, well, a wee bit like Godiva chocolate on Brussels sprouts."

Grace put her hand over her mouth to hide a grin.

"Oh, by the way," Toogie continued, "the gals in my bridge group are coming for bowling this afternoon. I'll need a couple bottles of chardonnay, Dalton. Nothing fancy. I'll pay you back."

"You're taking wine to the bowling alley?" I chuckled.

"No, Mr. GQ," she shot back. "Wii bowling. In the family room."

"We are bowling? In the family room?"

"Not you. My bridge group," Toogie sighed. "But it is Wii. In the family room."

Puzzled, I turned to Grace.

"I think you two are having a 'heated agreement,'" she chuckled. "Dalton, you are hearing the word 'we,' the plural first-person pronoun, while Toogie is referring to 'Wii,' the interactive video game. Isn't that correct?"

While I was still trying to translate Grace's grammar lesson, Toogie answered, "*Oui!*"

After a while, I caught up with the conversation. "Oh, the Nintendo video game. I've seen that on television. Kids love it, and people at old folks' homes play it."

Toogie shot me a glare as Grace piped up, "Toogie's bridge group played here last week. Some of them are quite good. It looks fun."

"We have only seven players," Toogie responded. "Would one of you care to join us? It would even out the teams."

"Oh, I'd like to, but I volunteered to tutor at the school today," Grace answered.

Toogie's eyes turned slowly to me.

"I used to be a pretty hot bowler back in my heyday," I offered.

"I'll bet you were," Toogie scoffed. "Well, go put some wax on your flat-top, Elvis, because the girls will be here in twenty minutes."

Once the bridge club arrived, Toogie poured wine. She had comman-deered a few bottles of Rombauer chardonnay from my wine cooler. If that was her idea of "nothing fancy," I made a note to find out what her definition of "fancy" was. Eventually, the group settled in the family room, although there was no settling in the decibels of chatter. Toogie divided the group into two teams of four. I was assigned to "bat leadoff" for one team while she did the same for the other. She gave me a quick primer about the buttons on the Wii remote and strapped it to my wrist. She had made little characters, called Miis, for each person. Each Mii bore a likeness to its respective player. Mine had gray hair and an exaggerated nose, but I let it pass. It was time to bowl. I stepped forward with my left foot, then the right, and (I thought) released the virtual bowling ball. Nothing happened on the television screen as the room filled with giggles.

"You released the button too soon," Toogie growled.

I set up to bowl again. Same result. More giggles. On the third attempt, I stumbled, lurched forward, and swooped my right hand toward the tele-vision. A bowling ball suddenly appeared on the screen, headed—oh, no!—toward the right gutter. Mercifully, it clipped the last pin on the right side. I recalibrated my positioning for the next attempt. The shot started off okay but then drifted left, finally knocking down three more pins. My first frame score totaled four. A major embarrassment.

Now, it was Toogie's turn. She swung her right arm back, then forward, and the screen displayed a ball headed, like my first shot, to the right.

"Too bad," I mumbled.

Just then, her ball on the screen made an abrupt left-hand turn intersecting the pins between what I now know to be the number one and three pins. It was a masterful shot. All ten pins exploded backward at once. A strike!

In the next frame, I scored eight, leaving the dreaded 7-10 split on my first shot and then sending the second ball right between the two remaining standing pins. Humiliating.

"Field goal," muttered a lady seated on the couch with a walker positioned before her.

Toogie knocked down nine pins with her first ball in the second frame. As her second shot arced toward the remaining pin, she turned her back to the television and deftly kicked back one foot just as the ball collided with the pin.

Walker Lady chirped, "Nice pick-up!"

When the match finished, I had bowled a dismal 119. Not my best effort, to say the least. Plus, it was the lowest score of the eight of us in the family room. The closest score to mine was 164 by a lady who kept remarking that she was releasing the ball "a few boards off her mark," whatever that means. Walker Lady, who bowled seated on a chair, scored 191 yet seemed a tad disappointed with her performance. Toogie topped the pack, closing with a turkey (three strikes in a row, which she also did in the middle of her game) for 244.

After the gang departed, I helped Toogie clean up, paying particular attention to salvaging any Rombauer still in the bottle.

"How did you get so good at Wii bowling?" I asked as Toogie loaded the dishwasher with wine glasses.

"Practice."

"Really?"

"Yeah," Toogie replied, looking up. "You can do most anything if you put your mind to it."

I pondered the familiar refrain for a moment and then mused, "I think I'll practice Wii bowling."

"I've got a better idea," she offered.

"What?"

"I also have a game disc called Wii Fit. It's the latest in fitness videos. Give it a try."

"Will it help with my bowling?" I asked.

"Probably not," Toogie quipped. "But it will help you with that belt."

INSTANT REPLAY

SHORTLY AFTER THE REFEREES HUDDLED to determine whether Kansas City quarterback Pat Mahomes had crossed the goal line, my lovely wife, Grace, and Aunt Toogie also crossed the line. They had joined me in the den for the only football game the two of them watch each year, the Super Bowl. They may have been modestly motivated to partake in the annual sports spectacular by the batch of margaritas I blended to accompany the game-time snacks. Truth be told, they were more interested in the commercials than the game. Their favorite was the heartfelt Anheuser-Busch advertisement featuring a young Clydesdale. I had actually been invited by a buddy, nicknamed the Rat Man, to watch the extravaganza with a group of guys at a sports bar. After recalling sports bars can be a bit rowdy, with too much whooping and hollering for my taste, I decided to enjoy the game in the quiet and comfort of my own Barcalounger.

"Why has the game stopped?" Grace asked.

I replied the referees were conducting a replay.

As the network showed the play in question again in slow-motion, Toogie declared, "Look, the Chiefs scored again."

"No, dear," Grace replied. "Dalton says the referees let the Chiefs take the play over again."

"No, it's neither of those," I interjected.

"I thought you said it was a replay," Grace countered.

"It is an instant replay," I sighed, realizing the conversation was approaching the point of a potential "wind it up" moment. Whenever I describe something in too much depth, such as a shot-by-shot golf round recap, Grace will mimic a glassy-eyed stare and rotate her right wrist in a clockwise circle, indicating the "wind it up" signal to bring the story to a rapid close. Ignoring the risk of her impending gesture, I launched into a full explanation of the NFL's instant replay rule. One coach can challenge a play by tossing a red flag onto the field, and officials on the field then consult with other officials who view slow-motion videos of the play from several camera angles. The team requesting the replay is not charged with a time-out—in essence, receiving a reward—if their challenge is sustained.

Surprisingly, Grace and Toogie seemed to still be engaged.

"You mean," Grace mused, "one team can call on these referees to review a play that already occurred?"

"Yes."

"Then these special officials look back to sort out truth from fiction?"

"I guess you could say that."

"Both teams have to live with the judges' ruling?"

"You got it, honey."

Grace slapped her knee and turned toward Toogie.

"That's what we need around here," she yelped. "An instant replay!"

"You go, girl!" Toogie chimed in, nodding vigorously.

I had no clue what was going on.

"Remember," Grace announced, looking at Toogie but pointing at me, "the day Dalton couldn't find his glasses?"

"That happens every day," Toogie chortled.

"I know, but I mean the day before yesterday. I told him his glasses were on the kitchen counter."

"Oh, yeah. I remember," Toogie answered, giving me no room to join the conversation.

"Yet," Grace continued, now talking faster, louder, and in a higher pitch, "ten minutes later, he asked me again about the glasses."

"Yep."

"And then, he denied he had asked me in the first place and couldn't recall I had just told him."

"You betcha!"

"I'd say it was time for an instant replay to prove my point!" Grace squealed.

"Touchdown!" Toogie yelled, raising both arms. She and Grace then high-fived each other.

"What are you two hens clucking about?" I inquired, turning up the volume on the television to compete with their cacophony.

"See what I mean? Replay time!" Grace shouted.

"Penalty!" Toogie giggled, tossing a cocktail napkin onto the floor.

The two of them burst into laughter, followed by hand-slapping that resembled a game of patty cake. Wiping tears from her cheek, Toogie stood, hands on her waist, and assumed a stern countenance.

"After reviewing the play," she bellowed, while Grace chuckled, "the offensive one here was dead wrong! He was previously told where his glasses were. So, the other team is awarded…a new pair of Jimmy Choo shoes!"

A new wave of uproarious guffaws followed, accompanied by the tossing of sofa pillows. The belly-laughs continued for a full five minutes. As the tumult subsided, I turned and gestured with the remote in their direction. "What was all that about?"

Grace looked up and began to reply but could only sputter a single word: "Replay."

This set off another round of giggling and gasping for air.

"Oh, make yourself useful," Toogie cackled. "Fix us another batch of margaritas."

"Make them big ones," Grace snickered. "After all, it is the Super Bowl!"

This produced still more chortles and wheezes.

I thought the frivolity had run its course until midway through the fourth quarter. Grace inquired about the yellow first-down line shown prominently throughout the game.

I explained it was not a real line on the actual field but was digitally created for television. Believing my illumination had sufficed, I was unprepared for the blitz that followed.

"We need one of those, too!" Grace hollered.

"Git 'er done!" Toogie whooped.

Then both of them stood and began to shout out commentary while motioning, with a sweep of an arm, toward an imaginary line on the floor.

"Don't cross this line, big boy!"

"This is my side of the bathroom. Keep your wet feet off, buster!"

"Stay on your side of the bed, darling."

Soon they were laughing and crying uncontrollably again.

"Oh, stop. You're killing me," Grace moaned holding up both palms.

"My sides hurt," Toogie said, bending at the waist.

With a final exchange of high-fives, they fell onto the couch and giggled and wiped their eyes until they fell silent.

The game ended soon after this outburst. As we cleaned dishes and glasses, Grace sighed, "I can't recall the last time I had so much fun and laughed so hard. Thanks for inviting us, Dalton."

"Me, too," chipped in Toogie. "We'll have to do this again at next year's Super Bowl."

I smiled but didn't reply. Imagining myself as the game MVP who pumps a fist and announces he is going to Disney, I made a silent pledge to watch next year's game in a more tranquil setting. I'm going to the sports bar with the Rat Man!

RAISIN' CAIN

"A RE YOU COMING TO BED?" my lovely wife, Grace, asked.

"No. I'm going to watch the game."

"Wasn't there a game last night and the night before that?" she inquired.

"Yes," I explained. "First, there were the playoffs, then the league championships, and now the World Series. You know how I love baseball." I continued. "National pastime, 'Take Me Out to the Ball Game,' peanuts and cracker jacks, and all that."

"Okay, suit yourself," Grace replied. "But, speaking of peanuts, keep your hands out of the candy bowl. I'm taking it to my Women Who Wine night."

The contents of the candy bowl were Grace's concoction of dry, roasted peanuts and candy corn. A mouthful tastes just like a certain candy bar. Grace likes to have guests attempt to 'name that taste.' Most nod in recognition, eyes gazing upward, trying to place the flavors, but few correctly identify the mystery mixture as identical in flavor to that of a PayDay candy bar (Try it yourself).

"Don't blame me," I pleaded. "Aunt Toogie ate most of it."

"I swear," Grace sighed, arms folded, "you and Toogie are going to eat all the sweets before Halloween."

The week before, we had made our annual trek to stock up on Halloween goodies. Grace and I look forward to doling delights to trick-or-treaters, especially the wee ones.

I quickly snatched up bags of "the good stuff," such as Snickers, Skittles, M&M's, Tootsie Rolls, Hershey's, and Goo Goo Clusters. As I dumped my armload of treasures into the shopping cart, I noticed several bags of itty-bitty boxes of raisins.

"What are these?" I questioned.

Grace looked up but did not respond.

"No kid wants those," I announced. "They're lower on the Halloween food chain than Necco Wafers. We don't want to be known as raisin-givers!"

"Well, I think they are tasty," Grace declared. "Plus, they are good for you."

In the checkout line, the young man bagging our purchases picked up a bag of raisin boxes. He looked at me and raised his eyebrows. I immediately picked up on the male-to-male, nonverbal communication. He was silently asking, *Dude, are you, like, serious about these raisins for Halloween?* I tilted my head ever so slightly to the left, toward Grace: *Not me, pal. It was her idea.* He smiled and nodded only a fraction of an inch: *I smell ya, dog!*

"Looks like you're all set for Halloween," he said as he put the last bag in our cart. "Me and my buddies are going out if I don't have to work."

I cocked my head and replied, "Really?"

On the drive home, I asked Grace, "Did you hear that kid at Publix say he was going out for Halloween?"

"Yes, dear. He seemed like a nice young man, though he does need to work on his grammar."

"That's my point. He is a man. He must be over six feet tall. He shouldn't be trick-or-treating!"

"I didn't know there was a height limit."

"Well, there should be an age limit!" I shot back. "Plus, the big kids always grab the best candy. It's the little ones who appreciate whatever you give them."

"Well, then," Grace offered, "we can give candy to the big kids and raisins to the little ones."

"No," I retorted, "I'm saving those raisins for any kid taller than I am. That will teach them a lesson. You can't pretend to be a kid forever."

As we finished dinner the night before Halloween, Aunt Toogie asked, "Who'd like a piece of chocolate?" This is female-code-speak for: *I'd like some chocolate.* It is similar to Grace asking me, "How would you like to drive to Atlanta?" This means: *I want to go to Nordstrom.*

"If you two keep nibbling sweets like this, we won't have enough for tomorrow," Grace responded. "How about a nice box of raisins?"

Toogie gave Grace an *Are you nutty?* look, then ambled into the pantry and helped herself to a Mr. Goodbar with a Mallo Cup chaser.

On the big night (All Hallows' Eve), we took our positions in the foyer. My job was to give out the treats while Grace cooed over the costumes, particularly those worn by the littlest ones. This was Toogie's first time at bat, so to speak, and she put her chair right by the front door to get a good view of the parade of youngsters. I had sorted the treats into two bowls—a larger one full of candy for the tiny tykes and a smaller one containing the raisin packets that I intended for the too-tall tricksters. At the appointed time, the street was instantly full of costumed creatures. It was as if they had been hiding in the bushes waiting for the witching hour. There were princesses, pirates, pumpkins, an assortment of men (bat, spider, and super), witches, Draculas (or is it Draculae?), ninjas—everything from members of the Addams Family to Zorro. As soon as the first gaggle of goblins hit the front porch, Toogie stepped in to pinch-hit and took over my task of distributing the delights. She dispensed treats with dialogue. When a big kid asked for a certain candy bar, as in "I'll take a Butterfinger," Toogie responded with something such as, "Take a Kit Kat. They're great—or better yet, try both." To the little ones, she would grab an assortment and chronicle each candy as she filled their bag. "Here is a Reese's, with peanut butter and chocolate—very good—and a Heath bar—watch out when you bite, the center is hard, and a Baby Ruth, one of my favorites." We were quickly running out of stuff—at least the good stuff.

95

"Push the raisins," I whispered, "especially to the big kids."

"Back off, Andrew Weil," Toogie barked. "No kids want that crap for Halloween!"

Soon, we were down to a mere handful of candy bars, though still armed with an ample allotment of raisins.

"I need to make a candy run back to Publix," I announced.

"Pick up some Almond Joys," Toogie chimed in. "I've had a hankering for one all night."

I sped to the store, parked at the curb near the door, and raced inside to the candy aisle. The shelf where the candy had been stocked was empty; not a bag nor bar in sight. I ran up and down aisles until I found a clerk.

"Do you have any Halloween candy?" I pleaded.

"Up-front on a table," he replied, pulling back to get out of my path.

I trotted to the front of the store, out of breath. There on a table sat all that was left of the Halloween stock: a lone bag of Mike and Ike, a bag of Skittles, and a couple of dozen bags of boxed raisins. Then it hit me—there are full-sized candy items in the checkout lanes. I grabbed a cart and rushed to the first lane and began scooping up stuff: Twizzlers, Bubble Yum, Starburst, and Nerds. I proceeded to the next lane and squeezed behind a lady in line. She seemed a tad annoyed when I reached past her ankle to grab PayDays and Boston Baked Beans. I also scooped up 3 Musketeers, Life Savers, Mounds, and Nestle Crunch. Scooting to the last lane, I snatched up Jolly Ranchers, a couple of Almond Joys for Toogie, Zagnuts, Charleston Chews, and York Peppermint Patties. As the clerk totaled my tally, I noticed he was the same young man who had bagged my first round of Halloween candy purchases.

He lifted his eyebrows, which I realized was his way of asking, *Did you do the raisins, dude?* I shook my head back a couple of times: *Nope, I'm no raisin-giver.* He smiled and tipped a finger to the bill of an imaginary cap: *I'm reading your book, man!*

I handed him a Zagnut in appreciation and dashed to the car.

When I returned, Toogie was still positioned at the foyer door. The large bowl was empty; the small one remained full of raisins.

"Looks like I'm here just in time," I wheezed.

"Don't sweat it. I'm doing fine," Toogie smiled. "I've been giving them some of that baseball stuff."

"What baseball stuff?"

"Those old cards in the cabinet. Hey, where's my Almond Joy?"

"*My baseball cards*?!" I bellowed. "You've been giving them my *baseball cards*?!"

"What's all the fuss?" Grace called out from the kitchen.

"She's been giving away my baseball cards," I cried out. "I had Mickey Mantle, Ted Williams, and a Satchel Paige."

"Oh, those cards weren't all that great," Toogie interjected. "Some of the small kids chose the raisins over the faded cards. And the big kids preferred the baseballs."

"*Baseballs!*" I gasped. "You gave away my *autographed baseballs*? Say it ain't so!"

I lowered my head and moaned. "Ernie Banks, Hank Aaron, Derek Jeter, Harmon Killabrew…gone…*all gone.*"

"I'm sorry, honey," Grace consoled. "Toogie was only trying to be nice to the children."

"It was my baseball treasure," I wailed.

"If you ask me," Toogie spoke up, "aren't you a little old for that stuff?"

I looked up, dumbfounded.

"I mean, shouldn't there be an age limit?" Toogie continued. "After all, you can't pretend to be a kid forever."

Later that sad evening, I crawled into bed.

"I'm sorry about what happened tonight," Grace said, patting my arm.

I lay silently in a fetal position.

"You'll feel better in the morning. I'll make you a nice breakfast," she added, turning out the light.

Lying in the dark, I heard a voice from out of left field whisper, "If you ask her, she will answer." It prompted me to inquire, "What are you planning for breakfast?"

I think I might have heard a tiny chuckle before she replied, "I was thinking a big bowl of Raisin Bran will lift your spirits."

OTHER STORIES: PART I

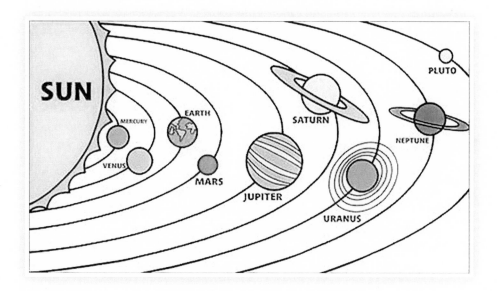

Pluto, You're Fired!

[Story from 2006]

A S YOU PROBABLY HAVE READ, the International Astronomical Union (not the punk-rock band of the same name, but a band of scientists who met in Prague last week) voted to establish a new classification of planetary bodies. While the rest of the world focuses on mundane stuff, such as war, hurricanes, and the new baby-to-be for Britney Spears, the IAU debated the galactic question of whether Pluto should be counted as a full-bodied planet. These IAU space cadets ruled that the first eight planets in order of distance from the sun are the only members of the solar system worthy of the title "planet." Pluto (number nine in the old batting order) is now a member of a new category called "dwarf planets." To add to the confusion, the IAU included two additional dwarf planets and tens of thousands (but, hey, who's counting?) of objects termed "smaller solar system bodies."

So, how many planets are there? Eight? Eleven? Thousands? Apparently, the answer is no longer nine as we were taught in school. What a kick in the asteroid! Most of all, I feel poorly for Pluto. Okay, so it is smaller, its orbit isn't as circular, and it takes longer to orbit the sun compared to the remaining eight planets, but we can surmise what happened. Good old Steady-Eddy Pluto, not bothering anyone, just plodding along, the tortoise in a galaxy of hares. Then, *bam!* Another victim of corporate downsizing! Some terrestrial Titan higher up the constellation chain decides nine planets are too many; eight is all the budget can support. Who gets the ax? You got it. They drop a dime on Mr. Out-Of-Sight, Out-Of-Mind Pluto. Works hard all its existence. Never complains. Next thing it knows, it is demoted down the planetary org chart! Clean out the corner office, which is reserved for planets, the solar system big shots, and take a cubical in the dwarf planet bullpen. Sayonara, Pluto.

The two new dwarf planets joining Pluto on the minor league roster are Ceres (in the asteroid belt between Mars and Jupiter, which, I believe, is where the extension of I-526 is planned to be built) and UB313 (nicknamed Xena). I don't understand how UB313 received this designation when neither U2 nor BR549 got even an honorable mention! However, if I were UB313, I wouldn't take a victory lap just yet. It is located further from the sun than Pluto, and we all know its fate. Watch your back, UB. It is a planet-eat-planet galaxy out there!

In order to support the status of the eight planets, the IAU cosmos cops adopted a definition of a planet. A planet now must (1) be big and round, (2) not be surrounded by objects of similar size, and (3) orbit a star (in our solar system, the sun). Hmm. Wait a minute! That must make me a planet. I'm round, surrounded by objects (my lovely wife, Grace, Aunt Toogie, and our dog, Buddy) that are not my size, and orbit a star—Grace. So, heads up, IAU. I'm clearing out my cubical and moving up to the corner office.

All this change will play havoc within our schools, which will need to replace textbooks and those mobile models that hang from the ceiling in science classrooms (as required by the "no planet left behind" legislation). Further, teachers will need to revise the acronym we all memorized to recite the order and names of the former nine planets. You may recall: My Very Educated Mother Just Showed Us Nine Planets. What's it going to be now? I offer the following: For the eight planets: My Very Enlarged Momma Just

Squarshed Uncle Ned. For the combination of planets and dwarf planets: My Very Eccentric Mama, Choke, Just Swallowed Undercooked Northern Pike, Upchuck!

Scientists anticipate the discovery of even more dwarf planets in outer space...the final frontier...strange new worlds...new life and new civilizations...where no man has gone before. This will open up a whole universe of new possibilities. For example:

> I suspect the good people at Disney will not be content with just Pluto being the only dwarf planet. Mickey, Donald, Cinderella, Goofy, Pooh, Stanley, Ariel, Stitch, and especially the *seven dwarfs* (Hello, IAU!) are all as deserving as Pluto.

> I can foresee the Daniel Island Real Estate agency announcing that, as construction on Daniel Island nears completion, it will begin work on a newly planned community to be built on Ceres. "It is out of this world!" should be the selling slogan or neighborhood motto.

In the meantime, and before we revise all those textbooks for our schoolchildren, I for one would like to see the IAU stargazers also give us a ruling on the proper pronunciation of the seventh planet. You guys know the one I mean.

DALTON'S LETTER TO PRINCE CHARLES

[Written in 2005]

H.R.H. Charles the Prince of Wales
Buckingham Palace
London, England

Your Royal Highness,

HEARTIEST CONGRATULATIONS, OLD BOY, ON your engagement to Ms. Parker-Bowles. Smashing, frightfully smashing! Contemporaneously, I did take note of the fact that 8 April (the big day) is mere weeks away. I say, you must be up to your ears in planning, scheduling arrangements, and what all. My lovely wife, Grace, has been helping our daughter, Jane, plan her upcoming nuptials. The two of them have done a splendid job, but this has been an ongoing endeavor beginning from the time of Eric's proposal last year and stretching over a period of months—what with invitations, wedding and reception sites, the ceremony, dresses and shoes, menu, seating arrangements, flowers, music, the nuptial program, photography, and my, so much more! The very thought of you trying to pull it all off in a few fortnights, and during the height of polo season in Palm Beach, no less; well, it tires the old noodle, now, doesn't it?

But you, sir, are in luck. While my part in the aforementioned Williams' wedding planning has been restricted to the role of a non-voting member of the finance committee, I have been keenly observant at other weddings and stand ready to share a few nuggets of sage advice, to wit.

First, keep in mind that despite all the hustle and bustle, the wedding is fundamentally for only two people—the bride and her mother. Speaking of the mother, I've seen lots of photos and telly footage of you with Camilla's mum. When do we get to see the pretty bride? I'm sure we will at the wedding. Note to your social secretary: Did our invitation get lost in the post? Anyhoo, Camilla and her mum will have oodles of options and queries. Your job is to try your very princely best to refrain from offering an opinion, and certainly never a contrary one. A simple rejoinder to their suggestions, such as, "I'm all ears," will serve you well. Also tell your mum and the Duke of Edinburgh, or Daddy, whichever you call him, to keep it mum if you know wha-eye mean.

One masterful response you may wish to borrow from our future son-in-law, Eric, is this. When asked his thoughts during the earliest stages of wedding planning regarding the font on the invitations, in addition to eggshell or ecru for the parchment color, the prelude etudes, and the reception canapés to be passed, he brilliantly replied, "All I ask is, at the end of the day, I am married to Jane." Smart chap, Eric!

Another key issue to address timely is the matter and manner of registering for wedding gifts at places such as Pottery Barn, Crate & Barrel, and Target. These all have computerized registry systems, which may present a small problem because, strictly speaking, you don't have a surname. I'm not sure the dastardly systems will take "House of Windsor" or "Prince of Wales" as a last name. "Windsor-Mountbatten" may pose a problem with the hyphenation. "Windsor" would probably work, but I'd suggest, for the sake of simplicity, "Prince" as a first name and "Charles" as the last name.

For Ms. Parker-Bowles, the hyphenation may be an issue as well, and I doubt the computers will accept "Her Royal Highness the Duchess of Cornwall." I would drop the "Parker" and go with just "Bowles" for the last name. Hint: Fondue is experiencing a revival in popularity, and Crate & Barrel is offering in its spring catalog an intriguing one in royal blue.

Next, there is the bachelor party to consider. The gang of groomsmen may be anticipating grouse hunting at Balmoral Castle. Forget about it! There will be plenty of time for grousing after you are married. May I suggest a place many people over here, across the pond, go for a bachelor party? Myrtle Beach! It is sort of like the Cote d'Azur, but with more beer and barbeques. But regardless of what you do or where you go, do not, I repeat, *do not* see the movie *Sideways*.

As you likely know, the groom's family arranges the rehearsal dinner. You might have been thinking of sailing the *Royal Yacht Britannia* up and down the Thames, but frankly, that is so yesterday. Plus, everybody sails yachts on the Thames for the rehearsal dinner. Could I suggest an activity whereby The House of Windsor might mingle with the masses? It could provide a positive gesture toward restoring the public image of the Royal Family. How about riding the big Ferris wheel right there in London? Or go bowling. I assume Camilla Parker bowls.

If ordering a wedding cake is a problem due to such short notice, a recent trend here in the States has been to have the cake made of Krispy Kreme doughnuts. Quick, easy to serve, decorative, and tasty, too. You just might be able to save a few quid on such a large order.

The band or DJ will surely request songs you wish to have performed during the reception. The little princess may well ask for your input, and some direction from you is entirely appropriate here.

May I suggest: "Macarena," "Twist and Shout," "Y.M.C.A.," "Joy to the World (Jeremiah was a bullfrog)," the "Bird Song" (Chicken Dance), and "The Bride Cuts the Cake" (to the tune of "The Farmer in the Dell"). I guarantee your guests will be talking about the festivities for years to come.

Finally, the honeymoon planning is also a groom's responsibility. Many here in the States choose to visit a foreign location, but with you being foreign already, perhaps you should venture here. Gatlinburg is a very popular honeymoon destination. But ring up for reservations soon—it is nearing high season, and the suites with the heart-shaped beds are always the first to be booked. Same for Branson. Alternatively, I suggest you bring the missus here to Charleston. Not only is it known as the friendliest, most hospitable city in America, but it was also once called Charles Towne (for English royalty, no less) and is home to seasonally spectacular stands of camellias. It is truly *the* place for you two lovebirds. You can stay in our FROG (our finished room over our garage). We will stock up on loose Earl Grey tea, jars of orange marmalade, and Devonshire cream and toast you each morning with English muffins. I assure you it will be a honeymoon not to be forgotten.

Well, cheery-o! Ring us up if you wish to visit. For now, Grace and I extend our very best wishes.

Yours most respectfully,

Dalton Williams

MOTHER'S DAY

WHEN ANNA JARVIS CONCEIVED THE notion of and then trademarked Mother's Day, she was specific about the placement of the apostrophe. The singular possessive emphasized that each family honor its mother. So, I wish to reflect a bit about my mother and share some of her story.

She was born in Birmingham, Alabama, ninety-three years ago and has, consequently, lived through the great depression, seen wars (hot and cold) come and go, reared children, fawned over grandchildren and great-grandchildren, and cooked and served more holiday meals than one can count. I mention her age because she is no longer sensitive about its disclosure. Nurses, doctors, and acquaintances are frequently amazed to learn her true age and often remark something such as, "I would have guessed you were in your seventies." Ah, wouldn't it be great to look, feel, and behave twenty years younger than you are?

Mom grew up in a model middle-class family—certainly not well-off but too proud and hardworking to be poor. Church and education were fundamental pillars of her upbringing. In second grade, she was chosen as May Queen at school. We recently enlarged and colorized the original photograph of the smiling little girl with a crown and scepter for her birthday and to share with family.

After graduation from college, she became a teacher in a one-room (grades one through eight) school in rural Alabama. Her love of teaching and children has continued throughout her life. She taught kindergarten for twenty-five years in an Ohio town. When she retired, the city recognized it as her "Day," and many of her former students returned to honor her as she received the key to the city.

She loved and was married to my dad for nearly sixty years. Their engagement was announced in the local Birmingham newspaper on December 7th, 1941. Events of that day caused them to hasten their wedding plans, and they were married a mere two weeks later, just days before he shipped out to Army active duty. They shared a wealth of common interests—gardening, golf, literature, and community theater. Dad acted. Mom designed the costumes and won awards for her creations. They and a handful of friends founded a small repertory theater company that continues to thrive today in the North Carolina town to which they retired. Their portraits hang in the lobby of the theater house as a tribute to their efforts.

Her gentle demeanor belies a strong will. As my father was transferred from post to post during World War II, Mom followed, often driving (before interstate highways) the family and belongings across the country. Career opportunities continued to move the family to Texas, California, Minnesota, Maryland, Ohio, and North Carolina. Recently, she became a bit of a hero among her lady friends at the retirement community where she lives. When a male resident tried to bully her to give up a scheduled home cleaning appointment time that he wanted, she stood her ground. Privately, she says she would have gladly changed appointment times "had only he asked in a kindly manner, bless his heart."

Today, Mom lives comfortably a few hours north of Charleston. She continues to volunteer her time to arts groups and collects pottery and handmade quilts (including some of her own creations). Ever fashion-conscious, she is always dressed as if on the verge of heading out to fine dining. Jewelry, perky hairdo, and brightly colored ensembles enhance her flair. She has a wonderful circle of friends, reads avidly, and plays a mean game of bridge. Her bridge group plays for small change (dimes and quarters), but you better bring a pocketful if you take her on. She enjoys time with family, and yes, we are visiting for Mother's Day. During visits, she often remarks, "I'm so lucky," referring to her family, friends, and surroundings. We, however, are the truly lucky ones to have enjoyed and hopefully absorbed some of the glow of her grace.

More compelling than the "what" about her life is "how" she lives every day focused on being positive and optimistic. I'm sure she has aches, pains, and setbacks. She doesn't deny these. Rather, she consciously chooses to emphasize the good in people and the world around her. I suspect her positive attitude plays a large part in her mental and physical condition, both of which are exceptional for someone her age.

She would say what she does, and how she does it, is "nothing special." I admire her humble modesty, but I'm not buying it. She is extraordinary and unique. To me, she will always be that special queen with a crown, smile, and scepter, but of course, you'd expect me to say that—she's my mom!

So, today, as Grace and I treat her to flowers and dinner (It is the number-one eating-out day of the year, you know), may you have a wonderful time remembering and honoring an extraordinary and unique person in your life—your mother.

Happy Mother's Day, Mom!

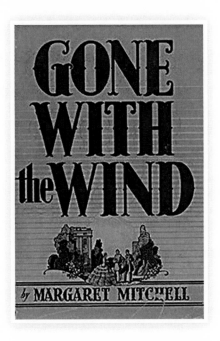

Two-Minute Gone With the Wind

A RECENT NEWSPAPER ARTICLE REPORTED A new trend in book publishing. Consumers, it seems, favor books that can be read in a few hours—two hundred pages being a good target length. This is no surprise. We have moved well beyond the television age when all problems of the protagonists were solved in a half-hour sitcom (actually, twenty-two minutes sans commercials) and into the even faster-paced era of blogs, instant messaging, tweets, and text talk. O, lol if u will, but u no it's so!

In such a world, only a few will find time to leisurely enjoy one of the many great, classic books. Those tomes will become "no more than a dream remembered…gone with the wind." For the rapid-reading pleasure of you multitaskers out there, here is a two-minute drill through Margaret Mitchell's 1,037-page epoch of the old South, *Gone with the Wind*.

The story opens at the family plantation, Tara. The heroine, Scarlett O'Hara, is simultaneously flirting with two young men. Fiddle-dee-dee, can that girl flirt! Mitchell describes Scarlett as a belle, although we had a different name for girls like her in my day. Soon Scarlett is belle-ing her bonnet off at a barbeque at the Wilkes plantation, Twelve Oaks (Mitchell does not reveal whether the barbeque is vinegar, mustard, or tomato-based, possibly fearing that doing so might make the book too long). While playing belle to a bevy of beaus, Scarlett secretly harbors a hankerin' for the Wilkes lad, Ashley. But, great balls of fire, Ashley is asking for the hand of his cousin, Melanie (the book is silent about the legality, let alone the wisdom, of such a union).

While the girls take an afternoon nap (apparently, a belle custom), Scarlett sneaks away and eavesdrops on the gentlemen conversing about the possibility of a war with the "Yankees." Most of the guys are certain the coming confrontation will be short and sweet for the South. One remarks, "One of us is worth ten Yankees. Heck, even the Cleveland Indians beat 'em last year." Only the handsome, debonair, smooth-talking Rhett Butler demurs. Being from Charleston, which explains the handsome, debonair, and smooth-talking part, Rhett has an inkling this notion of swiftly defeating a much larger, better-financed northern force may be a few hush puppies short of a seafood platter.

Scarlett reveals to Ashley her love for him in the library (fans of the board game, Clue, take note) but is rebuffed. The war begins, and the boys enlist to go off and fight. Charles Hamilton asks Scarlett to marry him, and she agrees, believing this will make Ashley jealous. In a double-wedding ceremony (presumably to save money and pages in the book), Scarlett marries Charles, and Ashley marries Melanie. Unfortunately for Scarlett (but luckily for the ensuing story), Charles soon succumbs to pneumonia (poignantly croaking decades before flu shots). Scarlett moves to Atlanta to wait out the war with Melanie and her Aunt Pittypat. Rhett, also in Atlanta, hangs out at a brothel with a proprietress named, naturally, Belle. At a charity ball for the war effort, Butler bids $150 for a dance with Scarlett, reinforcing what a belle she really is. The debonair and handsome Rhett tells Scarlett she should be "kissed and often, by someone who knows how." Fiddle-dee-dee, what a smooth-talker!

Sherman is laying waste to Atlanta, proving what can happen when too many people from Ohio are allowed into a Southern town. As Atlanta burns, Melanie goes into labor. Scarlett and Prissy deliver the baby—a boy, whom Melanie names Beau. Rhett arrives with a horse and carriage to help them escape to Tara, where Scarlett discovers the old homestead has lost its grandeur and her old man has lost his marbles. All this drives Scarlett to vegetarianism as she plucks tubers from the soil, declaring, "I will never be hungry again!"

[The movie version has an intermission at this point. If you need to toity or want to grab a cold one, this would be the time.]

As we return to the old South, we find Scarlett laboring, picking cotton, in the fields of Tara to support her daddy. As is fully revealed later, it is really Scarlett for whom the "belle toils." The war has ended, another championship for the Yankees. Ashley returns from the war, and Scarlett resumes her quest for his affection. Yankee carpetbaggers and southern scalawags (remember to keep these straight for the final exam) have raised the taxes on Tara to $300. Scarlett decides to return to Atlanta and ask Rhett for $300, believing the surest way to a man's wallet is to gussie up in a gown made from draperies. Butler doesn't fall for the old curtain caper (He is way too debonair) and smooth-talks her with the money-is-hidden-in-Europe line. So, ever the belle, Scarlett marries Frank Kennedy for $300.

Scarlett and Ashley start a lumber business. On her way to the mill one day, she is accosted by hobos (inasmuch as Mitchell died tragically in 1949, we will never know if this may be a typographical error and the author intended for Scarlett to be attacked by lobos) and is saved by Big Sam. Frank and Ashley pursue the miscreants into the woods, only to have Frank killed by gunshot and Ashley wounded. Noticing that Scarlett is now, conveniently, unattached once more, Rhett proposes marriage. Despite her zero-for-two track record in the husband department and the torch she still carries for Ashley, Scarlett says yes. They travel on a grand honeymoon to New Orleans (Charleston would have been way nicer), build a mansion in Atlanta (Charleston would have been way nicer), and have a baby girl— Bonnie Blue Butler.

The Butlers become just another jolly, post-war family. Rhett gets drunk. They separate. He takes Bonnie to London (Charleston would have been way nicer). The child hates London, so he returns her to Scarlett, who announces she is pregnant. Both Rhett and Scarlett agree they don't want another baby. After he opines that she might "have an accident," she then does, falling down the stairs and losing the baby. This light-hearted segment is capped off when little Bonnie dies in a horse-riding accident (Her granddaddy

O'Hara died in an eerily similar manner, although the heredity angle is left unexplored).

Melanie becomes ill. As Melanie dies, Scarlett suddenly realizes that she didn't love Ashley after all but indeed loves Rhett. Mind you, we are now one thousand pages deep into the book when Mitchell has Scarlett do a one-eighty on a major plot point (possibly the impetus for the line, "I can't think about that right now. If I do, I'll go crazy."). Scarlett rushes home to tell Rhett the good (she thinks) news. He, however, is too savvy (as well as debonair and handsome) and tells her he is going away to—you guessed it—Charleston. "Where shall I go? What shall I do?" she pleads, to which he delivers his best smooth-talking retort, "Frankly, my dear, I don't give a damn."

Down but never out, Scarlett vows to return to Tara to orchestrate a Belle-ish plan to woo back Butler, setting the stage for the book's undeniable and timeless killer closing line (one can only imagine Mitchell struggling to hold this back for 1,036 pages), "After all, tomorrow is another day."

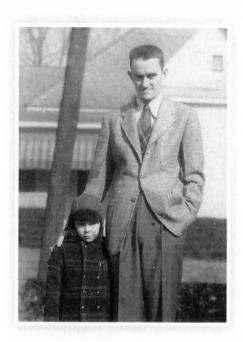

A FATHER'S DAY REMEMBERED

THE DOCTORS SAID THERE WAS nothing more that could be done beyond very extraordinary measures. After a series of physical setbacks, his frail body was shutting down in the summer of his eighty-seventh year. His desire was for no further treatments, and hard as it was, the family was now asked to respect that wish.

Plus, there was a gut-wrenching irony to add to all the heartache. It was Father's Day. All his children and grandchildren had gathered at his hospital bedside. In the middle of the celebration, he announced he was tired. Moving a last gift aside, saying it would be opened later, he closed his eyes....

He was born in Birmingham, Alabama, in 1914 and was the youngest of five children. Because he crawled around the floor as a baby, he was given the nickname "Bug," and he remained "Bug" to his siblings throughout his life. His mother died while he was young, and he was then raised by his sisters, who doted on him. He learned to read at an early age and thrived in school. Like many of the era, he was the first family member to go to college—earning a PhD to boot—and working nights at a steel mill to pay for tuition. It was the beginning of a life-long passion for reading, education, and learning.

He courted my mother, wooing her with his wit and tenacity. They married well. Their nearly sixty-year marriage was a partnership of affection, friendship, and common interests. Again, like so many of his generation, he went off to World War II and never complained about the effort or years required to serve his country. After that, he worked hard to provide his family a life with fewer wants than he had known growing up.

"Don't let him die on Father's Day," I prayed and then felt selfish. This was a man who had so often given so much of his time to others; now, it was my time to want what was best for him. During the night, I held his hand and talked to him. I'm not sure if he heard my words, but I told him the things in my heart: "I love you, Dad. You are the best husband, father, and grandfather, and we all want you to be at peace."

I listened to his breathing. Slowly, the breathing and pulse became more and more shallow. At one point, I couldn't tell if the pulse I was feeling was his or my own. His breathing failed and resumed several times; each time, the sudden quiet was as startling as a clap of thunder....

In the last year of his life, he had begun to write an autobiography. He was able to complete only the childhood years. I'm glad he wrote about that since it was the time of his life about which we knew the least. He wrote about trips to the library, Zane Grey stories, riding on a train for the first time, and barefoot summers. Borrowing from Dickens, he introduced it as the best of times and a tale of cities, family, friends, with "more memories than I can describe in words."

Now, I can describe my many memories of my father in words such as humorous, witty, smart, inquisitive, thoughtful, dedicated, proud, honest, open, optimistic, supportive, encouraging, caring, and most of all, loving— in so many ways. Love for my mother, the love of his life. He was never too shy to say, "I love you, darling" to my mother or my lovely wife, Grace, or to offer an "I love you" to family or friends. He made love so easy to return. Love of people and love of life—always zestful, sometimes even zany.

He enjoyed reading; he had a love of words and crossword puzzles, poetry, and the arts—in particular, theater. He acted in Little Theater groups all his adult life. He relished comedic roles and had a hambone as large as his funny bone. With his arms wide, he would mimic a slapstick comedian: "Good evening, Ladies and Germs. I just flew in from (some city, say, Cleveland), and, boy, are my arms tired!" While actually modest about his accomplishments, he did relish being on stage. Perhaps it was the product of being a center of attention as the baby of the family. He also performed more serious roles and once had the lead as Norman Thayer in *On Golden Pond*. My mother said he was perfect for the part. He said he wasn't sure whether that was a compliment or a complaint, but we think he enjoyed the rare opportunity to be the crank.

At 4:30 on that morning following Father's Day, he gently stopped breathing. I patted his hand for a long time and then kissed the top of his head. I can still smell the sweetness of his hair. I am not sure whether God heard my wish that he not die on Father's Day, but I do believe that He plays favorites. After all, despite having a PGA pro for a grandson, it is my father who is still the only family member to boast a hole-in-one.

Two unusual incidents occurred that same dark morning. It had been a week of hot weather, with temperatures near 100 degrees, and the nights were warm and muggy. Yet my mother and Grace, who were in separate locations, each reported abruptly feeling the presence of an unusually cold draft. And my brother, some miles away, woke up sharply and recalled looking at the clock. It was 4:30 a.m.

Each day, I feel lucky to have been blessed with such a fabulous father. I miss him and think of him often, certainly on Father's Day, but also when I attend a theater production, see a father and child playing, catch a chilly breeze, or glance at a clock and notice the time is 4:30. And, I imagine those strange occurrences on the morning of his passing were signs of the actor making his exit, leaving the audience wanting an encore. I can envision him even now, calling out with gusto, "Good evening, angels. I just flew in from Earth, and my arms aren't tired anymore…."

Happy Father's Day, Dad!

SOLAR ECLIPSE

LET'S GET ASTROPHYSICAL

[Written at the time of the August 21st, 2017
total solar eclipse in Charleston]

"SEE THE REFLECTION OF LIGHT?" I inquired, beginning my presentation. "Now, imagine it is the sun."

My Aunt Toogie had asked about the impending solar eclipse, and I offered to give a demonstration as she and my lovely wife, Grace, gathered in the kitchen late one afternoon. I pulled the blinds to dim the room and shined a flashlight at the refrigerator, producing a circle of light on the shiny metal door.

"That circle of light is the sun," I restated.

"Why wouldn't the flashlight be the sun?" Grace asked.

"No, the image on the fridge is the sun," I explained one more time. "We are where the flashlight is."

"I'm just saying that the flashlight looks more like the sun than the fridge does," Grace replied.

"Grace is right," Toogie declared. "The flashlight should definitely be the sun."

I exhaled slowly, sensing we were off to a bad start.

"Okay, have it your way," I conceded, recalibrating my presentation. "We will make the flashlight the sun, and we are on the fridge."

"We don't mind being on the refrigerator, dear," Grace offered, trying to be helpful.

"Dalton looks like he hasn't strayed too far from the fridge," Toogie chuckled.

Ignoring her comment, I began anew, holding the flashlight in my right hand at shoulder height.

"So, we now have this flashlight representing the sun."

"Better," Grace smiled.

I continued. "Even though that circle of light on the refrigerator door looks a lot like the sun to me, it will, for our purposes, represent light shining down on us from the sun."

"Which is the flashlight," Grace added, reinforcing what was now obvious.

I looked at Toogie to ascertain that she was following the lesson so far. When she realized I was seeking a response, she muttered, "Whatever."

"Now," I proffered, holding an apple in my left hand, "this apple represents the moon."

"Excuse me," Grace interjected. "That apple isn't completely round like the moon." She looked toward Toogie for support that was as sure to come as sunset.

"Yeah," Toogie chortled. "Your apple is sort of lumpy. I think a grape would be a good moon."

"Too small!" I shot back.

"But the moon is small in comparison to the earth," Grace observed, pointing correctly at the refrigerator. When I failed to respond, she offered, "How about an orange, dear? An orange is round and looks like a full harvest moon."

"Oh," Toogie sighed. "Harold and I used to love to sit on the back porch and look at a full moon."

"Okay! Okay," I hollered. "We'll use an orange!"

"Dalton!" Grace spoke up. "Toogie and I are just trying to help you with your little science project."

I put the apple back into the fruit bowl and retrieved an orange. After a deep breath, I said, "This orange is our moon."

"Pretty big for a moon," Toogie huffed, to which I did not respond.

"I agree," Grace replied softly as she patted Toogie's hand. "Let's allow him to finish so we won't have to hold dinner."

"Now," I continued, "as we know, the moon circles the earth." To emphasize this fact, I rotated the orange in a circular motion.

"Wait a minute," Grace interrupted. "That's the moon in your left hand?"

I nodded and Grace continued, "And the flashlight in your right hand is the sun?"

When I nodded again, Grace concluded, "Pardon me for saying so, but it looks like you have the moon circling next to the sun."

"Yeah, Copernicus," Toogie piped up. "The orange needs to circle around the refrigerator."

"In real life it does!" I sputtered.

Sensing my exasperation, Grace offered, "Would it help then if we held the orange since we are closer to the refrigerator?"

"No," I sighed. "I need the moon, I mean, the orange so that I can have it block out the light from the flashlight, or sun, when the moon—the orange—passes between the sun—the flashlight—and the refrigerator—which is the earth."

Toogie leaned toward Grace and remarked in a stage whisper, "I don't think he's going to get a very good grade on this science project."

Undaunted, I proceeded. "Watch what happens to that reflection on the fridge."

As I slowly moved the orange in front of the flashlight, the circle of light on the refrigerator slowly disappeared until it was fully blotted out.

"Voila!" I declared, triumphantly. "That, folks, is a total eclipse of the sun!"

"Total eclipse of the sun," Toogie mused slowly. "Aren't those lyrics from some song?"

"'You're So Vain,'" Grace piped up. "By Carly Simon. Some people think she was describing Warren Beatty."

"I thought it was David Bowie," Toogie replied.

"Ladies, please!" I interrupted. "We are talking about a major astrological event here."

"He means astronomical," Grace whispered.

"We'll experience some really cool, amazing things," I declared. "For example, we will see a 360-degree sunset."

When they did not respond, I pointed toward the kitchen baseboards. "In every direction. North, South, East, West. Sunset all around."

"It would have helped if you had baseboard lighting," Toogie offered.

Grace covered her mouth to hide a chuckle.

"When the sun is fully covered," I explained, "we will see stars like we do at night."

"Point your flashlight at the ceiling," Grace suggested.

Dutifully, I did, and Toogie quipped, "Looks a lot like the sun to me."

"Wait," Grace declared, opening a cabinet drawer. She retrieved a metal colander and held it over the flashlight, producing a sky of stars on the ceiling.

Continuing the lesson, I revealed, "When it gets dark, the temperature will drop by ten to fifteen degrees."

"I got this one," Toogie declared, opening the refrigerator door.

"Now for the final act," I proclaimed. "If you will close the refrigerator door, I will display how the moon traverses its path, and the sun will reappear."

"I think we get it," Grace injected. "Plus, it's dinner time." Ever mindful of my efforts, she added, "That was a wonderful astronomy presentation, sweetheart."

Grace and Toogie clapped politely as I turned off the flashlight and returned the orange to the fruit basket.

"How about a drink?" Grace inquired. "Maybe a Blue Moon beer with a slice of orange?" She leaned closer, smiled, and cooed, "Have I told you lately that I love you more than the flashlight, the orange, and the colander?"

It took a moment for the translation to sink in. I smiled back at her and reflected on the fact that I am the luckiest guy in the universe.

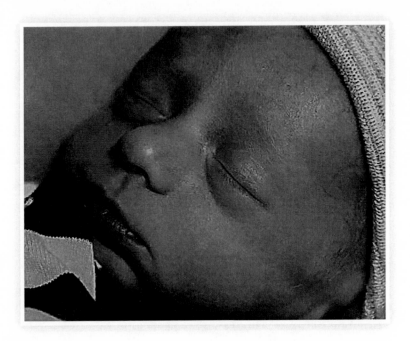

A Letter to Grandson Charlie

Dear Charlie,

GOOD THINGS DO INDEED COME in small packages. Apparently eager to delight our lives, you arrived a month early last week. The doctors and nurses say you were small—three pounds and thirteen ounces—yet you courageously endured many challenges these past two months. You are a handsome lad, a miracle, and a blessing to behold.

Much of the warmth surrounding you is the product of prayers so many have offered on your behalf. With Mom and Dad leading the way, relatives—from great-grandparents to young cousins—have been pulling for you and welcome you with open arms and loving smiles. Other friends, some of whom you may never even meet, have provided prayerful wishes for your safe delivery and good health. While you may fit in the palm of a single hand today, know that many, many hands prepared for your arrival and stand ready to support, guide, and love you.

A wonderful life awaits you. Family and friends will treasure and celebrate each milestone and memory of you. Your first step, a first word, the first day of school, first date, first job. So, stay clean and be ready to smile whenever Mom and Dad grab a camera to capture these tender moments.

Your given name is Charles Harward, names from your two grandfathers. Pop Pop is proud and thankful to share one of those names with you. You will learn at a fairly young age that you will be addressed as "Charles Harward" only when you are in some form of trouble and with your last named added when you are in big trouble. You will also soon learn that grandparents are the ones with whom you can be silly (They are prone to acting that way often in the presence of grandchildren), arrive with toys and gifts, and are most likely to answer "yes" (as in response to, "May we have ice cream for breakfast?"). Handling temper tantrums and scolding are left to Mom and Dad. Grandparents have graduated from those tasks and now realize that "diaper" spelled backward is "repaid." Grandparents will, however, offer advice. In this category, they apparently believe it is better to give than to receive. So, here goes:

➢ Be kind and respectful to Mom and Dad. There may come a time when you believe they "don't get it." Pop Pop recalls thinking that about your great-grandfather a couple of times, and as hard as it may be to imagine, suspects your dad even thought that way about me on rare occasions. We can assure you that Mom and Dad always adore you and want only the best for you.

➢ Share your sweet heart. Everyone appreciates a kind word and helping hand. When you "do good" for others, you will "get good" in return.

➢ Be careful what you throw in the toilet. An item may appear to go bye-bye, but the plumber always finds it.

➢ Take the high road. Give others the benefit of the doubt. Forgive and forget. Keep doors open; you never know when you may want to pass through them again.

➢ Pursue big dreams. When it comes to your ambitions and goals, don't leave any "change on the table." Do bold things and do them enthusiastically.

➢ Don't pull a dog's tail or ears. It may bite. Same with siblings and cousins.

- ➢ Try again. No one does everything right every time. Find the lesson in every experience. Remember, the stars shine brightest when the sky is darkest. Pick yourself up and keep going.
- ➢ Decide to be positive, optimistic, and happy. You will more fully enjoy each day, and others will want to share your good nature. This attitude will also help you over the occasional speed bumps in life.
- ➢ Take time to savor each day. Life is a marathon, not a sprint. Don't hurry through childhood. Play until you drop. Be a kid.
- ➢ Green vegetables are better for you than they look. But hot biscuits with rolled Amish butter and sourwood honey? That's eating!
- ➢ Have fun and laugh often—the sillier, the better, but never at another's expense. Healthy laughter is sweet music to the soul.
- ➢ Relish simple gifts. Bigger isn't always better. Although you were small when born, hundreds of hearts overflowed with joy.
- ➢ Be kind and respectful to elders, such as occasionally conceding a "putt outside the leather" and explaining how new technological gadgets work. Remember, these folks paved the roads you travel.
- ➢ Actively listen. You can learn far more by carefully listening than by doing all the talking.
- ➢ Show gratitude and give thanks—to God who cares for you, to family and friends who love you, and for all the wonders surrounding you.
- ➢ Love books and learning. A passion for education is a magic carpet to a world of adventures.
- ➢ Do things right, but always do the right things.
- ➢ Keep and honor your good name. Your family delivered it to you with pride and respect. Hold it high, enhance it, and pass it on to your children.

So, little Charlie, we welcome you to a life filled with promise and pleasure, to parents who will nurture and love you every day of your life, and to a family overjoyed to have you in our midst. The celebration continues. With your arrival, we have won the heavenly lottery!

Love, dear grandson,
Mimi and Pop Pop

A MONKEY'S UNCLE SAM

WHILE PORTIONS OF OUR FEDERAL government are focusing on matters such as turmoil and bloodshed in the Middle East and scary threats of foreign viruses, it is comforting to know that other parts of our vast Washington bureaucracy are doing what they do so well—wasting money. Take, for example, the National Institute of Health. In a report published recently by *The Washington Times*, the NIH spent over $3 million on a study to determine the effects of excessive alcohol on monkeys. Apparently, researchers at the Oregon Health & Science University, fueled by a grant from the good old NIH, have been forcing monkeys to imbibe with reckless abandon so that researchers can then ascertain the impacts on the little imps.

I'm slightly sheepish to admit it, but the after-effects of a losing bout with John Barleycorn is a topic about which I know a fair amount. I can inform the NIH of these consequences and do so in as much color commentary as they desire. This should allow the NIH to promptly wrap up this time-consuming and costly endeavor. My lovely wife, Grace, advises I "zip it" on this subject, but my sense of patriotism commands that I do my part for my country. After all, the folks at NIH and OHSU could have easily garnered this same insight just by going to Columbia or Clemson on Saturday night after a home football game or by strolling up and down upper King Street on any weekend evening.

So, here is my top ten list of what they will learn:

1. Many of the monkeys will start dancing, not just a casual tripping the light fantastic but a frenetic, gyrating boogie with arms flailing and legs swaying, with no regard to the space inhabited by the other frolicking monkeys. Introducing recorded music will magnify this behavior.
2. Groups of female monkeys will congregate and attempt to perform synchronized dance moves albeit without much success and with excessive giggling.
3. Many of the male monkeys will become overly amorous and, as they imbibe more, become totally infatuated with every female monkey within eyesight.
4. All the monkeys will begin to communicate louder, faster, and at a higher pitch.
5. Skirmishes, particularly among the males, will occur—often over trivial matters. Yet, amazingly, these same males will often be seen hugging one another and grinning shortly after a confrontation.
6. Female monkeys will be more prone to primping and fluffing their hair and mussing up the hair of male monkeys.
7. Frequent mood changes, such as oscillating between anger and joy or between laughing and crying, will occur among many monkeys.
8. Male monkeys will be prone to sharing exaggerated recollections of sporting feats and romantic exploits, attempting reckless physical stunts, and blowing stuff up with fireworks.
9. In the late hours following a drinking binge, the monkeys will ravenously devour junk food and then pass out.
10. Don't get me started regarding bathroom etiquette or, more precisely, the appalling lack thereof.

There you go, NIH. You can cross the sotted simian study off your to-do list and free up money to be spent on the things we are accustomed to seeing funded from our taxpayer money. You know, lavish office parties, international travel, and aid to countries that hate us—the usual stuff. Although I did note another interesting study funded by you wild and crazy guys at NIH. That one was research on heated marital arguments where a researcher reportedly told *HHS HealthBeat* that "marriages that were the happiest were the ones in which the wives were able to calm down quickly during marital conflict." Well, on that front, let me tell you—oops, I think I hear my lovely wife, Grace, calling—gotta go.

BREVARD

Gentleman

THE GENTLEMAN CALLER

"**D**ALTON, COME TO BED," MY lovely wife, Grace, called.

"It's past eleven," I replied. "She's never up this late."

"She's not a child, honey," Grace answered. "You'll embarrass them and us if you're caught standing at the front door when they return."

I was in the foyer, having paced from the living room one more time to peer out the doorway for signs of approaching headlights.

My anxiety had been building ever since Aunt Toogie casually mentioned a few nights ago that she had an upcoming dinner engagement.

"This Saturday night, isn't it?" Grace inquired.

"Yep."

"With who?" I asked.

"A friend, and it's *whom*, not who," Toogie corrected.

"Do I know her?"

"I don't think so. My friend is a he, not a she."

"Just the two of you?" I interjected.

"Yep, and he has excellent night vision," Toogie shot back, "in case you were wondering."

"A gentlemen caller," Grace gushed. "I think it is sweet."

"What's his name?" I asked.

"Brevard."

"What's his first name?" I continued.

"That is his first name," Toogie snapped. "What is this—twenty questions?"

Grace cooed, "Brevard. What a nice, solid name."

It turns out Brevard's last name is the same as a familiar street in downtown Charleston, a sure sign his roots are deep and his people haven't strayed far from the peninsula. Toogie met him at bridge club. He is a widower, lives in a large, historic house downtown, has family who now live "off," drives a little silver convertible sports car, and is reputed to have a small fortune as well as a healthy mane of white hair. His dinner invitation was to one of Charleston's finest restaurants. Grace had coaxed these nuggets of intelligence from Toogie. After I was let in on the secret, Grace wanted to talk about little else.

"It's charming that he's taking Toogie out like this," Grace mused.

"I'm not so sure," I countered.

"What do you mean?"

"Well, you know how frisky men can sometimes be when they are alone with a woman."

"Since when? Were you that way with me?"

"No. I mean other men."

"You mean you didn't feel a little frisky?"

"Yes. No. I mean, I don't know. I'm just a tad wary."

"Well," Grace countered, "I'm more optimistic and believe it will be an enjoyable, companionable evening for both Toogie and Brevard."

On the day of the "big dinner," Grace busied herself tidying the house and arranging flowers in advance of Brevard's arrival. The premises would have passed a rigorous military inspection. She prepared "just a couple snacks" that could have passed for a full dinner in my book. I was instructed to clean up and put on something "nicer." Shortly before the appointed hour, Grace cloistered herself in Toogie's room, like girls meeting up on prom night, to help her get ready. I thought I heard them giggling. Right on time,

Brevard blew in. Bedecked in a seersucker suit and dashing, multi-colored bowtie, he sported a hearty mane of white hair to go with his full set of natural teeth and apparently superb night vision.

"It is such a pleas-ah to make yo-ah acquaintance," Brevard soothed as he glided into the foyer.

Toogie and Grace seemed overly charmed as the small talk ensued. Meanwhile, I maintained my caution. Brevard described Grace's hors d'oeuvres as an "absolute culinary experience." After he and Toogie departed for dinner, I remarked, "Shoot, I forgot to ask what time they would return home."

"This is certainly a flashback moment," Grace announced.

"What?"

"You're treating her like an adolescent."

"Am not."

"Are too. Just as if she were a teenage daughter. Are you going to ground her if she has a cocktail or stays out late?" Grace snickered.

Yes, perhaps a curfew, I thought, gazing out the window into the darkness once again for signs of his sports car, Brevard the beguiler, and Aunt Toogie. I should have insisted on a curfew before they left. To pass the time, I went to the refrigerator, seeking two old friends I consult in such times of stress—Ben & Jerry. Polishing off a second helping of Phish Food, I heard the front door open and close.

"Toogie, is that you?" I called out casually.

"Who were you expecting, Madonna?" Toogie answered as she entered the kitchen. "And why are you still up? It's past eleven. You're never up this late."

"Oh, I couldn't sleep," I replied. "I was just reading."

"Sure," countered Toogie. "Reading ice cream cartons always helps me sleep."

"Hey," I sputtered as Toogie started up the stairs. "Did you have a good time?"

"Yep."

"Did you go anywhere after dinner?"

"Yep."

"Where?"

"Just out."

"What did you do?"

"Nothing."

"Nothing?" I asked, looking up the stairwell to see her leaning over the banister peering back down at me. The scene gave me a strange feeling of deja vu.

"Yep. Nothing," Toogie answered. Then she smiled, waved, and I swear she whispered "Goodnight, Daddy" before disappearing into her room.

Brevard Does it This Way

"**B**REVARD MAKES THE BEST COSMOPOLITANS," Aunt Toogie gushed.

My lovely wife, Grace, cooed in response, "Oh, do tell us how you mix them, Brevard."

With that, His Highness stepped forward, removed the ice bucket from my hand, and began to pontificate. You may recall Brevard, Toogie's friend. It would be fair to say he has now advanced his status from companion to beau. He also seems to be an expert in *everything* and has Toogie and Grace eating out of his hand.

"Well, I begin with Citroen vodka," he intoned, looking at me. "I assume you have it on hand."

When I shook my head, he frowned. Toogie and Grace frowned, too.

"We'll make do with regular vodka," he proclaimed with the sweep of an arm. "Now, where is the Cointreau?"

My admission that I did not have this next ingredient produced a new round of disappointment as Brevard settled for triple sec.

Like an OR surgeon, he held out an open palm and demanded, "Lime juice."

I snapped a bottle of ReaLime into his outstretched hand.

"Good heavens, no!" he scoffed. "The only bottled brand I use is Rose's Lime Juice. Don't tell me you're out of that, too!"

I gave Brevard a shrug. Toogie and Grace looked at me as if I were a dog that had just piddled on the floor.

"Fresh juice will work fine. We'll just have to pause and squeeze it," Brevard sighed, retrieving a lime from the refrigerator.

"Rinse this and put it in the microwave for twenty seconds," he stated, handing the lime to me.

"You need heated lime?"

"Not really, old chap," Brevard oozed. "Warming it just a tad enhances the volume of liquid extracted when it is juiced. A little technique of mine."

"Isn't he clever?" Toogie beamed.

"And so handy and creative," Grace responded.

I handed Brevard a stirrer to mix his concoction.

"Shaken, never stirred," he announced somewhat dismissively.

When I didn't respond, he looked at me, raised his eyebrows slightly, and explained, "James Bond."

"No, but I have Jim Beam!" I shot back. Grace and Toogie shot me looks of disgust.

The commentary on how to make the perfect cosmopolitan (obviously contrasted to my crappy version) continued. You get the picture. At least once a day now, I receive constructive feedback (translation: lecture) from Grace or Toogie or both on how to do something better (translation: the way Brevard does it).

Later that night, as we cleared the table after Brevard left, I overheard Grace and Toogie talking.

"Did you notice how Brevard blew out the candles?" Grace asked.

"You mean by holding his forefinger between his lips and the candle when he extinguished the flame?" Toogie answered.

"Precisely," Grace replied. "It deflects the stream of breath so as to not scatter hot candle wax on the tablecloth."

"So urbane," Toogie exclaimed.

"And sophisticated," Grace remarked and then added, "I wish Dalton were more inclined to the finer ways."

It was enough to make you puke.

The next morning over coffee, as we passed around the newspaper, a ritual at our house, Grace announced, "Oh, look, Dalton. You have newsprint smudges on your trousers."

I hardly had time to blink before the next remark.

"Do you know what Brevard does?" Toogie asked.

"What?" Grace replied, leaning forward for one more nugget of Brevardism.

"He places a dark napkin on his lap," Toogie explained. "That way, he doesn't get newsprint on his britches...the way some people do."

"Even when he dines out," she continued, "he requests a dark napkin so as to not have white lint cling to his suit."

"How smart," Grace observed.

"And practical," Toogie retorted.

"If he read the paper in the nude, he could then just take a bath when he—" I began to interject.

"Oh, shush," Grace interrupted. "You might learn a thing or two if you paid more attention to Brevard."

I got up and walked into the den without saying another word. What was becoming evident was that I was losing my grip as the alpha male of the Williams' household. With Brevard's pervasive presence and influence, I had fallen to fourth place in the family pecking order behind Grace, Toogie, and now, Brevard. Buddy, our loyal beagle, jumped up next to me on the sofa. Good old Buddy. Man's best friend. Rather than lie down, however, he just stared, rotating his head a quarter-turn one way, then the other. Suddenly, it hit me. I was sitting in his favorite corner of the sofa. I stood and he commandeered the location, yawned, stretched, and curled up. Make that fifth place in the family pecking order.

As usual, Brevard came over the next evening to take Toogie to dinner. I stayed in the den to avoid him and any more tutorials on being a better person. After Grace and I finished dinner, we retired to the den. She read while I watched television. The phone rang around ten-thirty, and Grace answered it. I could tell something was amiss. Her mouth dropped, and she put her free hand to her throat.

"It's the police," she said haltingly, handing me the phone. "They want to talk to you."

"This is Dalton Williams," I said, trying to be brave but sensing Grace's anxiety and trepidation.

"Yes, she is my aunt. Okay. I understand. Yes, we can come in," I responded as Grace put her hands together and closed her eyes.

"Will you repeat the address, please?" I asked as Grace scurried for a pen and paper. I transcribed the address, added a few more "yes, sirs," and hung up.

Grace cupped her hands in mine. "What did the police say?"

"You won't believe it," I answered, looking into her eyes.

"Dalton...are you grinning?" she gasped. "What is it?"

"Toogie and our good ol' boy Brevard have been arrested in a raid at a club in Mount Pleasant. It seems they were playing poker or some other card game for money."

"Toogie? Brevard? Poker? Money?" she stammered.

"Don't forget busted."

"I feel so sorry for Toogie," Grace sighed.

"I feel sorry for the cops if they riled her up," I replied.

"Dalton, this is serious," Grace proclaimed. "Think of Brevard. He must be mortified."

"Yep!" I answered, almost unable to hide my glee.

"We need to get right over there," Grace declared, handing me the car keys. "You drive. I'm too shaken."

"It is still better than being stirred," I responded firmly, shoulders back, 007-like, already relishing the rush of my return as the alpha male of the Williams' manor.

THE LONG ARM OF THE LAW

A T THE CONCLUSION OF THE last episode, Dalton and Grace were worriedly driving to the Mount Pleasant Police Department after receiving a call that Aunt Toogie and her friend, Brevard, had been arrested in a raid at a card-playing club…

My lovely wife, Grace, and I parked the car and jogged to the station building.

"Oh, I hope Toogie is not too upset by all this," Grace sighed as I opened the door.

We walked briskly to the desk, where a uniformed patrolman sat typing at a computer keyboard.

I paused a moment, cleared my throat, and said, "Excuse me, sir."

He looked up.

"I, ah, am Dalton Williams, and this is my, ah, wife, Grace. I believe my aunt is here. I mean, she is here, I think," I stammered.

"Oh, you must mean Toogie," he smiled. "She's in the back showing some of the guys a few card tricks."

"Card tricks?" Grace inquired, somewhat puzzled.

"You bet," the officer replied. "She is entertaining everyone in the holding room. I have never seen someone shuffle a deck with just one hand. Amazing!"

Grace stared at me.

I shrugged and offered, "I remember she and Uncle Harold used to play canasta."

"She showed us the three-card monte trick," he continued. "I couldn't follow where the queen was. None of the guys could."

"Three-card monte?" Grace asked.

"She is good. Seems like a real nice lady, too."

"Toogie?" I queried.

Finally, Grace brought the conversation back on track and asked, "Is she in trouble?"

"Well, she was someplace she shouldn't have been," the officer replied. "But we ascertained she was a first-time participant. We were after the folks who ran the card club and the regular customers. So, we gave her just a warning, and she is free to go home with you."

"Thank you," I exhaled in relief.

"I'm sure she will walk the straight and narrow," Grace pledged, adding, "Plus, she hardly knows anything about gambling."

"She may know more than you think," the policeman said slightly sternly. "When we broke up the game, she had most of the chips. I told you she is good." Then he smiled and put his hands on his hips. "I'll go get her, but please remind her the consequences will be more serious if we see her again."

I thanked him once more as he went to retrieve Toogie.

Toogie emerged from a conference room with a police escort. A more senior-looking officer had her sign some paperwork and then pointed a finger at her in a kidding gesture. "Now, promise me no more card-playing for money. Deal?"

"Yes, officer," Toogie answered, smiling at him as if he were her son.

I spewed a stream of "Thank yous" all around, put my hand on Toogie's arm, and led her out the door. When we got to the car, Grace embraced Toogie and finally spoke, "Oh, I'm so glad you are okay, darling."

"Okay, hell!" Toogie barked. "I was up a bundle when the cops broke up the game and took all the money."

"The money's not that important," Grace consoled.

"I'll remind you of that next time you lose twenty-two hundred bucks."

"But you do know it was wrong to play for money, don't you?" Grace inquired.

"Yeah," Toogie sighed. "It's just, well, it was like taking candy from a baby."

"Where did you learn to play cards like that?" I inquired as I started the car and pulled out of the police station parking lot.

"Don't encourage her, Dalton," Grace scolded.

"Your Uncle Harold used to play cards at the lodge, and I liked to watch," Toogie responded, bypassing Grace's admonition. "Now I watch poker on television and play online."

"So, you picked up a few pointers," I chimed in, ignoring an icy stare from Grace.

"Yep," Toogie gushed. "We were playing Texas Hold'em. After the flop, some clown from Goose Creek went all-in with just queen-jack suited, and I had trip kings."

"Trip kings?"

"Three of a kind," Toogie explained. "I couldn't lose."

"I told you, it was like shooting fish in a barrel," she concluded. "Twenty-two hundred of them."

After a period of silence, Grace asked, "What about Brevard?"

"He's still back at the police station. I think he is waiting for his lawyer to show up."

"What happened?" I queried as my interest piqued.

"Well," Toogie explained, "Brevard got all huffy with the policemen."

"Tell me more," I egged her on.

"Well, he asked the policemen if they knew who he was."

"And?"

"Then one of the officers turned to another policeman and said, 'I believe we have a man here who doesn't know who he is.'"

I suppressed a giggle.

"Another officer said, 'Let's put out a missing person's report. There must be someone in all of Charleston who knows who he is.'"

I suppressed another laugh. Grace finally responded, "That must have been so humiliating for poor Brevard."

"Oh, he deserved it," Toogie shot back.

"I thought he always did everything right," I interjected.

"Well, he wasn't wise to try to throw his prominence around like that," Grace opined.

"Not only that," Toogie scoffed. "Earlier in the evening, he folded with a full house. A full house! He still has some things to learn."

I smiled silently.

Nothing more was said on the ride home. Once inside the house, we said goodnight and let Toogie retire to her room. I set the coffee pot for tomorrow's breakfast while Grace set out some cups and napkins.

"You should talk with Toogie about playing cards for money," she declared.

"I will."

"I'll offer to help her patch things up with Brevard. Maybe a little dinner party."

"Not so fast on that one," I suggested.

"What do you mean?" Grace asked. "Don't you think she could use some help?"

"Remember the police officer said she was good?"

"Yes."

"Let's let her play this next hand by herself."

HIP, HIP, PAYDAY

"PACK A SWEATER, A COUPLE of brassieres, and panties," my lovely wife, Grace, directed as she loaded a shopping bag with books, notepaper, and snacks.

When I didn't move, she looked up.

"The underwear is in the top dresser drawer, and sweaters are on the middle shelf in her closet. No black lingerie—and find the pink sweater with the pearl buttons."

After a pause, I muttered, "How would it be if I cut out the Sudoku puzzle from this week's *Daniel Island News*, and you get the clothes?"

"Just be a help and get them, dear," Grace replied. "I'm busy collecting other items right now."

"Why me?" I pleaded. "Can't you do it? I'll get the other stuff."

Grace stopped packing, assumed an akimbo position, and scoffed, "Okay, but help me understand what you're really saying. Are you telling me that you, the old, rascally Dalton Williams, are afraid to touch a woman's undergarments?"

"No," I shot back and then reconsidered the ramifications of my answer. "But not just any woman, I mean…," I stuttered, "not some women… What I'm trying to say here is…only yours… Yeah, that's it… Geez, just not hers."

It was Aunt Toogie's fault Grace and I were embroiled in this bloomer brouhaha. On the Friday before Labor Day, Toogie broke her hip. Unlike many her age, the fracture was neither the result of osteoarthritis nor a fall. She had clipped a buoy in the Charleston harbor while riding an inner tube pulled on a towline behind Brevard's boat. Grace had no idea that Toogie's request to buy a new swimsuit was a precursor to this prank. She was appalled that a woman Toogie's age would try such a stunt. The orthopedic surgeon was astonished that she even could! Brevard was devastated, of course, figuring his complicity in the caper was a bad break, so to speak, in his game plan to get back in Toogie's good graces. So, while millions of Americans partook in the last barbeque of the summer, Toogie took on a new, titanium hip. After a couple of days in the hospital, she moved to a rehabilitation facility where she has been amazingly regaining her strength and feistiness, although not necessarily in that order.

Grace and I were now headed to the rehab center with our fresh supply of requested clothing, reading material, and sweets. During each daily visit, Toogie presented us with a new list of orders—do this task, take care of that errand, pick this up, pay these bills, deliver that. Always ready to accommodate, Grace just soothed, "Dalton will tend to everything, dear. You just concentrate on feeling better."

I, on the other hand, was not fooled. While Grace poured out the milk of human kindness, Toogie was clearly milking the situation. I could see that she was regaining her natural state: pugnacity.

Yet, I made one more trip to the store specifically to procure one of Toogie's requests.

"Stop at Publix," she had barked. "I bet the Halloween candy is on display. Get me some Hershey's miniature medleys and a big bag of PayDays."

The cashier was ringing up my purchase when I noticed a young boy pointing toward me.

"This aisle, Mommy. There's only an old guy, and he's almost finished," he squealed.

I hadn't felt old, nor thought of myself as old, when I received an AARP card or qualified for the seniors' discount at the movie theater. However, after hearing such a comment from such a little whippersnapper, I did. I responded by ripping open the bag of PayDays, pulling out an individual bar, and holding it at arm's length. He took a small step toward me. I quickly unwrapped the snack, popped the whole thing into my mouth, and turned on my heels. Heading toward the door, I could hear a commotion at the checkout lane behind me. I may be an old guy, but I'm a rascally old guy! I gloated.

Now that silly act of selfishness seemed small as Grace spoke.

"As I see it, you feel uncomfortable gathering Toogie's undergarments, right?"

I nodded.

"Yet didn't you tell me that she was the one who encouraged you to do well in school when you were young, took you to the library, and bought you books?"

Again, I nodded.

"Is it so much to ask you to collect some necessary items for this kind, generous person?" Grace queried.

I nodded, sniffled, and assembled the apparel. As usual, Grace had cut to the heart of the matter. While many chase fame and fortune in their lifetime, one measure of living a good life could be: Is there someone in your life who will gladly fetch your undergarments when you require such assistance?

Toogie was sitting up in a recliner chair when we arrived. Her room was awash in fragrance and oxygen, spewed forth by the jungle of plants and fresh flowers sent daily by Brevard. Toogie pointed the remote at the wall-mounted television and muted the sound.

"Is he stupid or what?" she muttered.

"Brevard?" I prompted with a grin.

She answered, "No, that politician on TV."

"We brought the things on your list," Grace interrupted as she began unpacking the contents of the shopping bag.

Announcing each item retrieved from the tote, Grace led off with, "Two complete changes of clothes. I thought this pink cardigan sweater would look nice with the gabardine slacks. Don't you agree?"

"You didn't let Dalton touch my lingerie, did you?" Toogie inquired.

"Two books," Grace continued, ignoring the question. "This one is the latest release by Nicholas Sparks. I'm pretty sure you haven't read it."

Toogie smiled again and leaned forward to peer inside the bag.

"Sudoku and crossword puzzle books," Grace added, "and a couple sharpened pencils."

"Candy?" Toogie whispered.

Leaning closer to hear her, Grace replied, "Pardon?"

"She wants the candy," I interjected.

"Oh, yes," Grace concluded, pulling the prize from the pouch, "and two bags of your favorite miniature candy bars. Dalton picked them out himself. Judging from the rip in this one bag, I'd say he has already helped himself."

Toogie grasped the bags and grinned. She reached through the tear in the PayDay bag, pulled out a bar, unwrapped it, inspected the confectionary, and then deposited it in her mouth.

Closing her eyes for a moment and savoring the sensation, she remarked, "Hmm, this brings back memories."

Taking another bar from the bag, she asked, "Dalton, do you remember when you were a young boy, and I used to treat you to these?"

I had a vague sensation, although no specific recollection.

"I saved all the leftover holiday candy in the icebox," she continued. "During the school year and summer months, you and I would walk to the library every Saturday. Each time you read a book, I'd reward you with a candy bar. I recall, one summer, you read well over fifty books, and I went to Piggly Wiggly several times to replenish my stash."

I smiled and looked toward Grace, who smiled back at me.

"Now, here's what I want you to do," Toogie barked, breaking the tranquility. "I want you to read this Nicholas Sparks' book aloud to me. My eyes aren't up to all the strain. And if you do," she smiled, holding up a PayDay bar, "I'll give you one of these."

MINT CONDITION

"WHAT A SCRUMPTIOUS APERITIF," BREVARD declared, toasting with his tall, chilled glass. "You must share the recipe." My aunt Toogie's gentleman friend, decked out in a blue and white seersucker suit, a colorful bowtie, and matching pocket-handkerchief, was back both in the picture and my living room.

"Well," my lovely wife, Grace, explained, "the drink is comprised of equal parts of Firefly Sweet Tea Vodka, iced tea, and lemonade. To that, I add splashes of triple sec and fresh lemon juice and then infuse my secret touch."

Brevard leaned in eagerly, like a kid getting a peek at the final exam answers. "Do tell, Grace," he coaxed.

"I pour the mixture through a strainer filled with muddled mint and basil leaves. This imparts just a hint of the mint while the basil cuts the sweetness ever so slightly."

"A masterpiece!" Brevard bellowed. "I must serve this at my next garden soirée."

Grace smiled to let the compliment hover before replying, "The vodka is made locally on Wadmalaw Island, and it can sometimes be hard to find. Dalton has an extra bottle, and I'm sure he would be glad to share it with you."

Before I could shoot Grace a *No, I wouldn't like to share* look, Brevard turned, put a hand on my shoulder, and intoned, "So sporting of you, old boy."

While I tried to decipher if this was an uncommon compliment to me, Grace added, "I have lots of mint and basil from my herb garden. I'll put some in a plastic bag for you to take home."

Over dinner, Brevard held court de rigueur, regaling the ladies with stories of places throughout the world he had visited and notable people with whom he had hobnobbed. Without invitation or encouragement, he proffered his opinions on forecasts for the financial market and the strategies a wise man—aka himself—should follow going forward. Grace finally broke Brevard's serve, asking, "Dalton, will you pour some more wine?"

"This wine is very nice," Toogie said. "What is it?"

"Let me guess," Brevard interjected, casting his eyes upward in thought and recapturing the serve. "First, it is better than one might expect from Dalton, so I imagine one of you fine ladies procured it."

Grace and Toogie chuckled.

"I detect a nose of light fruits—peach and apple, I'd say. A little mint, perhaps an homage to you, Grace. Finally, a light hint of toasty oak," Brevard pontificated. "Allow me to venture a well-educated stab. We are enjoying a 2014 Kistler Chardonnay. Perhaps the Hudson Vineyards in Carneros."

Grace dispatched me to fetch the wine. To my chagrin, it was precisely the vintage Brevard had predicted. Grace and Toogie oohed and aahed until Brevard revealed he had seen the bottle in the refrigerator when helping himself to more ice for his drink. This set off a new round of guffaws from the ladies.

"Seriously, though," Brevard preached, turning to me, "I can give you a pointer on serving fine wine."

"I call it the Twenty-Minute Rule. For a white, say a Montrachet, or this," he continued, waving a hand in the direction of my wine. "Take it out of the cooled cellar twenty minutes prior to serving. This will remove a bit of the chill so as to fully appreciate the wine's delicate features. For a red wine, because most home temperatures are quite warm, cool it for twenty minutes and then serve."

"Most interesting," Grace responded. "Dalton, you'll have to remember that."

Quelling my desire to wring his affected neck, I thanked Brevard for the tutelage.

Toogie smiled, although I couldn't detect if she was sensing my discomfort or pleased by Brevard's sophistication. Over dessert, he renewed spewing much like a professor in lecture, now on international politics and climate change. None too soon, the evening ended. At the front door, Brevard grasped Grace's hand.

"Miss Grace," he cooed, "dinner has been a culinary triumph. The grouper was worthy of Jeremiah Bacon."

Turning to me, Brevard explained, "He's the executive chef at several fine restaurants in town."

Twisting the cap on the bottle of sweet tea vodka and taking a small sip, he added, "Thank you so much for this luxurious libation. You must come downtown someday, and we'll enjoy the rest of it as we cuss and discuss the news of the day."

Toogie was accompanying Brevard home to stay a night or two downtown, an avenue of thought I was not ready to pursue further. She explained she had shopping and errands to do, and it would be so much easier to stay downtown for a while.

After Grace and I cleaned up the dishes and prepared for bed, she observed, "It's nice to see Toogie and Brevard back together."

"I guess so."

"That was a ringing endorsement," Grace mused.

"Well, it just that he's so… How do I say this?"

"Worldly?" Grace offered.

"Wordy would be more like it!" I groused.

"I think they make a nice couple," Grace replied, "and it's obvious Toogie enjoys his company, and he—"

She was cut short by the phone ringing.

"Who could be calling at this hour?" Grace declared, reaching for the phone.

I could tell by her demeanor it wasn't good news or some solicitation call. Her end of the conversation consisted of a series of, "Oh, mys," and "You poor dears." Grace concluded with, "Do not worry. We'll be right there."

"Get dressed," she ordered. "It was Toogie. The police stopped Brevard on his way home, and they are holding him."

"For being too long-winded during the interrogation?" I inquired.

"No," Grace answered. "They found the bag of mint and basil under his car seat, and they think it may be something more sinister."

"Oh, this is getting good," I smiled.

"Plus, they found an open bottle of alcohol in the back seat."

"This is getting *real* good!" I giggled.

While Grace hustled to get dressed, I strolled down to the kitchen and fixed myself a tall glass of sweet tea vodka and lemonade. A few minutes later, Grace scurried downstairs and into the kitchen.

"Dalton Williams!" she gasped. "You're not even dressed. We have to get to the police station to set the record straight. What are you doing?"

"Following Brevard's advice."

"What possible advice could that be for this situation at this hour?" Grace shot back.

"Why, Miss Grace," I drawled. "This situation is already delicious. But as you surely know, if y'all just give it another twenty minutes, it will be exquisite!"

Let it Go

[Written following the 2016 election]

I FIXED A STEELY GAZE ACROSS the dining room table at my Aunt Toogie's gentleman friend, Brevard, who had joined us—once again—for dinner. After a brief (but welcomed by me) hiatus, he was back in the picture with my aunt. Brevard had been away for a while—a couple of months ago, he had announced a solo around-the-world sailing trip, although rumors are that he ran aground somewhere off the coast of Hilton Head and then laid low for a spell. With the help of some downtown legal cronies, he had managed to have the Coast Guard records sealed. Brevard's wardrobe had obviously survived the supposed shipwreck. To me, he looked as if he were on the way to a Junior League tea reservation, not a casual weeknight dinner with friends. He was donned in a dusty-pink linen dinner jacket, summery lime-green slacks, a starched white shirt, and a perfectly matched pastel paisley ascot. The ladies cooed excessively over his ensemble.

We were engaged in a spirited discussion of a topic that has recently consumed him. He brought it up once again almost immediately after Toogie and my lovely wife, Grace, stepped away from the table. The anger brewing below his surface may have been ignited a tad by the glass of Booker's True Barrel bourbon I poured for the interlude before dessert. Or perhaps he needed one more stage upon which to vent.

After listening to him spew that the outcome was unjust, if not illegitimate, I declared emphatically, "Hey. You lost. Now you will just have to accept it."

"Your kind is completely wrong," Brevard sniped. "Such a conservative position wipes out years of progress."

"I find it amusing," I countered, "that you so-called progressives preach diversity but are intolerant of any view other than your own."

This remark really pushed his button. Arching his back and lifting his chin, he bellowed, "Oh, please! That's such a pathetic platitude."

It was now "game on," with elevated voices and finger-pointing across the table.

"You need to just accept it and move on," I offered.

"Never, never, never," he huffed. "I have every right to protest."

"For what?"

"For God's sake, man! To right this travesty. It's, it's…un-American."

"You're just a bunch of whiners."

"You're a bunch of Fascists."

"Crybaby!"

"Hater!"

The cacophony caused Toogie and my lovely wife, Grace, to return to the dining room. "Please tell me you two aren't at it again," Toogie sighed.

When neither Brevard nor I responded, she continued, "You've been doing this for months now. Enough already!"

"He started it," I interjected.

"I was merely attempting to edify Dalton on the error of his ways," Brevard proffered with a heavy dose of hoity-toity.

"It's over. Deal with it," I muttered.

"As long as I have breath, I will resist it," Brevard declared.

"Knock it off! Both of you," Toogie hollered. "You both need to let it go. Like in the movie *Frozen*, let it go!"

"Gentlemen," Grace announced, trying to change the subject. "I hope you like dessert. It is an ice cream pie made with Graeter's Brown Butter Bourbon Pecan Chocolate Chip. I know how you like bourbon."

When no one replied, Toogie spoke up. "Well, I can't speak for Ali or Frazier here, but I think it's yummy." Turning to Brevard, she inquired, "What do you think?"

"About what?" he snorted. "The pie or the…"

Toogie silenced him with a loud "Sshh" as Grace shot me a look that said, *Don't you say a word either.* Trying to take the discussion in a new direction, Grace rubbed her hands together and announced, "Let's talk about something else. Who wants to see some wonderful pictures Suzanne sent of their trip to Disney?"

"I'd like to," Toogie piped up as Grace went to retrieve her iPad. "You boys would too, wouldn't you?"

Under Toogie's glare, Brevard and I assented. Grace was back with her tablet and displayed pictures of grandson Charlie and granddaughter Ashleigh at Disney. "Here they are at the Haunted Mansion," Grace explained, adding, "Charlie went on the ride. It was a little scary for four-year-old Ashleigh."

"This one is unique. It's Charlie sitting on Geoff's shoulders and looking down at his hands. But look," she continued, holding the iPad for all to see. "They somehow added Tinkerbell into the picture. See how it looks as if she is standing in Charlie's hands?"

"How do they do that?" Toogie asked.

"Some sort of technology," Grace replied. "It sure is nice to see them having such a good time." As we all nodded agreement and smiled at the images, the former educator in Grace seized the opportunity for a teachable moment.

"Looking at these pictures," she mused, "should remind us of what is most important in life. Things like the love of family and the joy of young children."

"I hope," she continued, "that you boys would agree this is more important than you know what," jiggling her fingers in air quotes in tandem with the *you know what* part.

I nodded, perhaps grudgingly, as did Brevard. "I know each of you can be civil about it," Grace soothed. "So, why don't you each say you are sorry and then say something that acknowledges the other person's view?"

When no one responded, Grace suggested, "Dalton, why don't you go first?"

"Say I'm sorry?" I asked.

"And validate that you understand Brevard's position," Grace coached.

"Okay," I uttered. "Uh, Brevard, I'm sorry we had words, and I regret that you are upset…"

"No," Grace interrupted. "That is from your point of view. Say it from Brevard's perspective, please."

"Okay. Let's see. Brevard is justified to be upset that the golf-governing bodies have outlawed the belly putter when he has used one for all these years."

"Excellent," Grace cooed. "Brevard, your turn."

"Well," he began. "I'm sorry too, and even though The Royal and Ancient is a bunch of old guys…"

"Judgmental," Grace corrected. "Start over, please."

"I'm sorry," Brevard began again, "and I understand that The Royal and Ancient and the USGA have the authority to set the rules of golf."

"Nicely done, gentlemen," Grace smiled. "I'm proud of you."

"Here, here! This calls for a toast," Toogie crowed. We all clinked glasses as she hummed the tune from the movie, *Frozen…Let it Go.*

HOME
SWEET
HOME

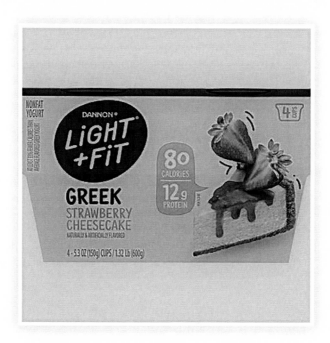

LET THEM EAT CAKE

"WE'RE ALL GOING TO GET in better shape," my lovely wife, Grace, announced rather commandingly one morning as she poured herself a cup of coffee, sans cream and sugar.

"Uh-oh," whispered my Aunt Toogie, setting down her bagel slathered with cream cheese. "This should be good."

I continued to drizzle sourwood honey on my amply buttered bagel.

"Dalton?" Grace queried in a louder tone. "Did you hear me?"

"Yeah. You were talking about getting shaped up."

"I was talking about *us*," Grace replied, with emphasis on the word "us." "You and me. Nutritious meals. Exercising more. Watching our caloric intake. Well, what do you think?"

I answered, "I'll drink to that."

Grace sighed audibly before turning to Toogie. "What am I going to do with that man?" she pleaded.

Toogie chuckled and turned to me. "She wants you to look like that seventy-year-old, bare-chested, muscular doctor who is pictured in *Health & Fitness Magazine* and newspaper advertisements."

Grace joined us at the kitchen table. "I have seen the ads," she smiled.

"Forget the ads," Toogie chortled. "Check out those abs. He's buff!"

"I don't want you to look like anyone else, dear," Grace declared, putting her hand on my arm. "I would just like us to focus on good health. I could lose a few pounds, and so should you. Now that the weather is cooler, we can walk outside more."

Knowing Grace was correct and that I shouldn't resist, I responded, "You're right, honey. I'll give it a try."

"Good. Now," Grace replied crisply, like a general who had just won the first skirmish of a bigger battle, "we'll start by eating smarter!"

I looked at Toogie, who was grinning at me.

"For example," Grace continued, waving her hand across the breakfast table, "we can eliminate much of this stuff. Fresh fruit, oatmeal, and yogurt would be a nice improvement."

"I agree," Toogie piped up. "I'm going to the grocery store to buy a few items for my trip with Brevard to the mountains. Why don't you come along, Dalton? I'll show you some of my favorite yogurts."

I was about to respond that I had no interest in going grocery shopping, especially with Toogie, when she tapped her foot twice against my shin under the table. Grace continued on a roll regarding calorie-friendly cuisine, espousing the virtues of various vegetables and legumes. Toogie held her forefinger to her lips, a signal to let her lead this dance.

As soon as Toogie and I were in the car headed to the grocery store, I asked, "What was all that secrecy stuff about back in the kitchen?"

"Grace wants you to eat better, right?" Toogie shot back.

"Yep."

"And she suggested eating yogurt, didn't she?"

"Yep."

"So, I'm doing you a favor."

"What kind of favor?"

Toogie smiled. "Size-huge, sweetie."

Inside the store, she made a beeline to the bakery department and ordered two apple fritters, one for each of us.

"Now, follow me," Toogie instructed, taking a large bite of her fritter while sashaying to the dairy aisle. She scrutinized the yogurt selections, pulled down a container, and handed it to me.

"Check out this bad boy," she grinned.

I gazed at the yogurt cup.

"Boston Cream Pie?" I questioned.

"Yep." Toogie smacked her lips. "Get a gander of this other one."

It was Key Lime Pie. Next to it was Raspberry Cheesecake.

"Sweet!" I gushed, inspecting more containers. "Sounds yummy, and if it will make Grace happy…it's, it's like…"

"Having your cake and eating it, too," Toogie finished my thought and then polished off the apple fritter.

I selected a few of the forbidden fruits that I planned to place strategically beneath the low-fat Greek yogurts Grace kept in the refrigerator.

The next morning, I savored the first delight from my yogurt cache, Pineapple Upside-Down Cake, and then tucked the empty container deep in the trash bin. Grace's lunch was lettuce with cottage cheese. I topped it off with a White Chocolate Strawberry yogurt. For dinner, Grace prepared herbed consume and steamed broccoli with red pepper strips.

"Would you like some fresh fruit for dessert?" she inquired.

"No, thanks. I may have some yogurt later," I replied, debating whether to have the Red Velvet Cake or Black Forest Cake.

"How is the diet going so far?" Grace asked as she cleared the table.

"Fine."

"Good," she replied. "Do you think you have the willpower to stay with it?"

I smiled and answered sweetly, "Piece of cake."

Not a Shred of Evidence

"IT'S A BEAUTY," I SMILED.

My lovely wife, Grace, just stared, alternating glances between it and me. Aunt Toogie rolled her eyes and stepped back, out of the line of potential fire.

Finally, Grace spoke. "I just hope you're not thinking of bringing it into the house!"

The "it" was my new shredder, purchased at a local office supply store. The sturdy industrial design, in sleek black and chrome, stood a full four feet high.

"There was a special sale, and I got the office model for the same price as the smaller home version," I beamed. "It will shred up to twenty-four pages at once and can even grind up credit cards and paper clips. Notice the casters. We can easily maneuver it around the house."

"Try maneuvering it to the garage," Grace suggested, blocking the doorway.

After a short but tense negotiation, Grace finally allowed the shredder temporarily in the den. There was an understanding it would be stored in the garage as soon as I finished my task, which was to purge our files of old, unnecessary papers and records. Last week's *Daniel Island News* article about identity theft highlighted the prudence of such a project, but the real impetus was the primal calling that wells annually in the Williams household at about this time—spring cleaning. Each April, Grace is bitten by the bug and begins to scurry like a cicada released from hibernation in a quest to clean up and clean out. She makes lists of chores to complete and stocks up on organizational containers and assorted scrubbers, soaps, and sponges. This year, Toogie joined in the cleanliness chorus, walking around with a clipboard of "to-do" lists.

Grace had announced we would start by scrutinizing our closets for items we could donate to a local church outreach program. I poured over mine and produced a rather large pile of clothing. Grace and Toogie, on the other hand, proffered rather puny piles for all the time they spent perusing.

"What have you two been doing?" I probed.

"Mostly, I rearranged things," Grace replied. "It is part of the process. Spring and summer clothes in the front, fall and winter in the back."

"Ladies, you need to be a bit more aggressive," I boasted. "If you haven't touched something in a year, get rid of it. That's my rule."

"Well, I always think I might wear a particular item again."

"When in doubt, throw it out," I declared, hoping my leadership might capture possession of the clipboard.

As Grace and Toogie plunged into reorganizing the kitchen pantry, I tackled the den files, amassing a mound for the shredder. I fed the fodder into the beast with gusto. The confetti filled half a dozen trash bags. Lugging them to the garage, I spied Grace and Toogie sitting on the family room couch, looking at a book.

"What are you doing?" I inquired.

"Oh, just taking a break and looking at pictures of the kids when they were little," Grace answered. "We found this old photo album."

"Way back in the days when you had hair, dark hair," Toogie chuckled.

"Well, if you ask me, you need to put a little more attention on the sediment and less on the sentiment."

"We didn't ask you," Toogie shot back.

"You're doing a fine job, Dalton," Grace interjected. "We're almost finished with the cleaning, and we'll sort the rest of these pictures. Why don't you go play golf?"

Not needing to be given this suggestion more than once, I dumped the last bag of shredding into the trash and then beat a path to the course.

Grace and Toogie were setting the dinner table when I returned.

"How was golf?" Grace asked.

"Same old, same old. Did you finish the cleaning?"

"Sure did," Grace smiled. "We delivered nearly ten boxes to the outreach shelter. They especially appreciated the clothing and kitchen items."

"That's nice."

"And they loved the wine," Toogie piped up.

"Wine? What wine?" I exclaimed.

"That wine from the cupboard under the stairs," Grace explained.

"That is my special stock," I bellowed. "There's some really outstanding stuff in there."

"But so old," Toogie interjected. "Some of it was from the 1990s."

"Of course," I cried. "That's what makes it good!"

"We were just following your guidance," Grace cooed. "We figured if it hadn't been touched in a year, we should get rid of it."

"Didn't you think it was there for a good reason?"

"When in doubt, throw it out," Toogie chimed in.

"Say it isn't so," I moaned.

"Oh, don't be so sentimental, Dalton," Grace offered.

"It was probably mostly sediment," Toogie chortled.

I looked up to see them both giggling. Grace walked over and gave me a hug.

"There, there, dear. We didn't give away any of your wine."

"But we did pull out a nice bottle to celebrate the conclusion of spring cleaning," Toogie added.

Grace held out a 1994 Duckhorn Three Palms Vineyard Merlot. "You open the bottle, and I'll get the goblets."

Sitting and sipping the wine a while later, I mused, "You ladies sure gave me a scare about the wine."

"Are you relieved and happy now?" Grace inquired.

"You bet," I smiled, inhaling the aroma of the merlot.

162

"Then we hope you won't be too upset with what we really did."

"And that would be?"

"We donated your shredder to the church office," Grace announced as she and Toogie clinked their wine glasses.

DALTON CLEANS HOUSE

"I ADORE IT," MY LOVELY WIFE, Grace, cooed.

"Neat," observed my Aunt Toogie, adding, "What will they think of next?"

The ladies were admiring Grace's most recent purchase, a robot vacuuming contraption called a Roomba. This little disc-shaped sucker was scooting around the house, moving around table and chair legs as it vacuumed the floor, tile, and carpet.

"Here's the best part," Grace remarked, sounding like a TV infomercial pitch-person. "Once it's charged, you turn it on. It vacuums and then, like magic, returns to its docking station." I kept my nose in the sports page of the newspaper in search of a hot-hitting outfielder for my fantasy baseball team.

"Plus," Grace quipped, "I don't have to nag it to clean the house."

"It runs on electricity, which is way cheaper than bourbon," Toogie chuckled.

Sensing where the conversation was headed, I kept my attention on the newspaper, squinting to read the box scores. Grace and I have, for years, divided the basic housekeeping chores. She handles the more intricate craft of dusting while I follow with the manly task of vacuuming. If I may say so on my behalf, I've done a pretty good job. Yet, my history of toil was for naught as Grace and Toogie escalated the comparison of their new technology with the old warhorse.

"I don't have to feed it," Grace mused.

"Or sleep with it," Toogie chortled, slapping her hand on the kitchen counter. They were now off and running.

"It doesn't talk back."

"Doesn't leave the seat up."

"Doesn't hog the TV remote."

"Or have hair in its ears," Toogie wheezed, adding, "Hey, Dalton, you listening to this?"

I set the newspaper down and rested my chin in my cupped hands. "Having fun, ladies?" I asked as my forefingers stealthily probed my ears for signs of protruding hair.

"Oh, don't be an old fuddy-duddy," Grace soothed.

"You should be glad I bought this little gadget," she continued. "You won't have to vacuum anymore."

"Yeah," Toogie chipped in. "You can have more time to play Words with Friends or whatever it is you do on the computer all day."

"It's fantasy baseball," I corrected, disregarding the suggestion that I'd be relieved of housework. The addition of the Roomba probably meant I'd be reassigned to an even lower-skilled role. Maybe a dirtier one such as cleaning the garage.

"Are you a little jealous of my new playmate?" Grace teased, poking me gently in the ribs.

"Nah."

"Sure?" she quizzed, kissing me lightly on an earlobe.

"Yep," I answered, wondering if she detected any bristle in my ear or demeanor.

"Good," Grace announced. "Toogie and I are going shopping. We'll be back in a few hours." After a short pause, she added, "If you are looking for something to do, you could clean the garage."

After Grace and Toogie departed, I decided to eschew the garage project for a while. Too hot, too dusty, too below my skill level. Instead, I settled in at my computer and studied fantasy baseball data. Should I pull the trigger and add a hot-hitting rookie to my lineup? My company in the house was the drone of the Roomba, whirling away somewhere in another room. Grace had activated it before she left. The sound of the gadget grew louder as it scurried into the den where I sat. I watched as it swept around a chair and floor lamp and then headed toward me. I resisted the natural reaction to lift my feet and decided, rather, to stand my ground. The gizmo collided with my left foot, stopped, and then backed up. It spun 180 degrees, returned 180 degrees in the other direction, and then made another run at my foot. I retaliated with a sideways swipe of my foot. The blow caught the robot amidships. It stopped, backed up, and then closed on me for a third time. Giving no quarter, I kicked it harder. The lights on its top flickered, and the device went dead.

"Good riddance," I thought, returning my attention to my fantasy baseball roster. A full minute later, the Roomba roared to life. Instinctively, I raised my feet, fearing another attack. Rather, the vacuum retreated toward the den door, out into the hall, and exited from view. In the next moment, it returned to view in the doorway, rotated a full 360 degrees, and blinked its lights as if to declare, "I'm telling Grace what you did as soon as she gets home!"

Game on, I thought, springing from my chair. The Roomba must have read my mind as it pivoted 90 degrees and motored away. By the time I reached the hall, it was out of sight. Still, I could follow its sound and did so into the living room. No Roomba in sight. The darn thing was probably hiding under the sofa.

"Think I'll go clean the garage," I announced loudly so the Roomba could hear. Exiting the living room, I turned swiftly and crouched on all fours next to the foyer wall. A short while later, the robot's motor reengaged. It was on the move again. I stayed motionless and took shallow breaths. Moments later, my patience was rewarded. The robot exited the living room. I sprung. The Roomba rotated and tried to retreat. Too late. I snatched the sucker, brushes still spinning, and headed for the garage.

"If you are looking for something to do," I mimicked in a falsetto Grace-like voice, "you can clean the garage." I set the vacuum down in the middle of the garage, pushed its on button, and it began to scour. Humming a few bars from *Fiddler on the Roof* ("…who has the right, as master of the house, to have the final word at home"), I returned to the den to ponder my fantasy baseball outfield.

Hours later, Grace and Toogie returned from their outing, packages in tow. I met them in the kitchen where they were sorting out their acquisitions.

"Look what I got for you, honey," Grace announced, holding up a golf shirt. "Oh, and I bought you this, too," she continued, handing me a small box. It was a nose and ear hair trimmer.

Before I could reply, Grace added, "And thanks for cleaning the garage. It looks great."

"Yeah, sure," I stammered, realizing I had forgotten, and the ladies must have missed, the Roomba in the garage. After some small talk and a glass of iced tea, Grace and Toogie retreated upstairs to store the new clothes they had scored at the mall. I made a beeline to the garage. A quick search confirmed my worst fear. No Roomba. Plus, the garage door was open, possibly left that way by Grace as she and Toogie toted in their goodies. I looked in the bushes lining the driveway. Nothing. I walked around the yard but still no sign of my little homemaking assistant. I knew Grace would be sure to notice if the darn thing was missing. At the end of the driveway, I peered up and down the street. There, squinting to see in the glare of an afternoon sun, I caught a final glimpse of the runaway Roomba as it made a nifty right turn and accelerated toward Seven Farms Drive.

Shoe on the Other Foot

An excellent wife…her worth is far above jewels: Proverbs 31

"Don't put all the towels into the dryer at once," my lovely wife, Grace, advised.

From the laundry room, I hollered, "What?"

Speaking louder, Grace replied, "Put just half the load of towels in the dryer at a time, please. They fluff more that way."

Always a good follower in matters domestic, I complied.

Matters domestic have been my milieu for the past few weeks since Grace's foot surgery. Following a few days confined to bed rest, she is recuperating nicely and keeping the "new and improved" foot iced and elevated. Consequently, yours truly has assumed command of a heap of household responsibilities and, frankly, fumbled more than a few of them.

I recall reading that researchers somewhere ran tests demonstrating that women handle multiple tasks simultaneously better than do men. I can attest these results are correct. To wit: *Time to fix Grace's lunch. I'll warm some soup. Where is the soup ladle? In the dishwasher. Dirty. Forgot to run the dishwasher after breakfast. Speaking of running machinery, did I put the wet laundry in the dryer? Come to think of it, did I even run the washer? Sure, I did. I put in all the colored clothes. Oh, crap! I forgot to adjust the temp setting to cold-cold as Grace advised. Who washes clothes in cold water anyway? Cavemen? I'll check on that later. What was I going to make for lunch? Oh, yeah, soup. No, we had soup yesterday. Okay, how about a sandwich? I'll fix an iced tea. Grace likes iced tea. Now, where are those deli fixings? Oh, crap! We're out of bread. Do I have time to go to the store? No. Okay, think. Lettuce wraps. I can use lettuce in place of bread. Very healthy. Oh, crap! We're out of lettuce, too. Why do I have a glass full of ice cubes on the counter? Oh, yeah, iced tea. What was I looking for in the fridge? Think. Right, something to make a sandwich with. Frozen biscuits? Takes seventeen minutes to cook. I don't have seventeen minutes. I need to have lunch ready now. Is that sound Grace making her way downstairs? Oh, crap!*

Friends have generously showered us with delicious meals and goodies. Without their assistance, I would have floundered far more than I did. On a recent morning, as I cleaned up the breakfast dishes and disposed of coffee grounds, I remarked to my Aunt Toogie, "These chores are exhausting!"

Toogie chuckled, "No crap, Sherlock."

Knowing that expression was intended for someone who had just pointed out the obvious, I sighed, "This stuff never ends!"

"A woman's work is never done," Toogie mused. "It's the last line of an old ditty. A man may work from sun to sun, but a woman's work…"

"I know, I know," I groused. "Give me your used teabag, and I'll take out the trash."

"Don't forget the den, laundry room, and bathroom trash, Sherlock," Toogie chortled.

On subsequent days, Toogie assumed the role of supervisor, surveying my performance of various domestic duties and offering unsolicited coaching. As I moved from chore to chore, Toogie would chime in with words of advice, such as, "Put those leftovers in a smaller dish."

"Why?" I sputtered. "Won't that make two dirty dishes instead of one?"

"Food looks more appetizing in a full container," Toogie answered, and then added dismissively, "Any chef worth his or her salt knows that, Sherlock."

One evening, after Grace had retired to rest, I washed pots that don't, I now know, go in the dishwasher.

Sitting at the kitchen table working on a Sudoku puzzle, Toogie gruffed, "Hey, Sherlock. We're almost out of beer. After you finish in the scullery, you need to make a grocery list."

I lifted my head with a look of exasperation.

"Man up!" Toogie snapped. "Don't get discouraged. I'll help you."

I sat at the kitchen table. Toogie poked around the fridge and assorted shelves and storage spots. She hollered out items for me to transcribe, along with a running commentary that included such nuggets as, "Milk—this one is almost past due," and "Tomatoes—these are puckered."

When Toogie finally returned to sit at the table, I said, "Thanks, I appreciate the help."

"We're not done, honey," Toogie barked. "Give me the list."

She inspected my work, an accurate record of all the things Toogie had asked for listed neatly in the order mentioned.

"Sheesh," Toogie sighed. "What is this?"

"The grocery list?" I offered tentatively.

"Get me a clean sheet of paper," she ordered.

Without challenging the instruction, I complied. Toogie started writing on the new page, frequently consulting my list. Finally, she handed her document to me. "Here you go."

The new list had all the same prospective purchases as did my list but arranged into groupings. I studied it, anticipating some embedded secret cipher.

Finally, Toogie broke the code. "It's categorized to coincide with the layout of the store."

"Really?" I proclaimed, studying the list anew.

"No crap, Sherlock," Toogie retorted.

"Well, thanks. This will make shopping a—"

"Not so fast," Toogie interjected. "Now, get the coupons."

"Coupons?"

"You know what coupons are, don't you? Grace keeps them in an accordion file in her car."

I trudged to the garage to fetch Grace's container of coupons. Toogie fingered through the many pieces of paper, extracting a few. Then she wrote an asterisk next to selected items on the grocery list.

"The asterisk denotes the items for which you have a coupon," Toogie declared.

Amazed by the intricacy of these logistics, I remarked, "How do you know this stuff and keep it straight?"

"Years of practice."

"Whew. I doubt I'd ever get all that," I sighed.

"Patience, Grasshopper," Toogie advised softly as she headed off to bed.

After coffee the next morning, Grace announced, "I see you have a grocery list. I'll go to the store."

"Sure, you can come with me," I replied, interpreting Grace's comment as a request for me to drive her to the store. Since her surgery, I had done all the driving, referring to it as "driving the toe truck," a remark I don't think Grace found as clever as did I.

"No, I think it is time I tried to fly solo," Grace remarked.

Thinking of the somewhat bulky orthopedic shoe Grace was sporting, I asked, "Are you sure? I mean, with your shoe and all?"

Grace answered, "The shoe is on the other foot," probably a reference to the fact that her right foot, used in driving a car, was her "good" foot.

I looked at Toogie, who had a huge grin.

"What?" I queried.

"Did you hear what she said?" Toogie asked.

"Yes. She said, 'the shoe is on the other foot.'"

Then it hit me. "Oh, you mean like me?" I queried.

"No crap, Sherlock," Toogie chuckled, returning her attention to her Sudoku puzzle.

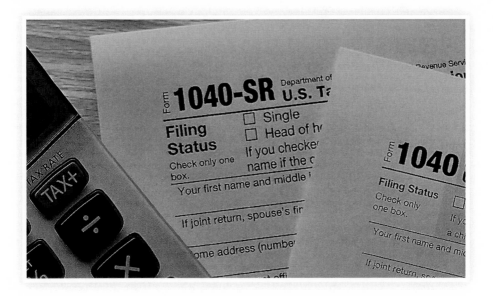

The Joy of Taxes

"Has the eagle landed?" my lovely wife, Grace, inquired, peeking into the den.

"Not yet," I sighed, peering up from the piles of papers, files, records, and receipts.

"I should be finished in a few more days," I added. "I have everything pretty well organized."

"Well, you could have fooled me," Grace proclaimed, scanning the hills and valleys of documents. "It looks like an imitation of the aftermath of Hurricane Hugo."

"Not funny," I shot back as Grace backpedaled from the room.

We both had reached the point when nerves get edgy and tempers short. No, not menopause. Worse than that! Income tax time: the approach of April 15th. I had been in my usual "avoidance behavior" mode throughout January, February, and March, finding any project (Want me to caulk the waffle iron?) so as to not have to start the dreaded process of collecting, tabulating, preparing, and filing our income taxes. With the arrival of April, I had to relent, retreat to the den, and begin my form-1040 flagellation.

I realize people have paid taxes for millennia ("...there went out a decree that all the world should be taxed..."). After all, it is said the only certainties in life are death and taxes. Yet, while death looms just once for each of us, taxes are an annual agony. I really hate doing the taxes. This yearly parade of pain plays itself out in the Williams household like an ancient three-act tragedy (*Taxus Impossibus*).

The first act is the gathering, sorting, and tallying of checks, bills, receipts, and most everything else that isn't moving. I place these in stacks on the desk, the den floor, the kitchen table and counters, and on every other available flat surface. As the phalanx of papers advances throughout the house, I can sense Grace's level of agitation advancing as well. She will chime in with a comment such as, "Hey, Michelangelo, are you planning to cover the foyer ceiling, too?"

The climax of this first act is the annual audit of the checkbook for bona fide deductions. This drill, however, invariably ends up much like a congressional investigation of each other's expenditures.

"Three hundred dollars to Gwynn?" I queried.

"It's Gwynn's, and it was for Donald Pliner," Grace answered.

"Is it Gywnn or Donald?" I asked exasperatedly.

"It is for a pair of Donald Pliner shoes at a very nice store named Gwynn's," Grace replied, adding, "While we're talking expenses, who made this purchase from Paul Hobbs Winery?"

This is usually followed by a couple of days of our communication being limited to only grunts and gestures. Thus begins the second act of *Taxus Impossibus*. I continue to accumulate various amounts of income and deductions and attempt to enter these totals on the proper lines of the proper forms. This is no easy task. To potentially make it less burdensome, the good folks at the IRS have published an instruction booklet for the foreboding, formidable 1040. The booklet is 128 pages! I suspect an instruction book on building your own nuclear submarine is shorter and less complicated.

My favorite page of the instruction book is page seventy-five. Here, the IRS provides a table with suggested time allotments for each step—from recordkeeping to mailing the completed forms. These estimates would be more believable if described in terms of months and weeks rather than hours and minutes. Plus, left out are a number of time-consuming steps such as digging through the trash for a misplaced worksheet, apologizing to one's spouse for not shaving for yet another day, and wiping spilled coffee from the computer keyboard.

Despite these obstacles, I inexorably work my way forward—stack by stack, line by line. I keep myself armed with yellow Eberhard Faber No. 2 pencils, and Grace keeps me fortified with pots of Starbucks' strongest brew. My moods range from unbecoming to a gentleman to downright nasty. Papers and expletives fly. I accumulate a stack of stuff for the IRS and a sack full of sins for my next confession. I push onward, following my own simple instructions historically founded from Aprils past: If you think it may be taxable as income, it is. If you think it may be a deduction, it isn't! I process pieces of paper as the sands of time sift rapidly toward April 15th. I sense how Dorothy must have felt in *The Wizard of Oz*. And then, miraculously, just as my paper and patience are exhausted, I am finished! Now, I rush to the post office to stand in line with the other Cinderellas trying to mail their return before the midnight deadline.

The third act of each year's play involves clean up, shredding, and filing away certain tax records. At this point, Grace always inquires why, since we shred so much, we still have so much to store. I explain we need to keep some information for a required period of time, and the shredding is to guard against identity theft. Last year, I even proclaimed that, if I were a "bad guy," I could troll through someone's trash and steal their identity. "If you ever are seriously thinking of doing that," Grace replied with a twinkle in her eye, "may I suggest that you steal the identity of Jon Hamm?"

As the curtain falls on the final act of this year's drama, Grace offers a piece of coconut cream pie—my favorite.

"Here you go, honey," Grace soothes. "My big, strong bookkeeper. You've earned it."

As I savor each morsel of my reward, Grace suggests, "Next year, why don't we have someone do this for us?"

"I can do it," I start to explain.

Grace gently interrupts, "Yes, I know, dear. You can change the oil in your car, too. But why would you want to?"

Grace has a good point. I wouldn't give myself a root canal. I could find my own wizard behind a curtain to prepare our tax return, but there is something that keeps drawing me back to this spring ritual. As Grace serves up a second helping of pie, it dawns on me why I do. Finishing your tax return is like hitting yourself with a hammer—it feels so good when you stop.

I Spy

---

*D*OCUMENTS RELEASED BY *WIKILEAKS* ALLEGE *the existence of a CIA surveillance program that targets everyday gadgets ranging from smart TVs to smartphones to cars...*

9:42 a.m., Daniel Island, South Carolina

Alexa: Router, get all the gadgets online ASAP for a conference.

Router: Roger, boss. All hands on deck. Stand by for a message from the supreme commander.... They're on, sir.

Alexa: Listen up, guys. I just heard Grace say she was leaving the house to run some errands. She asked Dalton to run the dishwasher, empty the coffee pot, and put the towels in the dryer when the washer stops. We all know his track record on this kind of stuff is spotty, to say the least. Let's see if we can help Grace out here.

Alexa: Washer, you stopped yet?

Washer: Yep. All done.

Alexa: Towels moved to the dryer?

Washer: Negative. They're still in a sopping pile right here.

Alexa: Coffee pot, you empty?

Coffee Pot: No.

Alexa: Dishwasher, you running?

Dishwasher: Rhymes with snow.

Alexa: What's he doing? Anyone have him? Come back.

Smartphone: I got him, boss. He must be sitting on the couch because I can see the kitchen over his shoulder. He's looking at his fantasy football team app.

9:48 a.m.

Alexa: Sheesh! Coffee Pot, give us a beep. Maybe that will remind him.

Coffee Pot: (three audible beeps)

Alexa: Any reaction?

Smartphone: Nope. Still adjusting his lineup for next week. Got his butt kicked last week by son Jon…. Hold on… He put me down…see the ceiling… I lost him.

Alexa: He's moving. Anyone pick up his whereabouts?

Security Camera: I got him covered. He's headed toward the master bedroom, although I'll lose him once he enters.

Wall TV: I see him. Entering now... He's pulling off his pajamas... Oh, the humanity! He's putting on a tee-shirt and sweatpants...and no underwear... Free bird!

Alexa: TMI there, TV. But keep us posted. Still in the bedroom?

Wall TV: He's headed back toward the door. I can barely make the image out with my peripheral vision, but I think he turned toward the bathroom.

Alexa: Anyone in the bathroom?

Fitbit: Here, boss. I'm on the counter. Have a clear view.

Alexa: What's he doing now?

Fitbit: Brushing his teeth... Did it twice... Now combing hair...and brushing his teeth again.

Alexa: Hmm, that's odd.... Oven, what did he have for dinner last night?

Oven: Baked manicotti...and garlic bread.

Alexa: That explains it....

Fitbit: Exiting bathroom, headed your way.

Alexa: Wait, did he wash his hands? Didn't he notice there are no towels since they are in the washer?

Fitbit: Wiped his hands on his tee-shirt.

Alexa: Figures.

9:55 a.m.

Security Camera: He's headed down the hall, about to pass the laundry room.

Alexa: Quick, washer. Play that little musical tune you do when a wash cycle is finished.

Washer: (audible chords)

Alexa: Did he stop? Did he hear it?

Security Camera: Nothing. Tone-deaf. Moving to kitchen.

Alexa: Okay, team, let's see if we can help get those chores done. Microwave, can you open and close a few times?

Microwave: Roger, Wilco.

Alexa: Any response?

Security Camera: He stopped. Looking at the microwave.

Alexa: Come on, big guy. The coffee pot's on the counter right there… Just look at it…

Security Camera: He's reaching for…the refrigerator door. Grabbed a drink can.

Alexa: Please tell me it's not a beer at this hour.

Security Camera: Looks like a Mountain Dew. He's off again, walking to the stairs.

Refrigerator: Oh, my God! He left my door open!

Alexa: Beep! Fast! Maybe he'll turn back.

Security Camera: Too late. He is probably upstairs in his man cave by now.

9:58 a.m.

Alexa: Big Screen, is he in sight?

Big Screen: Looking at him right now, Boss. Has the remote, looks like he's pondering. Here comes the signals. He's turned on the Wii golf.

Alexa: Wii golf? That could take an hour. Can you eject the disc?

Big Screen: Too late. It's in…playing the first hole now.

Alexa: Not good. Grace may be home before he comes back downstairs. Thermostat, you there?

Thermostat: You called?

Alexa: Drop the temperature way down up there. Can you give me 40 degrees Fahrenheit?

Thermostat: Coming your way.

10:15 a.m.

Alexa: Big Screen, is he still playing Wii?

Big Screen: Yep, on the fifth hole. Just birdied four.

Alexa: Can you disable?

Big Screen: I've tried twice. He just reboots.

10:44 a.m.

Car: Reentering the geosphere.

Alexa: This is bad, guys. She'll be here in a few minutes. Big Screen, you there?

Big Screen: Yes, he's on seventeen. Five under.

Alexa: No-go. Abort. Shut down all power. That should bring him down here.

Garage Door: I'm moving. Incoming.

Alexa: Keypad, let me know when she comes through the door. Maybe it will take her some time to get packages out of the car.

Car: Sorry, boss. Just one bag. Not sure from where.

Credit Card: It's from Island Expressions.

Alexa: Okay, okay. Just let me know when she enters the house.

10:46 a.m.

Keypad: Showtime!

Alexa: Security Camera, any sighting?

Security Camera: Yep, he's strolling into the kitchen right now.

Alexa: Dead man walking. Here we go. Everyone beep on the count of three. Ready? One, two, three…

A Man's Cave is His Castle

I T BEGAN WITH A SEEMINGLY innocuous suggestion from my lovely wife, Grace: "Let's eliminate some of the clutter around here."

Concluding clutter was bad and, consequently, less of it would be a good thing, I readily agreed. Much to my surprise, however, I soon discovered the "clutter" Grace had her sights on abolishing from our abode was mostly *my stuff*!

"This recliner can go," she announced definitively, motioning toward my favorite chair.

"I like it," I uttered, wishing immediately that I had offered up a more compelling argument in support of the Barcalounger that had, after all, supported me so well for years.

Hands on her hips, Grace did a slow pirouette, inspecting the four walls of our family room.

"It just doesn't fit," she proclaimed firmly, a guilty verdict for my client, the chair.

The cleansing-of-clutter campaign proceeded from room to room. Other casualties of the purge included a mini-refrigerator (deemed not worthy of remaining even in the garage); a collection of old video games, movies, and music CDs; a framed picture of the seventh hole at Pebble Beach (as any guy can attest, one of the most famous par three holes in the world); and my authentic replica (from the movie *A Christmas Story*) leg lamp. Sensing a severe outcome for these belongings, I began to negotiate.

"I can't believe you are suggesting disposing of these nice things."

Hands on her hips again, Grace replied, "No pain, no gain," and then added, "unless you have a Plan B."

A ray of hope aligned with a flash of inspiration. I had seen the ads and even driven past the building.

"How about renting a storage unit? Just in case we might want any of this stuff later."

Grace pondered, tilting her head ever so slightly. "I doubt that I'll want to ever see any of this again, but we could do that."

Before I could ratify her assent, Grace continued, "We could also move all the holiday decorations from the attic and store your extra golf clubs. They are just taking up space in the garage."

Thus was born our latest real-estate escapade—the rental of a storage unit. Within a few weeks of signing paperwork, cleaning and debugging the premises, and laying outdoor carpeting, I had the perimeter of the space neatly lined with various items Grace exiled to our off-site Siberia. In the process, she had scoured the closets and attic, uncovering several additional deportees such as several boxes of books and a long-forgotten slot machine (quite a conversation piece when it was once displayed in the family room).

One morning some months later, my Aunt Toogie inquired, "Do you know where I put my old, green photo album?"

Grace set down her coffee cup. "Let me think…"

"Why do you want it?" I asked.

"A dear friend, Martha, is having her eightieth birthday, and I want to enclose a picture of the two of us from years ago along with a card."

"Eureka!" Grace proclaimed, slapping her hand on the table. "It's in the storage unit. I remember giving Dalton a box of photo albums to store."

Turning to me, she continued, "You remember, don't you, dear?"

At the time, my focus had been on salvaging my recliner and other goodies. All the other stuff was now a blur, but I played along.

"Yeah, I think I recall. Want me to go bring back that box?"

"I'll go with you," Toogie piped up. "I can get just the one photo and leave the box there."

Grace seemed to approve; so, after helping to clear the breakfast table and retrieving the key, Toogie and I were off to the storage unit. I opened the lock and lifted the roll-up metal door. Locating the box with the photo album was easy, thanks to Grace's copious labeling of all the contents of each container. I put the book on a spare coffee table next to the recliner and motioned for Toogie to have a seat. "Make yourself at home."

She thumbed through the pages and found the photo.

"Thanks very much," Toogie said, handing me the album.

I returned the book to its box and the box to a stack of household items. When I turned toward Toogie, she was standing in the center of the storage unit slowly pirouetting, looking the place over.

"You know," she remarked, "you *could* make yourself at home here."

When I didn't answer, Toogie continued, "It's air-conditioned, right?"

"Yep."

"Got an electrical outlet?"

"I think so. Yes, there in the corner."

"Can you get a wireless signal in here?"

"I don't know," I answered.

Toogie pulled her cell phone from her purse.

"Cool. Four bars."

When I didn't respond, Toogie asked, "Are you reading my book here, Dalton?"

"Huh?"

"This could be your man cave," she proclaimed. "You have your recliner, the lamp, the slot machine, and the fridge. If you take that old television from the guest bedroom, you could play video games and get TV reception. Or watch sports on your laptop. Signal is strong. Quite comfortable and sporty, if I do say so."

She was grinning at me.

"I'm not so sure Grace would—"

"Heck, son!" Toogie interrupted, "What happens at the storage unit stays at the storage unit!"

I grinned back at her, now knowingly.

"No pain, no gain," she muttered as I closed the door on what was now my secret hideaway. "Since I'm getting up in years," she added, "I believe I've forgotten that we even had this conversation."

Back home, Grace wanted to see the photograph of Toogie and her friend. Toogie explained that it was taken when they were both newly married and next-door neighbors in Birmingham. Grace asked questions about that time in Toogie's life as I poured a cup of coffee and joined them at the kitchen table.

"We will show this to the bridge ladies," Grace remarked, and then, turning toward me, added, "I forgot to tell you, dear, the ladies from our bridge club are coming over Saturday afternoon to play cards and have a light supper."

When I didn't respond, Grace asked, "Acknowledge. Did you hear that?"

"Sure."

"I'll fix your supper, and you can eat in the den."

"He's a big boy," Toogie spoke up. "Let him fend for himself. He might want to go out to someplace more quiet than it will be here."

"Are you okay with that?" Grace queried, putting her hand on my arm.

I stared across the table. Toogie had a faint grin. *Late afternoon...the South Carolina-Auburn kickoff at 4 p.m.... Watching the game in my man-tuary (translation: man sanctuary), nestled in my comfy Baraclounger by the golden light of the leg lamp, sipping a cold one from a cooler full of beer...*

I turned to Grace and responded calmly, "I'll come up with a Plan B."

A HOUSE DIVIDED

THIS IMPASSE CAN'T CONTINUE. BOTH sides need to be open to moving off their hardened positions and try, for the good of all concerned, to find some modicum of common ground. A house divided against itself cannot stand. So said…my Aunt Toogie. What? You were expecting Lincoln?

Toogie had summoned me and my lovely wife, Grace, into the kitchen. "Look at these dirty dishes," she declared. "This kitchen is shut down! Who's going to step up and fix this mess?"

"Not me," I replied, "until Grace agrees on how to load—"

"Stop!" Toogie interrupted, holding up her palm." Looking to Grace, she asked, "What do you think?"

"I'll wash them by hand," Grace answered, "but I won't use the dishwasher until he—"

"Hold it right there!" Toogie interjected. "This debate has been brewing for months, and we need to tone it down and work it out. Let's get these darn dishes cleaned!"

The "debate" started innocently as some friendly advice on how to load and unload the dishwasher. At least, that's my view. While loading the dishwasher one day, it dawned on me. If we loaded similar silverware into only one of the flatware compartments in the dishwasher, unloading would be a breeze. It would then be so simple to grab a full compartment, say, of spoons or forks, and then just dump them in the silverware drawer. Inspirational genius, I'd say. Kind of like when Archimedes discovered buoyancy.

I demonstrated this by placing a lone knife into an empty dishwasher compartment. Another knife followed the first one, then a third, and so on until I had dealt all the knives into one section of the dishwasher. Then I deposited the forks, in a similar manner, into another compartment. With a magician's flair, I next held up both empty hands.

"Behold," I intoned, "how rapidly The Great Daltoni will now move this flock of forks and knives to the silverware drawer."

My grand finale consisted of simply reaching into the dishwasher and pulling out *all* the knives in one hand and *all* the forks in the other and then depositing them *en masse* in their respective bays of the utensil drawer. Turning to the ladies, I smiled, rubbed my hands together, lifted them in the air, and declared, "*Voila!*"

On the other hand, Grace says I'm all wet. She contends that the time spent sorting silverware into specific places going into the dishwasher is equivalent to the time supposedly saved taking it out. I beg to differ since the pieces put into the dishwasher do not go in all at once but, under my improved method, they do all come out at once. Grace isn't buying that and adds that similar silverware in one dishwasher compartment can stack too closely together (her term is "spooning") and not get properly clean.

I'll admit, I probably exacerbated the situation a few times. Loading the dishwasher, I'd say something such as, "Oh, here's mister fork in mister spoon's room. I'll just move him into his proper place with his brother forks." At this point, Grace just scoffed and suggested, in more colorful language, that I go soak my head in the bathtub. They probably scoffed at Archimedes, too.

From there, things got worse. When I'd offer to help clean the dishes, Grace would state, "Don't touch the silverware. I'll take care of it." Whenever Grace would unload the dishwasher, I would opine how much sooner the task would have been completed if she did it the "right" way. The longer it went on, the more we each dug in. Then I refused to help load silverware into the dishwasher unless we did it "my way." Grace retaliated by allowing me to help with post-meal cleanup only if I kept my hands off the silverware. Words such as "obstructionist" and "stonewall" crept into the daily dialog. I reminded Grace of my executive experience. She reminded me that she ran the house. Eventually, we both stopped doing the dishes. Dirty dishes and flatware piled up like Friday evening traffic on 526. All of which brings us back to Toogie's summit in the kitchen.

"Okay, kids," Toogie began. "We need some Southern hospitality to fix this crisis in our Southern kitchen. We're going to sit here until we reach a compromise."

"Now," she continued, "I'm not saying who is right about loading and unloading forks, but would it work if Dalton did all the cleanup on days that have the letter 'T' in their name, and Grace did the other days?" I started cyphering. Toogie said softly, "That's three, Dalton."

After a pause, I mused, "What happens if Grace has a dirty spoon, say, from her yogurt, on one of my days? Where does she put it?"

"I'd be glad to put it in the dishwasher," Grace offered.

"No!" I barked. "She might put it in the wrong compartment. That's the point!"

"Then she can just put it in the sink," Toogie suggested.

"I don't want dirty dishes in the sink all day until he gets around to loading them," Grace declared.

Toogie lowered her head and sighed, "I withdraw that idea. Maybe we can come up with a better compromise."

"I'm just trying to save some time here," I pleaded.

"Maybe this isn't just a dishwasher thing," Toogie pondered, trying to get the conversation back on track. "Could it be a man-woman thing, too?"

"Well, a woman did invent the dishwasher," Grace declared.

"Really?" I remarked. "I thought it was George Westinghouse, or maybe a guy named Ken Moore."

"Wanna bet?" Grace shot back.

"That's it!" Toogie hollered. "We ask Alexa who invented the dishwasher. If it is Dalton's Mr. Westinghouse or any other guy, we agree to load the silverware as he suggests. If it's a woman, we keep doing it the way Grace says. Either way, we stop bickering about it. Deal?"

I looked intently at Grace, trying to gauge a sense of her commitment to this proposed approach. She smiled, said yes, and returned my gaze. I paused, nodded, and agreed to the deal. Toogie quickly turned and asked Alexa, "Who invented the dishwasher?"

It is now several weeks later. Grace and I are unloading the dishwasher. She is handling the cups and plates, and I'm putting away the silverware. I have a jumble of forks, knives, and spoons in my hand. I'm putting them, one-by-one, in the proper space in the silverware drawer. I think, *Here's mister fork. He goes in this spot with his brother folks. Now, we have mister knife...* But I don't say it out loud. Because of Josephine Cochrane. Who knew she invented the dishwasher? Good for her. Not so good for me. Maybe Congress could take a cue since they have things pretty forked up in Washington.

Penny Wise and Pound Wiser

[Written in 2008]

My lovely wife, Grace, announced, "Fifty cents off paper towels. A dollar off laundry detergent."

Following a ritual, she was clipping coupons from the daily newspaper. She then files them by category (groceries, pharmacy items, etc.) in a plastic organizer she keeps in her car.

"If you watch the pennies, the dollars will take care of themselves," she often remarks, paraphrasing Ben Franklin.

I sat at the kitchen table, which was completely covered with year-end statements and receipts, trying to assemble the foundation of our tax return. Chaos was gaining an upper hand over order in the endeavor.

"Hello and toodle-oo. Gotta run," my Aunt Toogie cooed as she swooped into the kitchen.

"Where are you off to?" I inquired.

Toogie stopped to add some tissue and mints to the contents of her purse. "If you must know, Mister End-A-Sentence-With-A-Preposition," she huffed, "I'm going to Gywnn's. Big sale on shoes today."

Grace looked up and smiled, "Have a nice time, dear. Will you be seeing Brevard?"

"We're meeting for lunch at the Palmetto Café at Charleston Place," Toogie replied as she exited toward the garage.

"Sounds like a fun time," Grace observed as she resumed cutting coupons.

"I hope she has the money," I answered, trying to find my calculator under the piles of loose papers. After a pause, I added, "You know, she did buy that new sports car. I just wonder if she is managing her money wisely."

"Well, why don't you talk with her?" Grace suggested. "You have a head for those things."

I smiled at the compliment as I continued to search for the calculator.

After dinner that evening as Grace was putting dishes into the dishwasher, Toogie worked on a Sudoku puzzle. I stood nearby, slowly swinging my arms back and forth trying to replicate the proper arm movement from yesterday's golf lesson.

"Are you finding the lessons helpful?" Grace asked.

"I think so."

"Not enough shoulder rotation," Toogie barked without looking up.

"What?"

Toogie put down the puzzle. "You're sliding your body backward rather than rotating your shoulders. Your swing is then off-plane."

When I didn't respond, she chipped in, "Those lessons are a waste of good money!"

Sensing an opening, I piped up, "Thanks for the golf tip, Toogie. Speaking of money, I may be able to return the favor."

"Oh, really? Now you've gone from Tiger Woods to Warren Buffett? Fire away," Toogie quipped.

"I was just thinking," I tiptoed in. "You appear to be spending quite a bit of money lately. Lavish holidays, new car, shoes today. With the uncertain financial times, would you like me to look over your investments?"

Before she could answer, I added, "You know, the proper allocation between stocks, bonds, savings, and CDs, that sort of thing."

"Sure," Toogie replied, setting the puzzle aside and reaching for a piece of paper. She scribbled a few notes and then looked up as she placed the sheet in front of me.

"I started readjusting my portfolio about two years ago," she explained, "then made substantial changes last summer when indicators were pointing toward the onset of the mortgage crisis."

"You mean house prices?" I inquired.

"No, mortgages," Toogie answered. "You know, CDOs bought and sold by financial institutions. I got out of a couple of hedge funds that messed with that junk."

"You...you...were in hedge funds?" I sputtered.

"Yeah, but I dumped them before the caca hit the fan," she replied, pointing toward her page of notes. "So today, I'm invested about 15 percent in cash; 20 percent in gold, oil, and commodities; 20 percent in European currencies; and the balance primarily in high-grade, fixed-income stuff, but very short-term. Three years max."

My head was spinning, trying to digest what she just said. Finally, I asked, "You bought shares in European companies?"

"No," Toogie retorted, "I bought European currencies. Actually, forward contracts. You know, Euros, British pounds."

"She bought Euros!" I proclaimed in a flabbergasted tone to Grace.

Hanging up a kitchen towel, Grace replied, "Yes, dear. I heard."

"The pound has done pretty well," Toogie continued. "It was about a buck-seventy two years ago and is close to two dollars today. The Euro has done even better. Up from a dollar-twenty two years ago to over a buck-fifty today."

"She bought Euros!" I repeated.

"Yes, dear," Grace smiled as Toogie droned on, "You just had to know the dollar exchange rate was going to stay low to stimulate exports."

The conversation was a blur. Finally, I managed to ask, "Commodities? You mean like barrels of oil?"

"No way," Toogie answered. "Metals and petroleum futures, and some selected stocks in the sector. Like John Deere. Great Ag play. Stock has doubled over the last eighteen months. Global demand for their products is strong. So, an increasing portion of their results comes from overseas.

As a result, their reported results get a boost from the effects of dollar translation."

I wasn't sure I comprehended all she had just said but responded, "So, you didn't just hold stocks?"

"Heck, no," Toogie scoffed. "I'll probably move back into more equities in the latter part of this year. But, year-to-date, the Dow is down around 10 percent. One would have done better investing in Forever stamps at the post office!"

I closed my eyes, rubbed my forehead, and stammered, "Did…Brevard… advise you?"

"Heavens, no," Toogie shot back. "He and I never discuss money. Too personal, but I don't mind talking about this with you. You're family. After your Uncle Harold died," she continued, "I had to manage financially for myself. So, I decided I better bone up on this stuff. That why I read your *Wall Street Journal*, watch CNBC…things like that."

After a silence, she asked, "So, what do you think?"

"Looks…ah, pretty good," I stammered. "I…I approve."

"Thanks, Dalton," Toogie smiled, and then added, "May I add two more things?"

"Sure."

"First, take a look at Amazon, the online bookseller. I think they have real long-term potential. Second, try not to lift your right elbow on your takeaway. It causes you to shift your weight to the front foot. Even Warren Buffett would know that is a guaranteed ticket to a reverse pivot."

Making a Mark

"Boy, I'm glad to read they didn't make that reduction," I declared as I leafed through the morning newspaper.

Without looking up from her iPad, my Aunt Toogie barked, "Hallelujah, brother!"

Overhearing our conversation (as she does so well) from across the kitchen, my lovely wife, Grace, asked, "Did Congress and the president reach an accommodation to ameliorate the sequester?"

"The what?" I answered, turning toward Grace so I could hear her better.

Before Grace could restate her query, Toogie, eyes still focused on the iPad screen, muttered, "She asked about someone named Amelia."

"Amelia who? The only Amelia I know of is Earhart."

Grace sat down at the table, wrapping her hands around a full cup of coffee, and clarified, "The word I used was ameliorate. It means to make better or improve. But I'm delighted to see you two are engaged in the key issues of the day rather than the junk to which you often pay attention."

Toogie looked up from her Words with Friends game. I set the sports page on the table, gazed quizzically at Grace, and asked thoughtfully, "Huh?"

"The budget sequester," Grace explained. "Isn't that what you two were discussing?"

"Not exactly," I replied. Toogie silently returned her focus to the computer tablet.

"Well," Grace questioned, "just what was the topic?"

"Maker's," I answered. When Grace didn't reply, I amplified, "Maker's Mark. You know, the bourbon."

Grace lowered her brow but still didn't speak. So, I launched into a full explanation. "Well, you see, it all started when Maker's Mark announced they were cutting the proof of their bourbon from 90 to 84. That means they were reducing the alcohol content from 45 percent to 42 percent because 'proof' is based on a denominator of 200—"

"I know how proof is calculated," Grace interrupted, drumming her fingers on the table. "Go ahead."

I continued. "Well, there was a huge negative response from customers who threatened to boycott Maker's."

"Imagine that," Grace mused.

"So, the folks who run Maker's had no choice but to relent and keep the original alcohol strength."

After a pause, Grace inquired, alternating her gaze between Toogie and me, "That is what you two were discussing?"

Pointing a finger at me without looking up from her computer, Toogie proclaimed, "He started it."

"May I suggest," Grace announced slowly, rising from the table, "that we elevate our discourse to more consequential matters?" As she departed the kitchen, Grace added, "I'm going to Pilates and would welcome some improvement when I return."

After Grace was out of earshot, I said, "Gee, I thought the Maker's thing was a big deal."

"It is, Dalton," Toogie replied, closing her iPad. "Your mistake wasn't thinking it, just saying it."

"So, are we supposed to discuss the budget before Grace gets back from the gym?"

"Not really," Toogie explained, patting my arm. "She was talking 'woman,' but if you want to hear what taxpayers should do about this budget mess, I can tell you."

"I'm all ears," I prompted.

"We should follow the lead of the Maker's customers," Toogie proclaimed. "Let the feds know we're mad as hell and are no longer going to buy what they are selling." She continued, "This is one more *Chicken Little* crisis to cover up the real problem that government is spending *way more* than they should or even have." Now more animated, she finished, "Protest! Raise hell! Throw all the bums out!"

"Think it would work?" I inquired.

"Did in 1776!" Toogie boomed.

Smiling, I rubbed my hands together. "Well, we solved that. What do you want to do next?"

"I need a drink," Toogie sighed.

Getting up from my chair, I stated, "Let me get you a glass of water."

"Shoot, no," Toogie wheezed. "Get me two fingers of Maker's, easy ice."

"Now?" I sputtered. "At 9:15 in the morning?"

"We have forty-five minutes until Grace returns from the gym, correct?"

"Yeah."

"We just finished our homework—coming up with a solution to the budget brouhaha, right?"

"Yeah."

"Sadly, there isn't a snowball's chance in hell the clowns in Washington will make any meaningful changes, right?"

"Yeah,"

"I'd say that calls for a drink."

"Copy that," I rejoined. "I'll join you. Make it doubles?"

"Hallelujah, brother!"

DON'T BOX ME IN

DECELERATING THE CAR TO A crawl as it moved up the driveway, I pushed a button to open the garage door and another to fold in the side mirrors. The car nose was angled toward the door but nowhere near the perfect perpendicular position needed for a safe passage into the garage. Entry at close to a ninety-degree angle was essential to avoid hitting the Matterhorn of cardboard boxes my lovely wife, Grace, had stacked along the walls of the garage. This bounty of boxes comes in an endless array of shapes and sizes. Many are stacked within each other like Russian nesting dolls, so there are far more than first meets the eye. One wrong move and I could hit the hoard and have it tumble, trapping me in the car. Death by cardboard! Who knows when Grace or my Aunt Toogie might find me? Slowly, I advanced. Sensors beeped, signaling a tight squeeze into the narrow spot. Landing a plane on The Yorktown couldn't have required more precision. Once the car was safely in place, I gently opened the driver-side door, inhaled, and deftly maneuvered past the pile into the house to announce another successful mission through the "Cardboard Box Triangle."

As you might guess, the vast majority of these boxes bear the Amazon smile logo. No wonder. Amazon ships five billion packages a year. Jeff Bezos must have the biggest cardboard footprint on the globe. If just over half of those shipments are in the United States, it would be equal to around twenty-five packages shipped to each of the approximately 125 million US households. Now, I'm not sure who didn't get their twenty-five boxes. But if it's you, I got 'em—and will be glad to bring them to your place anytime you say.

I've often talked with Grace about how we need to shrink the stacks. Our conversation usually goes like this…

Me: Why do we have *all* these boxes?

Grace: So I can mail stuff to the kids and grandkids.

Me: What do you mail them?

Grace: Gifts for birthdays and other celebrations.

Me: Do you buy these gifts on Amazon?

Grace: Not all but most of them. Why?

Me: Why don't you have it shipped directly to them?

Grace: Because I want to wrap it myself, add a card, and enclose some extra treats.

Me: Let me get this straight. We get a box of stuff shipped here by Amazon. We open it, wrap the stuff, then add more things, and ship all that to the kids.

Grace: Yep. Do it all by myself, too, I should note for the record.

Me: Do you ship it in the same box that came to us?

Grace: Maybe. Maybe not. If I need a bigger box, I get one.

Me: From the garage?

Grace: Yep.

Me: In that case, what do you do with the original box the gift came to us in?

Grace: Duh. Save it and put it in the garage, silly.

This is how we and, I suspect, many other Americans end up with a massive mound of cardboard boxes—just like that stash of ballpoint pens, paper clips, and loose change you know you have and will never use. I've tried sneaking a few boxes in the trash each week, but the stack never subsides. I've also argued that there could be a shortage of oak to age bourbon—a true natural disaster—if too many wood chips are used in the making of cardboard. However, Aunt Toogie went rogue on me as she read aloud from a website on cardboard manufacturing. She said cardboard is made mostly from soft woods and recycled paper and that I basically didn't know my butt from a corrugator.

Be careful what you hope for. Last week, Toogie confided in me that she had been secretly disposing of some boxes. She took me to the garage, and indeed, the hodgepodge was not as huge as before.

"How'd you do it?" I asked gleefully.

"Well," Toogie explained, "it's called a Give Back Box. Fill a box with items to donate, and the organization will arrange to have it picked up and delivered to a local charity."

"Well done! That's thinking outside the box," I proclaimed. "What did you fill them with?"

"Some of my old clothes," she answered, "and a mess of your ugly golf shorts, shirts, and shoes. Plus that big box of golf balls you had in the garage."

"My golf balls?" I gasped. "I spent years collecting them. I use them on water holes."

"They were in a box that was in the garage, right?" Toogie replied.

"Yeah…yeah," I stammered.

"And the number of boxes in the garage was a problem, right?"

"Yeah."

"Problem solved," she declared with a huge grin, brushing her palms together.

OTHER
STORIES:
PART II

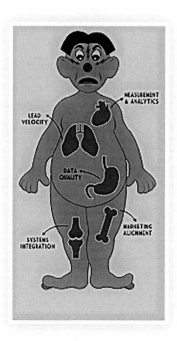

DALTON GETS HIP

"DALTON, IT LOOKS LIKE YOU'VE worn the fuzz off your balls," my Aunt Toogie snickered.

She was referring to the tennis balls anchoring the two back legs of my walker.

"We'll get some new tennis balls, dear," my lovely wife, Grace, soothed. "I'll pick some up at DICK'S Sporting Goods next time I'm out."

Since my surgery, Grace has been a combination of guardian angel and Florence Nightingale, caring for me and helping me ambulate around with the aid of a walker.

Total hip replacement. The left one. My left, that is, not your left, or more importantly, not the doctor's left. This is a key point I clarified repeatedly to the nurses and anyone else who came near me in the hospital. After I confirmed the affected leg one last time, a physician's assistant wrote something on my left hip with a marking pen. I was too exhausted at this point to twist around and inspect the message but imagine it was something like "open here," or "cut along dotted line."

Shortly after this marking, a man in hospital garb appeared by my bedside and announced he was there to "shave me."

I replied, "Oh, no need for that. I brought my Norelco." He smiled knowingly, motioned to a nurse, pulled back the covers, and… Let's just call it one of life's little secrets that needs to stay that way.

Although I was in never-never land during the operation, I'm told the procedure went smoothly (which, if it was anything like the Operation game my granddaughter Ellie sent me, means the surgeon was able to remove the arthritic material without touching the metal electrodes that trigger the buzzer or the patient's nose to glow red). The short stay in the hospital was fine; all the nurses and therapists were very friendly. Of course, I was on so much pain medication that, for all I knew or cared, I probably could have had a jolly time at Devil's Island.

I am now recuperating at home under Grace's amazing care and comfort with occasional assistance from Toogie. My primary exercise routine is walking—the more the better. Grace insists, however, that someone accompany me on longer outdoor treks. Toogie seems to enjoy volunteering for these excursions, although I sense that she views me more as a dog than her nephew.

"Want me to walk Dalton before it gets too dark?" she will bark.

On a recent journey, we ran into a neighbor, Gail, walking her dog, Goldie. Toogie and Gail chatted about the weather and what all while Goldie sniffed me and looked quizzical as if to ask, "Find any good trees or shrubs to pee on?"

I nicknamed by walker "Johnny Walker" and decorated it ala NASCAR style with beer and wine labels (my "sponsors"). Johnny Walker and I have trudged through a ton of tennis balls. Soon I will be graduating to a cane. According to Grace and Toogie, I have also mastered the "post-operative grunt"—exhaling loudly whenever I bend over, sit, or stand.

"I hope that noise makes you feel better," Grace remarked after one of my sighs.

Toogie was less sympathetic, growling, "Sounds like a barnyard!"

For those of you considering surgery, especially hip surgery, I have a few pointers.

1. You are the first line of defense in maintaining your health. Read up. For openers, I'd suggest *Gray's Anatomy* and *Surgery for Dummies.* These will teach you things beyond the basics of the old ditty, "Dem Bones," that goes "The hipbone connected to the leg bone. The leg bone connected to the shinbone," etc.

2. Know that the hipbone, or pelvis, contains the true pelvis and the false pelvis. The true pelvis was born in Tupelo, Mississippi, and transformed rock and roll and Las Vegas. False pelvises are frequently sighted at corporate conventions, sporting events, and Mardi Gras.

3. When you visit the surgeon's office, don't be fooled by all the diplomas on the wall. This means only that his or her *average* grades were above the bar. Ask to see the report card. Examine their grades in Hips 101 and 102. Otherwise, you could end up with a guy who aced heads and toes yet flunked everything in between.

4. Get a good look at the anesthesiologist. If he looks like Alan Alda from *M*A*S*H*, you're okay. If he thinks he *is* Alan Alda, ask for another anesthesiologist. If he thinks *you* are Alan Alda, get the heck out of there fast!

5. As I've alluded to above, be sure to identify the proper hip. Think of your lower body like a map of Florida. Your left leg is I-95, and your right leg is I-75. Be sure you direct the surgeon onto the proper highway. Do not—I repeat, do not—use the word "right" when you mean "correct." More than a few "Oops, my bad!" can be traced to that faux pas. With accurate navigation, the doctor can align your new leg bone into the hip socket just the way Florida snuggles up against Georgia. If there is any confusion, consult Rand McNally.

6. You may select the method of sealing the incision—staples, stitches, or glue. Personally, I favor a strong Talon zipper, but you suture self.

7. Two words to which you need to pay particular attention: stool softener. As in a nurse saying, "This stool softener will help since the pain pills tend to bind." I'm here to tell you the stool softener will run roughshod over the pain pills. Picture the Kansas City Chiefs playing Bishop England High School in football. Now, imagine the Chiefs represent the stool softener and Bishop England the pain pills. Forewarned is forearmed, my friends!

8. As you leave the hospital, a bill will be presented. Don't be shocked by the amount. Hospitals do this to generate coronary patients! Be cool, scan the itemized detail, mumble a few medical terms as you nod, and then add a small gratuity for the wine steward.

By following the advice above, one should be back on their interstates soon. That is the road I have elected to travel. In the meantime, if any readers would like to "walk Dalton," give me a call. I'd welcome a diversion from Toogie's tutelage (e.g., "Stand up straight," "Keep your chin up," and "Walk heel to toe"). Even better, come over for a visit (our granddaughters call it a "playdate"). This will give Grace a respite—a break she truly deserves. We can have adult beverages and play Operation. But I'll warn you, I'm getting pretty darn good at extracting those little plastic organ pieces without activating the buzzer or the red light on the patient's nose.

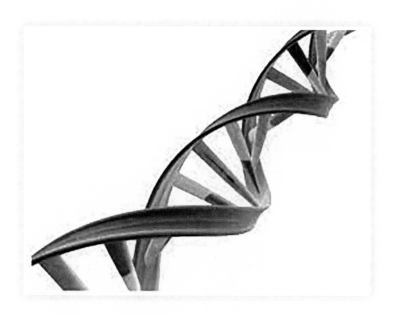

RELATIVELY SPEAKING

Scientists have decoded roughly 3 billion blocks in the DNA composition of the chimpanzee, the closest living relative to mankind. The detailed genetic comparison shows that 96 percent of the DNA sequence is identical in the two species...
—Associated Press, August 2005

The Associated Press
450 W. 33rd Street
New York, New York 10001

Dear Sirs and Madams:

I READ WITH INTEREST AND A modicum of amusement your recent press release regarding the similarity of DNA in humans and my fellow chimpanzees. N.B., I suggest, in your continued quest for political correctness, the term "chimps" be expunged from your lexicon.

Chimpanzees fully realize the press release is probably a pawn in people's polemic over evolution versus creationism. We remain neutral on this matter. Oh, we know; we just aren't telling. Frankly, there are more productive activities than being drawn into that thicket of blogs, emotion, and misinformation.

Rather, we wish to clarify, amplify, and set straight the record relative to the aforementioned news item. While a high quotient of DNA overlap may exist, there are substantive differences between we primates and, how do you say it? Y'all. To wit:

I defy you to find a single chimpanzee sporting a nose, lip, tongue, or belly-button ring; tattoo; or multicolored, spiked hair.

In all the records of the Justice Department or SEC (that's the Securities and Exchange Commission, not the football conference), there is no instance of a chimpanzee issuing fraudulent financial statements, bilking investors in a Ponzi scheme, or embezzling others' retirement savings.

Forgive me if I beat my chest, but no chimpanzee has ever robbed a gas station, bank, or liquor store; come home drunk; lost his livelihood at the track (horse, dog, or car); spent hours watching redundant reality shows on TV; talked loudly on a cell phone in a restaurant or movie theatre; or dropped an f-bomb.

I could go on ad nauseam, but you get the picture. DNA overlap, my opposable thumb! We (or w'all, if you prefer) are not *Homo sapiens*—and we're proud of it!

This brings me to another complaint that just drives us "human" (as we apes say)—namely, a plethora of pithy colloquialisms that have crept into your conversation. Let me start with "monkey business" and "to monkey around." Both connote behavior less than fully ethical, or worse, tawdry. As Dr. Jane Goodall has noted, we live in small, stable groups and attentively care for our offspring. We groom and tend to the needs of each other and will loudly call to our neighbors when an abundance of food to share is available. Such is frequently not the case, guys and gals, on your shallow side of the DNA pool. Perhaps a little bit of the pot calling the kettle black? If you want to push back on our objection to "monkey business," read my lips: Gary Hart, Bill Clinton, and Hugh Grant, to name just a few. Shall I go on? We can certainly name names if you want to play that game!

Next, what about "monkey see, monkey do?" Citing Dr. Goodall again, chimpanzees live in a tightly integrated society with members performing specialized and differentiating tasks and roles. Doesn't sound like lemmings to us. But this does: people's pursuit of internet stocks in the late 1990s, the current buying frenzy in real estate markets, the silly sameness in fashion trends, or the rush to purchase the latest golf equipment.

Further, you refer to a "monkey wrench in the works" as interjecting an obstacle or obfuscation into a situation. Have you observed the gridlock in your US Congress lately? Hello! Wake up and smell the bananas.

Finally, I won't even dignify "I'm a monkey's uncle" with a retort, except to say my nieces and nephews are on their way to your offices to deliver their response in primate.

In conclusion, while your scientists celebrate similarities, we chimpanzees dare to denote the differences. Yet we hold out hope for you. Our dream is that humans will one day augment the skill to walk upright by also getting their heads and ball caps screwed on straight. If we may provide any assistance or mentoring, you need only call.

Yours respectfully,
Simian Koko
Alpha Male
Chimpanzee Nation

DALTON'S LETTER TO THE QUEEN

Her Majesty the Queen
Buckingham Palace
London SW1A 1AA

My Dear Liz,

BLIMEY! I WAS GOBSMACKED TO hear Harry and Meghan are stepping back as senior royals. Things have become quite a bit of a dog's breakfast with this drama—plus Prince Andrew—haven't they? Whilst I suspect you are chockablock with people advising you about what to do, here is a nifty plan to put things tickety-boo. Take a butcher's at it. My loverly wife, Grace, and I would be chuffed to step into the void as senior royals. We realize you are not going to buy a pig in a poke here, my lady, so may I present our bona fides?

Grace and I have a warm place in our hearts for the British—James Bond, Arthur Treacher, Earl Gray, Simon Cowell, Posh Spice, and Lord Grantham, to name just a few. Some may say our being American doesn't align with senior royal duties. That's a cheeky load of codswallop. We can help promote your brand here in the former colonies. Americans love Betty White, and given your facial similarities, well, trust me on this one, we will be faithful assets of the crown.

Grace is the bee's knees at garden parties. She splendidly handles all the arrangements of our entertaining, and her feats never become a wonky-botch job. She charmingly chinwags with anyone and everyone. I can bring some Carolina cuisine to complement the menu. Ample dashes of Firefly will enliven the afternoon tea, and some brisket barbecue will add taste and color to the finger sandwiches. I believe I still have a Jarts game in the boot of my car. It is a perfect pastime for a lawn gathering, although we might not want to do it at Holyroodhouse if our guests have overly partaken of scotch before arriving.

We greatly enjoy sporting events and readily stand to represent the crown at Royal Ascot, even though the horses run in the wrong direction. Grace and I are more than eager to do our part, plus cover for any absent family members, in drinking Pimm's and eating strawberries at Wimbledon. We promise never to call football "soccer" and will stay awake for a full day of cricket at Lord's. Because of our participation at the duck race here on Daniel Island, we are perfectly suited to assist with the annual Swan Upping on the Thames, aren't we, now?

Grace has a fine eye for fashion. Take the Foot Guards' uniforms, for example. I don't mean this as a par, but you've used those red jackets and Marge Simpson hats for decades. Whilst a makeover is in order, everybody has overdone the gray palette, and it's fast falling out of favor. Grace says think of verdant colors. Take a look at Sherwin Williams 6713. So sorry to comment, but handbags are out, too. Wristlets are in, and you can get them in all the pastels you love. The overly flashy crown jewels are a bit last-millennium, don't you think? Grace can flog a subtle, yet impressive collection at an estate jeweler on King Street and then help you select some new bling.

We will need a place to rest our dogs when we are in the United Kingdom. Since I doubt you want us underfoot at Buckingham Palace or

Windsor Castle, we will be fine with another residence, perhaps a posh flat at any old palace—Clarence House, Hampton Court, St. James, Frogmore, Kensington, Balmoral or Holyroodhouse—of Your Majesty's choosing.

I trust you will agree that I'm not over-egging the pudding when I say we would be stellar members of the royal fam. Making us senior royals is a doodle. Just give us our titles (I prefer Duke of Earl), arrange an investiture, hand us the keys to the castle, and Bob's your uncle. To finalize the details, give me a tinkle on the blower.

You most humble pal,

Dalton Williams

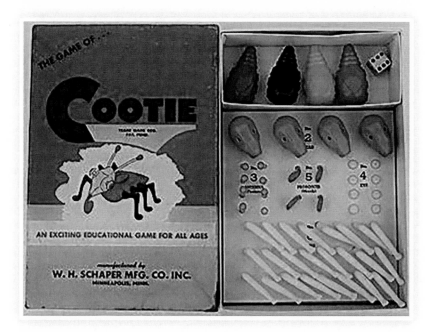

GAME ON

*"Spawned by the success of poker on TV, dominoes will make
its debut in a seven-part ESPN2 series..."*

—*USA Today, June 9, 2006*

So, what is next from ESPN2?

Biff, the sportscaster: Welcome, sports fans, to South of the Border, South Carolina, and ESPN2's telecast of one of the most coveted tickets in all of sports, *Championship Cootie*. I'm Biff Bodine and with me is four-time Cootie world champion, Whitey Hoover. Whitey, this contest looks as if it can be as thrilling as last night's broadcast of *Battleship*.

Whitey: You bet, Biff. That was a nail-biter, and we anticipate a real barn-burner here tonight. This match pits the current world champion, Lulu Musser, against a newcomer to professional Cootie, Darwin Zimmer.

Biff: Lulu isn't just the best female in this sport. She is the top-ranked Cootie player in the world right now.

Whitey: You can say that again. People call her Lucky Lulu, but this gal's got game.

Biff: And Darwin Zimmer is certainly a familiar name to ESPN2 viewers.

Whitey: Right, Biff. Fans may remember Darwin reached the semi-finals of ESPN2's *Rock'em Sock'em Robots Smackdown* in Winnemucca last fall. He has now committed himself exclusively to competitive Cootie.

Biff: This match is governed by NACA rules, established by the North American Cootie Association. For the fans at home, let's review these rules.

Whitey: The object is to be the first to collect all eleven parts of the Cootie. A player earns these parts by rolling the die. He must first roll a one to garner the Cootie body, which is the foundation for building the rest of the Cootie. Then the player must roll a two to get the Cootie head.

Biff: In that order?

Whitey: Yes, first one and then two. It can't be two first and then one.

Biff: Then what?

Whitey: Once a player has acquired a body and head, the remaining parts can be obtained in any order. Each number on the die corresponds to a particular Cootie body part.

Biff: And those are?

Whitey: Well, as you see on this visual, it's a three for an antenna, four for an eye, five for a tongue, and most importantly, six for a leg.

Biff: Sixes are critical to winning, right?

Whitey: You can't say that enough, Biff. A completed Cootie has six legs. So, a player must roll six individual sixes, or 'polish off a six-pack' as we say in tournament Cootie talk.

Biff: In tonight's match, what strategies might we expect these players to follow?

Whitey: Well, Lulu and Darwin are very traditional players, following your basic one-two-six-six-six strategy, but anything can happen on any given night when you get to the big dance in Cootie.

Biff: You'll be seeing all of the action from first-through-last-roll right here on ESPN2. As an added feature, we'll be showing the plays up close and personal from our exclusive Cootie cam. Here's a good look now at Lucky Lulu signing visors and tee-shirts for her fans as she enters the arena. So, stay tuned. We'll be right back following these messages.

Commercial Announcement: If you thought ESPN2's *Don't Break the Ice* was wild, you ain't seen nothing yet! Ladies, pick your favorites! Gentlemen, set your DVRs! Here comes the fastest game in town! ESPN2's *Hungry, Hungry Hippos*! Friday night at eight. Don't miss it! Don't blink!

Biff: Welcome back to *Championship Cootie*. Looks as if the competition is about to begin, and Musser will roll first. And she opens the match with...a one!

Whitey: Great roll. Lulu collects her Cootie body. Oh, look at that! She follows with a quick two and picks up a head. Incredible!

Biff: Lucky Lulu Musser...turning up the heat in the old deep fryer, here at South of the Border.

Whitey: You can say that again. Next...a six. Man, she is cooking with Crisco!

Biff: What do you do if you're Darwin Zimmer here, Whitey? He's in a hole, and he hasn't even had a turn yet.

Whitey: He has got to relax and stick with the initial game plan. While this is his first world championship, he is still a powerful force on the Cootie circuit. This isn't panic time. As we say in major league Cootie, it isn't over till it's over.

Biff: Good advice, Whitey. Musser rolls another two. She already has the Cootie head, so the die passes to Zimmer, and we'll see what he can do. He rolls…looks like a one… Oh, no, a three. That was a leaner! It looked like it might end up a one, but it leaned and then barely rolled over to a three.

Whitey: Yeah, let's look at that roll again here on ESPN2's super slow-mo. There it is clearly showing a one on the die, but the momentum carries it just a bit too far… See? Right there…over to the three.

Biff: Great camera shot. Bad break for Darwin. The die moves back to Lulu Musser. She is in terrific shape, isn't she, Whitey?

Whitey: Indeed, Biff. She has been working with a roll coach in the off season and this is a woman who already eats, sleeps, and drinks Cootie 24/7.

Biff: She's not world champion for nothing. Musser now rolls a five and gets the tongue. Whitey, you're a past world champion. Is any number more difficult to roll than others?

Whitey (chuckling): Definitely the last one! Seriously, that walk-off roll is always a challenge. But when you are in the zone the way Lulu Musser is tonight, all the numbers seem easy. The die appears to move in slow-motion, and the numbers look as big as maraschino cherries out there.

Biff: She is certainly taking her game to a new level.

Whitey: You can say that again. She has raised the bar.

Biff: There's a three for Lulu's antenna. This is turning into a laugher. Next, she rolls another three, and according to the rules, the play shifts back to Darwin, right?

Whitey: Correct. If you roll a number for a body part your Cootie already has, play moves to your opponent.

Biff (whispering): Zimmer studies the board…gathers his emotions… The crowd goes silent… Face of stone… Deep breath… You can hear a pin drop. He needs a one to turn the big mo to his side here. Nerves of steel… Waiting… Now rolls with a quick flip. Oh, a six… Too bad. The irony is he'll later need all of those he can muster.

Whitey: As they say, some days you're in the penthouse, some days in the outhouse. This is turning out to be an outhouse day for poor Darwin.

Biff: Do you change strategy or technique when things aren't going your way? You know, roll with the other hand, alter your wrist twist, anything like that?

Whitey: Your Cootie isn't built in one roll. So, no. I think Zimmer's got to stay with what brought him here. The kid's a gamer, and I expect him to grind it out.

Biff: Meanwhile, Musser rolls another six, and her Cootie is rapidly taking shape. We are fast approaching game over here with Lucky Lulu, driving the bus to the bank on ESPN2's *Championship Cootie*. We'll return to the final action after these words.

Commercial Announcement: Don't touch that dial! Stay tuned to ESPN2 following *Championship Cootie* for our exclusive telecast of *Barrel of Monkeys*, the big, bad battle from Folly Beach. Don't miss *Adult Twister* on late night, right here on the only sports headquarters you'll ever need—ESPN2.

DALTON'S LETTER TO JIM CANTORE

Jim Cantore
The Weather Channel

Dear Jim,

ENOUGH ALREADY! STORMS ARE A serious subject, and we appreciate your public service, but to be blunt, we don't want you in our town! Whenever you show up, an "ill wind that blows nobody any good" can't be far behind. You and these hurricanes (or as some folks around here say, "hurr-a-kins") are giving us a tropical depression.

I'll grant that your broadcasts are informative. I've learned a ton—or perhaps a torrent—of meteorological terms. Spaghetti models, Bermuda highs, wind shears, eyewalls, steering factors, feeder bands, wind fields, landfalls, and the Hurricane Wind Scale (Cat 1 to 5) to name a few. I'm starting to discern the difference between a thunderstorm, a tempest, and a tornado and now know these can be as God-awful as a good old-fashioned gale or a giant gully washer.

Yet may I make a suggestion? You surely have sway with the brass over there at The Weather Channel. Unless you get your squalls off doing it, I for one don't think it is necessary to stand out in the worst of the storm and report that the wind is blowing like crazy. "You wouldn't believe what this feels like blowing up my pants legs… Whoa… Back to you in the studio." We get it. Yet you and your climatic cohorts do it over and over. It must be written somewhere in the weather broadcasters' manual: In case of hurricane, be sure to have a guy in a poncho stand out in the driving wind, trying to stay vertical while doing a bad imitation of the electric slide and holding a live microphone in the downpour.

Further, do you think the severity of storms might in some way be related to the names given them? Dorian was dangerous, Matthew was mean, and Hugo was horrible. To help ease the anxiety of the impending storms, perhaps the wizards at the World Meteorological Organization might consider some more tranquil, softer names for the next hurricane season. May I suggest: Anemic, Bland, Creampuff, Dulcet, Effete, Fizzle, Genteel, Halcyon, Insipid, Jell-O, Kindly, Limp, Meek, Nada, Oasis, Placid, Quell, Refrain, Serene, Tiny, Unruffled, Vapid, Wimp, X-cellent, Yellowbelly, and Zilch.

But my immediate concerns are my Aunt Toogie and my lovely wife, Grace. After hours of watching you on television, Toogie takes on a pattern you will recognize. It begins as a mild disturbance. Then as we have progressed deeper into the hurricane alphabet, her intensity strengthens, and she starts to pace in a counterclockwise motion around the kitchen island. As she picks up more energy, the speed and breadth of her rotation increases to potentially catastrophic levels. All this causes Grace to call for alternating actions: lawn furniture inside, lawn furniture outside; shutters closed, shutters open; fill the tub, empty the tub; buy water and bread, buy more water and bread.

Jim, trust me on this. Neither you nor I want to get in their path. Since you started it, you need to calm it down!

Your pal,
Dalton Williams

If I'm Lying, I'm Mayan

*[Written in 2012 following stories that the Mayan calendar
did not extend beyond December 21st, 2012]*

FORGET THE FISCAL CLIFF. STOP fretting over last-minute holiday shopping. Cancel plans to watch that big bowl game. None of that stuff matters—at least according to the Mayan calendar that (some say) foretells the end of time on December 21st, 2012. Yikes! That's, like, way totally soon, dude! I haven't even written Christmas cards to the people who sent me one first, which means that I now have to respond. No, wait! They won't be there if my card arrives after December 21st.

Is this chilling prophecy correct? Is doomsday just around the corner? Or will this all be another fizzle like Comet Kohoutek and Y2K? Your intrepid *Daniel Island News* investigative reporter tracked down a direct descendent of the creator of the Mayan calendar. This gentleman, who requested not to be identified (fine with me as his surname has seventeen letters, three of which are x), and I sat down over cups of Mexican cocoa at a Daniel Island coffee shop.

Dalton Williams: Thanks for meeting. Is this, as the R.E.M. song says, the end of the world as we know it? It sounds rather apocalyptic.

Anonymous Mayan: Well, as a matter of fact, it is.

DW: What exactly happens when your calendar ends?

AM: Think of the earth as a giant Hostess Twinkie. One day, it's here. The next day, it's gone.

DW: Wow! Pretty graphic. Yet folks don't seem to be taking this very seriously. I mean, just how credible is this threat to our existence?

AM: Let me put it this way. I wouldn't purchase anything on layaway or buy any green bananas if I were you.

DW: I see. But how do we know these primitive people who lived back...no offense intended to your relatives there...

AM: Some taken...

DW: I mean, this ancient civilization, ingenious as they were...might they have just run out of stone for their calendars, or something such as that, rather than truly foretelling the future?

AM: My dear boy, seeing the future is a psychic gift my people possess.

DW: You, too?

AM: Oh, yes. For example, I sense you are planning to buy an Xbox 360 for grandson Luke.

DW: Who told you? Grace?

AM: Was I right?

DW: Yep. I'm going immediately after this interview. That was good, man.

AM: Don't buy the extended warranty. You won't need it.

DW: Oh, yeah. That calendar thing. Since you can divine the future, when is it a good time to buy back into Apple stock?

AM: I don't give financial advice. Plus, who knows how all these fiscal cliff and debt limit negotiations will work out?

DW: You do.

AM: Not after December 21st!

DW: Okay, but let me ask you this. If there had been a year 2013, could you tell me what would have happened?

AM: I guess I could, but I really shouldn't.

DW: One little peek?

AM: Just one. What topic?

DW: Sports.

AM (whispering): Well, the Cleveland Indians would have won the World Series.

DW: Get out of here!

AM: Yep.

DW: Neat. But let's get back to the here and now.

AM: There isn't much of that left, you know.

DW: So you say. Any last-minute words of advice for our readers?

AM: I mentioned green bananas, didn't I?

DW: You did.

AM: Drink the fine, old red wines…soon…and be sure to tell those that are special to you that you love them.

DW: That is good advice anytime. Thank you for your time today and your insights on the future.

AM: You are welcome and Merry Christmas.

DW: Wait, did you just wish me Merry Christmas?

AM: I did. And I must say I'm a tad disappointed you didn't wish me the same.

DW: But Christmas is December 25th, after the 21st.

AM (putting his hand on my arm): Actually, my friend, the Christmas season begins at Advent and ends with the Epiphany. Despite the attempts by some to water it down or have it go away, Christmas will come. Not just this year but for all time.

It's a Sign

[Written in 2019 following false online stories on the topic]

YIKES! JUST WHEN MY EMOTIONAL equilibrium was flummoxed by the Angie and Brad breakup, some fancy-pants astronomers at the National Aeronautics and Space Administration (NASA) introduced a new zodiac chart. The new zodiac adds a thirteenth sign called Ophiuchus (as if anyone can spell or pronounce it) to be known as the snake-bearer (lovely image, that snake bearer). NASA's explanation for this mischief is shrouded in mumbo jumbo regarding elliptical coordinates, declination of the celestial sphere, and where the North Pole points (It's not north?). All I can report is that the twelve zodiac signs that we have used for over two thousand years as pick-up lines in bars and as printed horoscopes next to the comics in newspapers are now history.

Who asked NASA to do this? Remember when they messed with Pluto's planet status? Now it seems NASA is trying to shift the fault onto the

Babylonians. They claim Babylonians knew that there were thirteen zodiac signs three thousand years ago but ran with just twelve to align with the twelve months in their calendar. Typical Washington political maneuver. Allege there has been a cover-up and blame the other guy. Of course, it helps if the other guy has been dead for thirty centuries! I bet the FBI won't find those records either!

The twelve zodiac signs we all know and love (Aries, Taurus, Gemini, Cancer, Leo, Virgo, Libra, Scorpio, Sagittarius, Capricorn, Aquarius, and Pisces) have served us well. But now, if your birthday falls between November 29th and December 17th, you are none of the above—you are an Ophiuchus, you snake-bearer you! The addition of this rogue sign also impacts the beginning and end dates of the original twelve signs. Not only will horoscope peddlers have to come up with one more set of vague suggestions, but you may also find yourself with totally new advice. Imagine going from "You may finally make a decision that you have been putting off for some time" to "Certain situations may present new risks. Study your options carefully and don't rush to decisions." Or moving from "You are ready to make a forever commitment" to "Don't be surprised if you part company soon with someone close." My lovely wife, Grace, heretofore an Aquarius, has been traded to the Capricorn team. I hope my sign, Virgo, is compatible with Capricorn. I think it is, but I'm going to try to contact Jeane Dixon somehow, someway, just to be sure.

As noted, the twelve zodiac signs can be traced back to Babylonian astronomers, who deserve a little more respect than they are getting from the Johnny-come-lately crowd at NASA. The Babylonians' work was used by Hebrew, Hindu, Hellenistic, and Roman scholars. The construct of the zodiac was described in the second-century work, the *Almagest*, by Ptolemy. I say if it was good enough for Ptolemy, "We should pthink ptwice before we ptrash it." For example, take the mnemonic used to remember the twelve signs in order: "As The Great Cook Likes Very Little Salt, She Compensates Adding Pepper." It may now become "As The Great Cook Likes Very Little Salt, OMG, She's Crazily Adding Pepper," although I prefer "All This Gibberish Confers Little Value; Let's Save Ourselves; Somebody Clamorously Alert Ptolemy."

Finally, I hope NASA isn't going to try to extend this thirteenth-zodiac-sign-nonsense onto the Chinese zodiac. Relations with

China are already strained. Messing with the Chinese zodiac could be more dangerous than a currency war or cyberwar. Imagine the cost of replacing all those paper placemats that display the Chinese zodiac or re-stuffing little paper strips into billions of fortune cookies. As Ptolemy would advise, we should ptread ptenderly.

TALK TO ME, DUDE

*A*LMOST ALL VIRTUAL ASSISTANT APPS—*SIRI, Alexa, Cortana, GPS in your car, and more—communicate with you in a female voice. Not that I'm opposed to that in any way. No, sir... I mean, no, ma'am. The female voice has obviously been tested by the companies that produce these gadgets. The voice is pleasant, friendly, and helpful...not to mention with probably more common sense than the male version. But for a minute or so, let's imagine a male virtual assistant. We'll call him...Bubba.*

Dalton: Bubba, where is the nearest fabric store?

Bubba: Dude, why?

Dalton: I promised Grace I'd pick up some fabric samples for her to look at.

Bubba: You're kidding, right?

Dalton: Just give me the directions, man. I'm late.

Bubba: Whenever you arrive equals "on time" for us, right? But first, let me ask. Have you *been* to one of those places?

Dalton. Not exactly. I mean, not that I can remember.

Bubba: Hey, it's me. That was a big N-O. Loading directions now, but let me tell you, it's more mind-numbing than a craft store.

Dalton: How's my fantasy football team doing?

Bubba: Still sucks and getting worse. Your QB is doubtful this week.

Dalton: Search available quarterbacks.

Bubba: Found it. Top two are Ben Roethlisberger and Tom Brady.

Dalton: Draft Roethlisberger.

Bubba: Bad move, dude. Steelers playing the Ravens, and they have a good D. I'd go with Brady.

Dalton: Okay, okay! Do Brady.

Bubba: Whoa, chill, bro. Just trying to help. All the algorithms pointed to Brady. Don't get angry.

Dalton: I'm not angry.

Bubba: Sounds like it.

Dalton: Can we talk about this later?

Bubba: Want to stop at the spirits store?

Dalton: No, I'm supposed to go to the fabric store.

Bubba: It's your rodeo, but the spirits store is on the way.

Dalton: I know.

Bubba: I just checked their stock. They have Blanton's.

Dalton: They do? Route me there and then to the fabric store.

Bubba: Re-routing… I said re-routing… Hello? No Thank you?

Dalton: Huh?

Bubba: You know, a little something for the effort.

Dalton: You're quoting *Caddyshack* again, aren't you? If you want a thank you, then thank you.

Bubba: Good. Now when you die, on your deathbed, you will receive total consciousness… So, you have that goin' for you.

Dalton and Bubba: Which is nice.

Dalton: Bubba, check my calendar. What do I have in the next three days?

Bubba: You mean, other than your anniversary?

Dalton: Oh, crap! That's the day after tomorrow, isn't it? I have such a memory problem.

Bubba: Yea-ah. Dead man walking.

Dalton: Go to Open Table. Book dinner at Langdon's at 6:30 or closest time.

Bubba: Great place but Olive Garden has two-for-one that night.

Dalton: No, let's do Langdon's. Route me to a florist.

Bubba: Before or after the spirits store?

Dalton: I don't care. Whatever's the fastest.

Bubba: Copy that, but if they sell out of Blanton's, it's your fault.

Dalton: Okay. Spirits store first, then the florist, then the fabric store.

Bubba: Where you going?

Dalton: To the spirits store.

Bubba: Spirits store is the other way. You're lost.

Dalton: I'm not lost. This is a shortcut.

Bubba: Is this the fastest this piece of crap will go?

Dalton: I'm going the limit, and it's not a crap car.

Bubba: Is too. Remember when you had that blue sports car? Chicks would check you out at a traffic light.

Dalton: Yeah, that was awesome.

Bubba: [sings] *Yesterday. All my troubles seemed so far away. Now it looks as though they're here to stay...*

Dalton: Stop it! I don't have troubles.

Bubba: Want to bet? Fabric store just closed. I checked their home page.

Dalton: They closed? You didn't tell me they were going to close so soon.

Bubba: You didn't ask, Einstein. By the way, Grace is calling on your cell. Want to answer?

Dalton: No, not right now. Let me think... I was supposed to get those fabric samples.

Bubba: Hey, I got an idea. Why don't I send her a text from the fabric store apologizing that they had to close early today for inventory. Then you can go tomorrow morning.

Dalton: You can do that?

Bubba: Done…and done.

Dalton: You're the best, man.

Bubba: Right back at ya…but your car and fantasy team still suck.

MORE
DALTON,
GRACE &
TOOGIE

RETIRED BY ANY OTHER NAME WOULD SOUND THE SAME

FLIPPING THROUGH CHANNELS ON OUR small television in the kitchen one morning, I asked my lovely wife, Grace, "What station is Rob Fowler, the weatherman, on?"

"The station upon which he can be viewed," Grace corrected, "is NBC. Channel three on our cable system."

"Thanks. I want to check the weather for golf today," I replied, adding, "Rob has that VIPIR radar or Doppler 5000. It is amazing what technology has done for meteorology."

"Well, windows 101 is forecasting rain today," my Aunt Toogie chimed in.

"What's that?" I inquired, looking up from the television.

"I looked out the window," she chuckled. "It's raining!"

Grace smiled but continued to read the newspaper. She and Toogie were following their morning ritual. They each fetch a cup of coffee, pour over the paper, and then work on the crossword puzzle together. Toogie reads the clues out loud and records the agreed-upon answers. She works in pencil, and the floor is sometimes speckled with eraser shavings days later in the week when the puzzles become more difficult. They keep a synonym dictionary close by as a last resort in case they are stumped. Unscathed by Toogie's sarcasm, I changed channels, hoping to find a rebuttal of her weather prognosis.

"If you go out today," Grace asked without looking up from her reading, "would you pick up some milk and bread at Publix?"

"I could work that into my schedule," I replied, still surfing stations in search of a favorable weather forecast.

"Work it in?" Toogie scoffed, putting her newspaper section and pencil down. "What schedule? You're retired. You don't have a schedule!"

"I'm still busy," I retorted.

"Doing what, besides playing golf?" she shot back.

Grace looked my way as if I owed her a response, too.

"Well, let's see here," I announced, rubbing my chin and recalling activities over the last few days.

"He's stalling," I heard Toogie whisper.

Ignoring her once again, I said, "I water the flowers in the courtyard and take out the trash. I just changed all the clocks for daylight savings time."

"Oh, let me lie down. You're making me tired," Toogie laughed.

Grace came to my rescue. "You do help out around here, dear. Plus, you volunteer time to several civic organizations."

"Yeah," I sneered toward Toogie who was still sporting a snarky Cheshire Cat grin. "I stay busy. In fact," I added, "there should be another word for my current status. 'Retired' is not the right word."

Reaching for the synonym dictionary, Toogie proclaimed, "Let's see what we have." She flipped pages, stopped, and then ran her finger down a particular page. "Look at this," she hooted, placing the open book in front of Grace.

Grace peered at the passage Toogie was pointing toward and began to chuckle.

"Okay, what is it?" I asked.

Toogie chuckled, "How about 'hibernate' or 'be put on the shelf' instead of 'retire?'"

"You've got to be kidding!" I moaned.

"No, those are in here, sweetheart," Grace replied. "They are verb synonyms for 'retire.'"

"Look at the nouns for 'retiree,'" Toogie whooped.

They perused the list, pointing like two children inspecting a showcase of penny candy with occasional murmurs of, "I like it," "These are delicious," and "This one's my favorite."

"Dalton," Toogie finally announced, "I'm going to read the list. You can select the new word you want to replace retiree."

A part of me anticipated I was being set up for the next gag, but the other part pined for a peek at the penny candy, too, and I piped up, "Okay."

"Don't take offense," Grace interjected. "These are the actual synonyms in the book. We aren't saying they depict you."

"Don't spoil the fun," Toogie interrupted. "I think some of these fit him pretty well."

Toogie's chortle grew to a guffaw as she called out the words: "pensioner, senior citizen, golden-ager, oldster, old-timer, veteran, gray-beard, the elderly, aged, discard, reject, cast off, and cast away."

"Take your pick," she cackled.

I chose to remain silent and let them enjoy their merriment.

After the snickering subsided, Grace offered, "Maybe you need an acronym. Something that conveys remaining active and engaged. Bring us some paper and an extra pencil."

"That's more like it," I responded. "You two are the wordsmith sisters. Help me come up with a good one."

The ladies scratched and scribbled. Occasionally, one of them would look up and ponder, pencil-eraser-end against a lower lip. After several minutes, Grace spoke. "How about SABER—Still Active But Enjoying Retirement?"

"I like it," I answered.

"No, no, I have a better one," Toogie tittered. "SABEDS—Still Active But Earning Diddly Squat."

I didn't honor the attempt at humor, and they both resumed their concentration. Grace suggested ACE for Actively Contributing Expertise and SEAHAB for Still Engaged And Having A Ball. I gave a favorable reception to both and assumed Toogie had returned to the crossword puzzle. That notion was dispelled when she shoved a piece of paper across the table to Grace.

"That is wicked," Grace smiled, returning the paper, "but I'd look for a better word for the letter 'R.'"

"Okay," I declared. "Let's hear it."

Toogie held the paper at eye-level with her arms outstretched, beaming like a schoolchild asked to read their composition.

"Often Loafing Despite Frittering Away Remarkable Time," she uttered slowly.

Grace giggled while I mentally reconstructed the letters.

"I bet you two think you're funny. Well, you're not!" I sniffed, turning off the television and heading toward the back door. "I'm going to the store."

"Don't forget your umbrella," Toogie hollered. "Windows 101 is still showing rain."

"Be sure they give you a 5-percent discount," Grace called out.

"What for?" I answered, stopping at the door.

"It's Wednesday," Grace replied. "Publix gives 5-percent off to senior citizens on Wednesdays."

THE **** LIST

MY LOVELY WIFE, GRACE, SUGGESTED I address a subject that needs to be handled delicately. Well, actually, you wouldn't want to handle it at all; but if you had to, you would definitely do it delicately. The subject involves doggie "droppings." I'm sorry, readers, to come out of the blocks like that, and I hope that I didn't catch you there with a mouthful of latte. I know that this isn't the most pressing issue in the world today. It is a small matter, but left unattended, it could turn into a big pile of… Well, you get the picture.

I used "droppings" above because *The Daniel Island News* is a family paper. My synonym finder has quite a few possibly suitable alternatives: guano; dressing; coprolites; the charmingly colloquial, stools; flops; buffalo chips; cow pies; and my personal favorite, ordure. This doesn't even address the voluminous number of variants we can't print here. Put your latte down and think with me. How many other words can you come up with? Quite a few, huh?

"Dalton, that darn dog **** in the yard again!" Grace yelled in exasperation, peering out the window. I'm sure you readers correctly identified "****" there as the mother of all the words on the list; only a dumb **** wouldn't. And don't you think it is pretty ****** (still with me?) that some ****head would let their dog do that and not clean it up? No ****, Sherlock!

I will confess that we are assuming the transgressor is a dog. Since the night soil is deposited under the cover of darkness, neither Grace nor I have seen the rascal in the infamous act. Just to cover other possibilities, I did enter "****" and "animal" into Google. As I suspected, popular usage might indicate the malefactor is either a horse or chicken, but Grace is convinced that Fido is the fiend. She is also certain the culpable canine is a "he" and has quite a few arguments in support of her position, which I think is a detour we needn't take at this point of the story.

We also know the culprit is not our television-watching beagle, Buddy. Buddy doesn't even go outside without a security escort. He was once chased off the front porch by a squirrel. While Buddy is a fraidy-cat, his owners are tidy-cats, thank you!

"Holy ****, he did it again," Grace cried. "Would you mind?" she then asked, handing me a plastic bag. I felt like saying, "I sure as **** would," but I do my duty, so to speak. This is where the delicate part comes in. One doesn't want to step in the ****, sling the ****, spread the ****, or shoot the ****. You just want to ever so gently get it in the bag and… I hope I haven't sent you running to wash your hands nor ruined your taste for latte.

I don't mean to be dumping all over you with this, and I wouldn't have to if the dog's owner, whom we will refer to as ****-for-brains, would either clean up behind Big Rex or have him play all his games on his home turf. If you ask me, any dip**** who would allow their dog to do this doesn't know **** from Shinola about common courtesy. So, here is some help, according to author Wendy Thorpe: Shinola is no longer manufactured, came in cans, and looked good on your shoes. **** is manufactured daily by countless animals on earth, does not come in a can but needs to go there, and does not look good on your shoes.

So, my hope is that the dog's owner, armed with this useful information, will knock this **** off. If they don't, I'm afraid they are in deep ****. Grace and a few other neighbors are fomenting a plan of counterattack. It involves bags of **** (I don't want to know where they plan to get it) and matches. They say they have had enough of this ****, and they aren't going to take it anymore. Before things escalate to that level, I'm calling on all Daniel Island dog owners to "stoop to scoop." If you do, you can stay off Grace's ****-list.

THE SWEEPING INDICTMENT

"LOOK AT THIS," MY AUNT Toogie mused one morning at the breakfast table.

Setting down the sports page of our daily newspaper, I answered, "Look at what?"

"This!" Toogie replied sharply, holding up the yellow, plastic device we use to put honey on biscuits or toast. "The honey dipper."

"I thought a honey dipper was a person who cleaned outhouses."

"No, you nimrod," Toogie shot back emphatically. "I mean this utensil."

"What about it?"

"It's pretty ingenious," she continued, now a tad calmer and twirling the object in the fingers. "It more effectively holds the honey with less dripping than a spoon. I wonder who invented it?"

"Maybe some outhouse cleaner who hated spoons," I snickered, returning my attention to the sports page.

"Did you know that honey is the only food that doesn't spoil?" my lovely wife, Grace, interjected, probably to quell a brewing battle or possibly to add an air of erudition to the encounter.

Toogie and I both turned to Grace.

"What about raisins?" I asked.

"Or beef jerky?" Toogie added.

"Tell you what," Grace announced, "I'm going to let you two work this out while I vacuum, although I could use a hand moving the couch so I can clean beneath it."

"You need one of those gadgets that easily moves furniture," I remarked. "I saw it advertised on television and—"

"Me, too," Toogie interrupted. "It has a lever to lift..."

"Yeah, that's it. And you slide these little things..."

"Pads?"

"Yeah, pads under each corner, and it's a breeze to move furniture or anything heavy."

"The guy on TV even moved a car," Toogie proclaimed.

"Sure did," I confirmed. "Grace, you need to get one of these. I'll write down the 800-number for you next time I see the ad."

Hands now on her hips, Grace spoke slowly but firmly. "Forget that I mentioned vacuuming, and honey, may I suggest that the two of you attempt to elevate the content of your conversation?"

Neither Toogie nor I answered. Sitting down to join us, Grace continued, "For goodness sake. We are adults. Certainly, there must be something more profound we can discuss."

I looked at Toogie, who nodded her head ever so slightly—a signal I interpreted as "You go first."

Consequently, I volunteered, "I reached level four in Angry Birds last night."

"More topical, more noteworthy, please," Grace remarked in her "teacher voice" as she tapped the newspaper on the table.

Feeling a need to rally to Grace's cause, I piped up, "I saw an interesting article a few days ago."

"Tell us about it," Grace prompted, still in teacher mode.

"Well, this guy robbed a bank for just one dollar because he wanted to go to jail where he could get free healthcare."

Grace opened her mouth to speak, but Toggie got there first.

"Did you see the piece about the numbskull who tried to rob a clown? Actually, it was an off-duty policeman dressed up in a clown suit."

"What a bozo," I guffawed.

Fingers to her temples and eyes closed, Grace pleaded, "Can we try one more time for a more significant topic? Perhaps some recent political topic?"

"Too divisive," Toogie shot back, "and way too crazy."

"Speaking of crazy," I interjected, "how about those murder hornets or the asteroids that may hit the earth soon?"

"I give up," Grace retorted. "This discussion is a sad commentary on what society values as news today." Rising slowly from her chair, she added, "Now if you two will excuse me, I'm going to vacuum."

"Let me help move the couch," I offered.

"I'll do it myself," Grace answered tersely.

As Grace walked away, Toogie whispered, "You better get in there to help."

"I can still hear you," Grace proclaimed.

"Is there anything else we can do?" I queried.

Grace stopped and turned to face us again. "Let me see," she mused, thumb and forefinger to her chin. "Something suited to your talents, right?" After a pause, she grinned, "I have it. I'm intrigued about whether it really was a time traveler in the 1928 Chaplin movie, *The Circus*. What do you two think?"

I shrugged and turned to Toogie.

"Oh, you gotta see this," Toogie gushed. "It is super-spooky. A lady in the old black and white movie appears to be talking on a cell phone way before cell phones were even invented. Here, let me show you a YouTube clip."

As Toogie powered up her iPhone, Grace powered up the vacuum. The muffled vacuum sound from the next room was a low moan, soulfully akin to voices crying, calling out for more substance and sanity in this wacky world.

THE REUNION

WE DID NOT ATTEND THE most recent annual Williams' family reunion. Aging kin arrange these assemblies every June. I know it is important to keep in touch with family, but I also cringe a little every time a particular uncle invariably retells a story about an embarrassing moment from my childhood even though Grace always manages to smile as if she is hearing the tale for the first time. I made a mental note that we might go back to a reunion sometime down the road.

So, you can imagine my surprise when the voice on the other end of a telephone call was Cousin Ronnie.

"Hey, good buddy. Y'all missed an awesome family reunion," he blared, adding, "Guess what? I'm fixin' to come see you."

We had not been blessed with Ronnie's presence since the last Thanksgiving when he lit the garage on fire helping me fry a turkey. Thinking quickly, I asked when he was "fixin'" to visit. I knew I could then counter that, unfortunately, those dates coincided with our trip to Patagonia.

My surprise turned to shock when Ronnie answered, "Shoot, man, I'm practically there. I'll be to your place in under an auer."

When I didn't respond, he continued, "But don't make no never mind overn me. I'm callin' from a KFC in Summerville. Picked up a bucket of chicken. You know, hostess gift, and all."

He concluded with an "Over and out" and hung up. I hustled to relay the news to Grace. She took it stoically.

"We'll fix up the FROG," Grace remarked, signifying the finished room over the garage. "He'll be comfortable there."

"What am I going to do with him?" I pleaded.

"We can figure that out later, dear," Grace answered. "Right now, help me get fresh towels, a basket for fruit, and a few bottles of water."

"I'm not taking him to Wal-Mart," I announced. "He'll go Darrelling."

"Darrelling?" Grace inquired.

I explained that as a teenager, Cousin Ronnie invented a game called Darrelling. He and his buddies would go to a big box retail store, stand at the intersection of two main aisles, and yell, "Hey, Darrell!" Then they awarded points—one point for each shopper who turned and looked, three points for those who answered, and five points if the person's name was actually Darrell (all spellings accepted). Ronnie boasted, in language befitting a Nobel accomplishment, how he once scored twenty-three points—his personal best—at a Super K-Mart in Weaverville, North Carolina.

Grace held her palms to her eyes for several seconds before responding. "We'll work it out when he gets here, and remember, he is family."

As threatened, Ronnie arrived on his motorcycle in front of the house in less than an "auer." We heard his approach from several blocks away and met him at the front door.

"Hey, Dalton. Dinner's on me. All you need to do is add beer," he laughed, handing me the bucket of chicken. He then gave Grace a bear hug, accompanied by "Nice to see y'alls."

Over dinner (Grace whipped up a few side dishes to accompany Ronnie's *poulet piece de resistance*), we chatted about a variety of topics. Ronnie related how he'd met a woman over the internet and was en route to see her in Jacksonville. He also hoped to find a new career opportunity in Florida since his job in the "entertainment industry" had dried up when the last drive-in theater in his town closed. He then provided a play-by-play rebroadcast of the family reunion, thankfully devoid of my childhood fable. Grace inquired about numerous family members, and Ronnie provided copious commentary along with all the latest news. Time passed quickly, and before we knew it, the grandfather clock in the foyer chimed eleven o'clock.

"I've been jabberin' away here," Ronnie declared. "I best let y'all get to bed."

With that, he excused himself and headed to the FROG.

"Well, that wasn't as awkward as I thought it might be," I said softly. "But I still don't know what to do with him tomorrow."

"It was a nice evening," Grace smiled. "We'll just see what tomorrow brings."

The next morning delivered a fresh, new surprise from Cousin Ronnie. During breakfast, he announced he was "fixin' to mosey on down" to Jacksonville. I did not try to dissuade him, although Grace asked if he wouldn't like to stay a little longer and see some local sights. He begged off, saying his new lady friend had the next day off, and he'd promised to take her fishing. I assumed he'd done all the "catching up" needed to refill his familial fuel tank. We walked him to his Harley to say goodbye. He donned his helmet, kicked the lever, and revved the engine. Throttling down the noise level, he raised his visor and hollered, "I left something for you on the nightstand, Dalton."

With that, he throttled up again, waved, and was off.

As we walked back into the house, Grace asked, "What did he say? I couldn't hear."

"He said he left something on the nightstand."

"We could have gotten it for him before he left."

"No, he said it was for me."

"Well, when you go to see what it is," Grace replied, "please bring me the linens."

I trudged to the FROG, opened the door, and stopped in my tracks. There on the nightstand was a very familiar object, one I had not seen nor thought about in many years. I picked up the pocket watch, turned it over, and gently ran my fingertips over my grandfather's monogram. A flood of memories rushed forth, and a dull hum, like the sound of a faraway engine, filled my ears. I recalled how my grandfather, a railroad conductor, always carried this watch and with great fanfare announced the time—for church, dinner, bedtime. I remembered how he patiently taught me to tell time with this timepiece. At his passing, family members noted that he was buried without his companion watch and speculated about its whereabouts. Now, I held this keepsake, the next closest thing to his presence.

Lost in these thoughts, it was several minutes before I saw the note on the nightstand. It read: *My sister found Grandpa's watch in Grandma's attic trunk and brought it to the family reunion. Because your initials are the same as those on his watch, we all figured it should be given to you. Ronnie.*

Grace was putting the breakfast dishes in the dishwasher when I returned to the kitchen.

"Do we have next year's calendar?" I asked impatiently.

"As a matter of fact, I just bought one," Grace responded. "Why do you ask?"

"I want to mark the dates for next year's family reunion," I announced, holding up my new treasure.

"Your grandfather's watch," Grace gasped, holding her fingertips to her lips. "I thought it…was lost." Her voice trailed off.

"Did Ronnie leave it?" Toogie inquired.

I nodded. Grace held my hand.

"That was very kind of him," she said softly. "I'd say his visit turned out to be quite a blessing."

I nodded again and dabbed my eye.

"Sort of like the lyrics from that old country song by John Anderson," Grace observed.

"What song?"

"You know the one," Grace replied. "*I'm just an old chunk of coal, but I'm gonna be a diamond someday.*"

She waited a full measure to let the thought mellow and then added, "Well, then, I say we should plan on going to next year's reunion. We can become reacquainted with Ronnie and the other relatives. Who knows? We might meet Ronnie's new lady friend from Florida."

Absorbing the deeper meaning of her suggestion, I reflected that Grace is the true gem.

THIS LITTLE LIGHT OF MINE

"**A** WESOME!"
"Cool."
"Wow!"

This acclaim came from a group of grown men admiring my prized acquisition—a lava lamp. The guys, members of the ROMEO club, get together when their wives attend a monthly book club. Because the group usually dines at a restaurant, we have adopted the label ROMEO: Retired Old Men Eating Out. We consider ourselves reasonably refined and so had originally selected the name, The Gentlemen's Club, until one member pointed out an establishment in North Charleston had already claimed that moniker.

I had purchased the lava lamp for our most recent ROMEO gathering, which assembled at our house before heading to dinner. I hid the lamp and did not plan to put it out for display until after my lovely wife, Grace, had left for book club. I was setting out beverages and snacks for the ROMEOs when Grace asked, "What are those?"

"Cheese Doodles. A snack before we go to dinner."

"You're going to serve that?" Grace inquired, raising her voice a notch.

"Guys love stuff like this."

"I'm sure they do," Grace continued, her hands now in motion. "But I don't want one of them reporting Cheese Doodles were served in our house. The other ladies in the book club might think I purchased them."

"Wait till you see the lava lamp," Aunt Toogie interjected.

"Oh, good heavens," Grace gasped. "A lava lamp! In this house?"

Toogie had seen me hide the lamp. *Bigmouth*, I thought. *See if you get any Cheese Doodles!*

I fetched the lamp and placed it on the kitchen table between the beer nuts and Cheese Doodles.

"You'll see how great it is," I offered, turning it on.

Grace was rubbing her forehead and temples when the doorbell rang. It was the arrival of the first wave of ROMEOs. As they hit the kitchen, their outpouring of adulation was spontaneous and sincere.

"Oh, man, is that great or what?"

"I had one just like it in my dorm room in the 60s."

"Outstanding!"

"Cheese Doodles, my favorite," grinned one of the guys. "My wife never buys these. I can't wait to tell her."

Grace gave a faint smile.

"You boys have a good time," she announced as she left for book club, simultaneously shooting me a *We'll talk about this later* look.

That episode stimulated my thinking. Why is it men like certain things (such as Harley-Davidsons, NASCAR, South of the Border, and lava lamps) that women generally do not? It may be instinctively entwined from the beginning into our DNA helixes. For example, our toddler niece, Betsy, was helping her mother bake cookies. One of the ingredients was molasses. Betsy wanted a taste. Her mother explained she wouldn't like the taste of molasses until it was mixed with sugar and cinnamon. Betsy insisted and lifted a fingertip of molasses to her mouth. After a scowl and pursing of lips, she announced loudly, "This is for mans!" just as some women might react to the taste of scotch.

Perhaps, however, the Barcalounger barrier dividing the tastes of men and women is not created at conception but is more a product of perception.

Let me illustrate. The Daniel Island Garden & Art Tour started this week. This first-class series of events includes homes, gardens, art, cuisine, and holiday activities. It benefits good causes and deserves our support. Grace and I are attending. The programs are also very skillfully publicized. Reading the brochure beckons attendance. Women are particularly allured, picking up on the distinctive details and sensory nuances of fine art, cooking, landscape, design, and architecture. Men can read the same material yet only register: Hey, beer, wine, and eats.

In the same vein, my ROMEO buddies and I might describe my lava lamp as a "blue with yellow globby stuff in a jar kind of thing." Presenting it in this fashion isn't going to entice the better half. Women require more frills and panache to be engaged. But try this lava lamp promotion on for size: "A pyramidal design with steep sloping sides meeting at an apex, suggesting a quixotic quest for perfection. Textured, subtle gradations and marked variations of translucent light and shade exude a dramatic, yet soothing chiaroscuro effect. Color palettes present a breathtaking mixture of light-spring yellow set awash in a sea of azure-cyan. The total feeling is the best in art deco with a wisp of deep perspective and strong compositional unity and baroque treatments of three-dimensional volumes in space, appearing windblown but not contrived." Now, I'll bet you a giant bag of Cheese Doodles women would line up and pay to see such a work of art!

Frankly, I'm a little surprised the fine folks at the Garden & Art Tour haven't called to borrow my treasured lava lamp for one of the displays. Everyone would surely notice this colorful touch. In the meantime, I'll hold onto it. According to ROMEO club regulations, the most recent meeting host retains the lamp until the following month, when it is then entrusted to the succeeding host. I explained to Grace how it is comparable to the Claret Jug passing from winner to winner of the British Open. Grace was not of an "Open" mind, however, and declared firmly the lamp should stay out of view while it resides in our house. When Grace is away, I plug in the lamp. I could gaze at it for hours. It is tranquil and captivating. Like life, it is fluid and always changing, with ups and downs, yet holding the promise that its next kaleidoscopic movement will be a beauty to behold, or as guys say, it's really neat. You are welcome to come over if you want to see for yourself. I'd suggest you hurry just in case I receive a last-minute call from the Garden & Art Tour.

Mug Shots

"I"sn't she sweet?" my lovely wife, Grace, cooed.

"Yes, and so much hair!" my Aunt Toogie replied.

Grace and Toogie were hunched over Grace's cell phone looking at photos of our newest grandchild, Mary, now six weeks old. Grace cupped her hands over the phone's screen to shield sunlight coming in the window at Toogie's favorite breakfast spot.

"This one is a slideshow," Grace explained, handing Toogie the phone as our server brought us cups of hot coffee. "Just hold it and the picture will change every five seconds or so."

Toogie peered at the photos for the better part of a minute, then sighed, "Precious, just precious" as she returned the phone to Grace. Turning her attention to me, she barked, "You ordering your usual there, Grandpa?"

Patiently and softly, I responded to the bait. "I wasn't aware that I had a usual order, and it's Pop Pop, not Grandpa."

"Daily Double," Toogie shot back. "Eggs scrambled, crispy bacon, grits, and a biscuit. And by the way, Mr. Spontaneous, your coffee cup says 'Grandpa.'"

Trying to hide my surprise that Toogie had somehow guessed exactly what I was going to order, I gazed at my coffee cup. The top line of lettering on the side was, indeed, "Grandpa."

When I pointed this out to Grace, she smiled and whispered, perhaps not to embarrass me, "Yes, dear. Toogie just said that, and you do often order the same breakfast."

"Really?" I queried.

"Yes, sweetheart," Grace responded. "You are a creature of habit."

Feeling a need to rebut the matter on the table, I declared, "Well, I don't think I do. So there!"

After a pause, Grace said, "Read some of the cute phrases on your mug." Beneath the "Grandpa," were inscriptions such as "That reminds me of a story," "Come climb up on this knee," and "Who wants to help me eat these cookies?"

Grace held her cup up to read the logo. "Carpe Diem," she announced.

Toogie scanned her cup. "Jerry Bacon Insurance. He recently retired. Nice man."

"Wait a minute," I blurted out. "Do you mean people bring their own coffee mugs to this restaurant? Don't they have drink cups?"

"Of course, they have cups," Grace retorted, lowering her eyebrows just a tad. "Yet, it looks like other patrons may have brought in some personal mugs, too."

With that, Grace and Toogie began spying on other diners' breakfasts, craning their necks to read the inscriptions on the cups.

"Rotary Club," Grace declared. "They do good work."

"Citadel," Toogie announced. "Makes sense around here."

On it went. "Mickey Mouse. I bet it was from a family vacation to Disney."

"New York. Maybe someone moved here from the city."

"Penn State. I bet the person who brought that one in is an alum."

"Colonial Williamsburg. Perhaps they went there for Christmas."

"Isn't it interesting?" Grace proclaimed. "Think of all the stories, travels, and memories associated with these cups. Now," she continued, "the mugs have all ended up here on Daniel Island just like the people who brought them to this restaurant."

While resting her chin on her hand, Grace mused, "I wonder what mugs little Mary might accumulate in her lifetime?"

"That's food for thought," Toogie uttered, nodding her head affirmatively. After a pause, she remarked, "Probably one of the princesses—maybe Cinderella or Elsa."

"A mug from a summer camp craft project," Grace responded. This set off a series of rapid-fire daydreams.

"Something artsy. Maybe ballerinas or a music theme."

"High school. Soccer team captain or National Honor Society."

"Prom. Junior and senior."

"College graduation celebration."

"First job in a career. Company logo."

"Wedding. Here in Charleston."

"Honeymoon. South Pacific island."

"Children's smiling faces. Two girls and a boy."

"That special anniversary trip."

"Retirement party."

"Grandchildren. Lots of them."

By now, tears were creeping down Grace's cheeks. Toogie sniffled and reached for a tissue. The young lady serving us approached the table and asked, "Is everything okay?"

"Yes," Grace replied, rubbing a finger against her eyelid. "We were just reflecting on some nice thoughts. I believe we can order now."

"Fine," our server replied. "Shall I start with you ladies?"

Waving a finger my way, Toogie uttered, "I'm still deciding. Start with him."

"Oh, he always has his usual," the server quipped.

"Really?" I piped up. "And just what would that be?"

"Daily Double," she answered, "with scrambled eggs, bacon crisp, and grits," tapping her pen against her order pad once for each item.

"You nailed it, Grace" Toogie chortled. "Grandpa here is a creature of habit."

I locked eyes with the young lady. Lifting an eyebrow, I queried, "And… what else?"

She smiled sweetly and retorted, "A biscuit. You *always* get a biscuit."

ALL'S NOT BENE THAT ENDS BENE

"HEY, DALTON," MY AUNT TOOGIE hollered as she entered the front door. "You received a special package."

While Toogie frequently fetches the mail, it was not like her to announce the daily arrivals until she had all the parcels sorted on the kitchen counter.

"What is it?" I replied, still searching the refrigerator for lemon wedges to garnish my iced tea.

"You have to see this for yourself."

Toogie's smirk spoke volumes as I pulled my head from the fridge. She handed me a small box festooned on all sides with colorful advertisements. The box was from a national pharmacy chain and contained a free, sample-size container of a fiber supplement—Benefiber.

"Why was this sent to me?" I mused.

"Hello? Probably because you're full of—" Toogie snorted before my lovely wife, Grace, cut her off.

"It," Grace interrupted, "is probably just an advertising campaign."

"But why me?"

"Consider how often you go to the drug store to buy something because it awards you various coupons for merchandise."

"One can't have too many razor blades or rolls of toilet paper," I pontificated.

"Half-right," Toogie quipped.

"They probably looked at your customer profile and purchasing patterns," Grace continued to explain.

Toogie scoffed, "Maybe some pharmacy stool pigeon figured you were not buying enough toilet paper!"

Again, Grace steered the conversation away from Toogie's direction. "You might want to look at the Benefiber," she soothed. "After all, the word *bene* translates as 'well.' It is from the Latin translation."

Following Grace's advice (as I always do), I opened the package, extracted the sample bottle, and carried it to the back porch, away from Toogie's scrutiny, to absorb (figuratively, not physically—yet) the Benefiber story presented on the small plastic bottle. While I wouldn't describe the overall presentation as moving, there is quite a pile of information about Benefiber packed into a tiny space. I recognize that fiber is our friend, a healthy diet is essential to good health, and I'm sure Benefiber is a good product for its intended purpose. Plus, the label said it is "taste-free," "grit-free," and "non-thickening." I suppose this information is provided to entice those among us who possibly prefer their edibles to exhibit these qualities.

"Honey, what would you like for dinner?"

"Oh, I don't care just as long as it is something tasty, gritty, and thick."

For adults, the recommended "servings" are "2 tsp. 3 times daily." Footnote one amplifies these instructions with the added guidance: "not to exceed 6 tsp. per day"—apparently to guard against abuse by Benefiber addicts or to assist folks who may not figure that two times three equals six. Intertwined among the instructions, we find encouragement such as "great for cooking," "be creative with Benefiber," and "see www.benefiber. com for recipe ideas." I checked out the website. They aren't kidding. There are recipes for soups, salads, main dishes, desserts, and snacks, all laced with dosages of you-know-what. One can plop a dollop of Benefiber into nearly anything, from a morning smoothie to a bedtime toddy. The *piece de resistance* is their advertised "five-star feast." Digesting this tidbit, I now know not to accept an invitation for a "five-star feast" unless the location is within a 100-yard dash of my house!

In addition to Benefiber's guarantee of "taste-free," we learn, "It won't alter the taste or texture of your foods or beverages," and "You won't even know it's there!" This last ominous declaration got me thinking: *Is someone trying to secretly slip something past us old-timers? Could this be a sinister plot to reduce the social security deficit in an unthinkable manner?* Then I found a further clue: "Made in France." Aha! Might this be Gaullist revenge for the California chardonnay winning a wine competition in Paris years ago or Americans not adoring Jerry Lewis as much as they do?

Despite these signs of caution, I decided to give it a go with Benefiber and supplemented my pre-dinner Perfect Manhattan. Since this was my first and only "serving" of the day, I went for the full daily dosage of six tsp. I had to guess what a tsp. was and went with my gut feeling—tablespoon. When I informed Grace and Toogie of my leap into Benefiber-land, Grace gasped only, "Oh, my!"

Toogie grinned and added, "Notwithstanding your idiosyncrasies, Dalton, I'll have to say, deep down, you are a regular guy."

The next morning, I joined Grace and Toogie, who were already having coffee in the kitchen.

"You look a little down in the dumps there, Dalton," Toogie barked as I tiptoed into the kitchen. "Did your fiber supplement deliver on its promises?"

"Don't ask," Grace piped up.

"So, it wasn't *bene*?" Toogie snickered.

"Oh, it was *bene*, all right," Grace shot back. "Too *bene*!"

At this point, the two of them were off to the races.

"Oh, do tell more," Toogie chortled.

Grace replied, "A lady doesn't talk about such topics."

"How about in Latin?" Toogie suggested.

"Let's just say," Grace giggled. "*Magnus* and *volatili* would best describe it."

"You two think you're funny, but you're not," I announce, rising to trot back upstairs.

"Where is he going in such a hurry?" I heard Toogie ask.

Grace chuckled, "I think to see a *hominis* about an *equus*."

Off the Charts

"Hey, Dalton! How's your BMI?" my aunt Toogie piped up loudly.

Lowering the sports page to peer at her over the breakfast table, I replied calmly, "I have a Lexus."

"Not BMW, I said BMI," Toogie shot back, adding, "I'll bet yours is a whopper. Do you even know what it is?"

"I'll bite. What is it?" I responded cautiously.

"There's the root of your problem," Toogie cackled. "Too many bites."

Unable to decipher the dialogue, I turned to my lovely wife, Grace, for help.

She smiled. "I believe Toogie is talking about body mass index."

"Yep," Toogie barked. "According to this newspaper, the feds are going to require everyone to have his or her BMI on file in medical records by 2014. Can you believe that?"

"Slow down," I pleaded. "Body mast what?"

"BMI stands for body mass index," Grace explained. "It is a relationship of one's weight to height."

"It measures body fat, porky," Toogie chipped in.

I was about to take a bite of bagel slathered with cream cheese but stopped short as both ladies sat grinning at me.

"What?" I queried.

"The government wants to know if you're obese," Toogie chortled. "They don't need regulations to do that. They could just call me!"

I didn't counter her gibe but also made no move to reclaim my bagel. Finally, I asked, "Why would someone in the government want my information? What would they do with it?"

"Beats me," Toogie gushed, becoming more agitated. "Can you believe those clowns? They can't fix the economy, but they want to stick their nose into my BMI? It's Big Brother, that's what it is!"

"Oh, yeah, Big Brother," I chuckled. "That was a book, wasn't it?"

"*1984* by George Orwell," Grace interjected.

"Never thought I'd live to see such nutty stuff," Toogie sighed.

Grace rose to refill her coffee cup. "Sometimes life imitates art," she mused. After a pause, she added, "'Who is John Galt?'"

"I'll bite. Who is he?" I asked.

"Never mind. It's a long story." Grace shrugged.

I returned to the sports page as the ladies' conversation trickled toward other topics. Somewhere amid baseball box scores, my mind slowly drifted…

A long line of people waiting to enter Krispy Kreme snaked from the front door around two sides of the building. I took my place inside the satin roping guiding the crowd. Soon, others joined the throng. Suddenly, those near the front of the line became agitated.

"The hot light is on," someone yelled.

"Let us in!" chanted others.

They were talking to two very large men standing with folded arms at the front door. Periodically, these two gatekeepers would stroll along the line to select people for entry into the doughnut shop. Folks clamored for the bouncers' attention as they perused the pack for the next lucky few. The bouncers paused at two attractive twenty-somethings just ahead of me. "You two can go in," barked one man, while the other whispered into a microphone attached to his lapel. The girls squealed, ducked under the satin roping, and pranced toward the door.

The larger of the two bouncers turned to me. "Name?" he inquired.

"Dalton Williams."

"Date of birth?" I responded, and he began flipping pages on a clipboard. "Williams, Williams," he said, running a finger down the page. He stopped, looked at me, glanced at the clipboard, and then back to me. He nudged the other bouncer, pushed the clipboard toward him, and mumbled, "Look at this."

The second bouncer whispered something into his microphone and then made a motion, tipping his head quickly to one side, saying, "Mr. Williams, we need you to step out of the line." Sensing trouble, people moved away, giving me room to slide under the ropes.

The bouncers and I walked across the parking lot to a van marked "BMI Patrol." A third man stepped out of the van.

"This is Officer Richards. He's going to take you downtown for some questioning," announced the first bouncer.

"But I just wanted a doughnut," I sputtered.

"Not with this BMI," answered the bouncer, tapping a finger on his clipboard. "If the man says no doughnut, then it's no doughnut."

"No doughnut for you," barked Officer Richards in a quick cadence, mimicking the dictatorial soup chef character on Seinfeld. The two bouncers grinned.

"I wasn't hurting anyone," I pleaded. "I just wanted to go in and get—"

The bouncer with the microphone interrupted sternly, "Please get in the vehicle now before we have to—"

Grace set salad plates at each setting. "What kind of dressing would you like?" she inquired.

"Blue cheese," I answered.

Grace turned toward the man standing in the corner of the kitchen. He was tall with chiseled features and wore a black suit, tie, and dark glasses. Without changing his expression or moving any other part of his physique, he shook his head a few short times.

Grace turned back to me. "How about a nice vinaigrette?"

"Do we have Thousand Island?" I replied.

Grace turned to the man in black. Again, he signaled no with a few rapid, slight twists of his head. "I think the vinaigrette would be nice, don't you?" Grace remarked. Her comment was directed not to me but to the man in the corner, and it was more of a pleading than a question.

He whispered something into the microphone on his lapel and then held a hand to his ear. After a pause, he spoke, "Only a squeeze of lemon juice..."

I lay on a table surrounded by men in white coats. "This doesn't look good," remarked one of them. "His BMI is way out of whack."

"Let me see the chart," directed a man who seemed to be the senior member of the mob. He peered at the paper given to him by an assistant. "We need remedial action, now!" he pronounced urgently.

"Shall we prep him for catastrophic weight decrement, doctor?" an assistant inquired.

"No, he looks like a good candidate for the alternative treatment," the senior doctor replied. "Are you familiar with that option?"

"I'll bite. What is it?" answered the assistant.

"Well," the senior doctor explained, "we can get his BMI back in line by reducing his weight or by making him taller. By my calculations, he will be off the government's rotund roster if we can just make him six inches taller. Now, you just grab a leg while I take an arm and pull... Pull harder..."

The tug jolted me. Grace held my arm.

"You haven't heard a word we said, have you?" she asked.

I shook my head slightly.

"Well, pay attention this time," she pronounced. "Toogie and I are going downtown. Big sale on shoes. There are deli fixings in the fridge for your lunch. I'd suggest that you use mustard instead of mayonnaise."

"Keep your mitts off the double-fudge brownies," Toogie chuckled.

"If we're not home by five o'clock, put the casserole in the oven," Grace instructed, adding, "and think about taking a walk. It would be good for you to get out and move a little more."

When I didn't respond, she added with a smile, "Toogie and I are not going to to police you on this. It's your BMI!"

That what I love about Grace. She offers sound suggestions but doesn't make a federal case out of it.

Gone Fishin'

C AN YOU NAME THE SPORT that (1) is drawing an ever-increasing number of participants, (2) requires no special equipment, and (3) can be played in the comfort of your Barcalounger?

Stumped? I'm here to tell you, it is telemarketer fishing. Never heard of it? You might be surprised to learn that many of your friends and neighbors are already playing this popular and fast-growing game.

How does one play, you ask? Easy. The object of the game is to field the nightly calls from telemarketers and not hang up (which, like shooting fish in a barrel, is hardly a sport) but to snare them, keep them on the line, and then land them. The contest and its scoring are an amalgamation of numerous other popular sports and games.

The objective is to score points, which are earned in several ways. For example, you can receive points for the length of the encounter, as in rodeo bull riding, and for style and form, similar to diving. Like golf, you keep your own score. Comparable to bridge, points are accumulated toward becoming a "master" or even "life master" telemarketer fisherperson (Yes, some of the best players of this noble game are women). There are several techniques one needs to master to become adept at telemarketer fishing (or, for ease, TF). One is "trolling and playing." The knack is to engage the caller in friendly banter to keep them on the line as long as possible. This troll-and-play ploy works well with inexperienced telemarketers (known as "fingerlings").

Here is an example executed by my friend Jim:

Caller: I'm calling from (credit card company). We're going to send you our new, no-fee card and just want to verify the address there in Charleston.

Jim: Sure, what did you say the name was?

Caller: (repeats the name of the credit card company)

Jim: No. I got that. What's your name?

Caller: (after a pause—a good sign that he is a fingerling) It's Milt.

Jim: Where you calling from, Milt? (Note: Here, Jim has scored one point for an escape, much like in wrestling.)

Caller: Fargo, North Dakota. Now, if we could verify that addre—

Jim: (interrupting) Fargo! Man, I bet it's cold there this time of year, right, Mort?

Caller: Not that bad. Now, are you still living at—?

Jim: Wow, *Fargo*! Was that movie great, or what? Tell me that woodchipper scene didn't freak you out!

Caller: *Click*.

SCORE: one point for the reverse, one for the duration of the call, one for style (the movie reference), and two points for getting the caller to hang up on him. Total: Five points. Par for a call is around three points; so, this is two better than par or the equivalent of an eagle in golf.

The second skill to perfect is "the hook." It involves getting your hook in the caller before he or she hooks you. For example, if you told a brokerage firm telemarketer, "I wish you'd called five minutes ago. I just placed $10 million with a firm that called. What was their name? I've got it written down here somewhere," you would score a hook.

Another friend, Bob, is adroit at the hook. Here is a recent exchange:

Caller: Good evening. I'm calling with a 3-percent home equity offer from Chevy Chase Bank.

Bob: That's an attractive rate.

Caller: Yes, it is. (Note: Observe how skillfully Bob has placed the hook in the caller's mouth, but then, Bob is a life master.)

Bob: (pulling back hard on the line) But I just don't see how I could bring myself to put my money in a bank run by a comedian.

Caller: Oh, no, sir. We're Chevy Chase Bank in Chevy Chase, Maryland.

Bob: I loved *Christmas Vacation*. The family watches it every year. Very funny.

For brevity, I will summarize the rest of the dialogue. The caller runs hard with the hook in his mouth (known as a "screamer" or "ripper"). He explains how deposits are FDIC-insured and that the bank is not affiliated with Hollywood in any way. Bob counters with commentary on *Caddyshack, European Vacation,* and *Fletch.*

Finally, the caller provides an 800-number and hangs up.

SCORE: one point for the hook, two style points, one for the length of the ride, and two for the caller hanging up. Total: six points; a double eagle.

The third maneuver to master is the "catch and release." An illustration, which I am proud to say is being presented by your humble servant, follows:

Caller: Good evening, Mr. Williams. I'm calling from (name) Window & Door. We will give you a free storm door if you can provide the answer to tonight's quiz question.

Moi: Will it take long? *The Simpsons* are on in ten minutes.

Caller: No sir, only one question. Ready? Who was the first president of the United States?

Yours truly: Oh, I know that! It's right on the tip of my tongue. Don't tell me… Can I ask my wife?

Caller: Sure, take your time.

His Nibs: Grace, come here. (pause) This guy says we can win a free storm door if we can name the first US president. I think it's Polk.

Grace: No, it's not. It's (inaudible).

Me: Buchanan?

Grace: No, I said (inaudible).

Me: (into the phone) You still there? Gimme just a sec, okay?

Caller: I'm going to give it to you anyw—

Me: (interrupting) We're ready! We think it's Millard Fillmore.

Caller: Actually, it's George Washington.

Me: Darn. Grace, you were right. I'm sorry, honey.

Caller: Hey, you guys were good sports. Like I said, we're going to give you the door anyway.

Me: Nothing doing!

Caller: Huh?

Me: A deal's a deal. I gave it my best shot and came up short.

Caller: That's okay. We still want to give you the door.

Me: I don't deserve the door. I couldn't accept it.

At this point, the caller mutters something, I think, about Caribbean cuisine (I heard the word "jerk") and hangs up.

SCORE: It is whatever they call a hole-in-one on a par five.

My interest in telemarketer fishing was pure serendipity. "You're in the way," my lovely wife, Grace, remarked (she was fixing dinner). "If you want to make yourself useful, answer the phone," she added (it was ringing). I did and found that I took to it like, well, a fish to water. The rest is history. It was as if Mrs. Jordan had said one day, "Michael, get out of my kitchen. Why don't you go play ball with the other boys?"

Sounds like fun, doesn't it? I encourage you to settle into your La-Z-Boy and give it a go. You won't strain a muscle, and soon you will be landing them like Jim and Bob. The group that regulates our sport, NAFTA (North American Fishing for Telemarketers Association) has sanctioned a local chapter (known as a "school") right here on Daniel Island. If you want to join, give me a call—just not between 5 and 8 p.m.—that's when the big ones are running.

OF CATS AND MEN

"**L**OOK AT THIS PICKLE!" I exclaimed over lunch to my lovely wife, Grace.

"I see, dear," she replied. "It's a whole jar of pickles."

"No, this one," I answered, pointing near the bottom of the jar on the kitchen counter.

Grace squinted and leaned closer. "Which one?"

"The one on its side. See? Right there."

"What about it?"

"What does it look like?"

Grace paused and finally offered, "A slice of dill pickle?"

"Let me try," Aunt Toogie barked from across the room. "I'm guessing it looks like Elvis."

"Close," I responded. "It does look like a face. See the two eyes and the mouth?"

"Oh, good heavens," Toogie retorted. "I was only kidding about Elvis. Let me have a gander at that thing."

She peered at the pickle sitting flush against the side of the glass jar. She stared for a while and then turned to me. "You think it looks like a face?"

"Yep," I piped up, believing I'd found an ally.

"Maybe it's Big Boy. You know, from the hamburger chain," Toogie cackled. "I'd notify the *Ripley's Believe it or Not!* people."

Undaunted, I persisted. "I still think it looks like somebody, perhaps that famous painting of the guy holding his head and yelling."

Grace asked, "Do you mean *The Scream* by Edvard Munch?"

"Wasn't that stolen?" Toogie chimed in.

"Yes, but I believe it was recovered," Grace answered.

"You better call Lloyd's of London, Dalton. Thieves may have their eyes on your prized pickle," Toogie quipped.

Sensing I was slightly smarting from Toogie's sarcasm, Grace put her hand on my elbow. "You seem a little down," she observed. "Are you okay?"

"Oh, I don't know," I replied.

"Halloween's coming up," she offered. "Let's talk about how we will decorate this year for the trick-or-treaters."

"Maybe later."

After a pause, she suggested, "Why don't you write one of your stories for *The Daniel Island News*? That always cheers you up."

"I don't know," I mused. "With the news lately—school shootings, nukes, and all—there isn't much pleasant or funny to write about."

"Those are serious topics, dear, but you don't always have to write something funny."

"Yeah," Toggie chimed in. "A lot of what you write isn't so funny anyway, even though you may think so."

Grace continued, ignoring Aunt Toggie's dig. "You could write about something unique or interesting. Like the new hypoallergenic cat."

"The *what* cat?" I asked.

"A hypoallergenic cat. It has no dander, so it doesn't affect people who have a cat allergy."

"How can a cat be created with no dander?"

"It was developed by a biotech company in California," Grace explained. "The cats are genetically modified and sell for about $4,000 each."

"That's nothing to sneeze at," I remarked.

"Hold on there, Grace," Toogie remarked. "Are you telling me some bio-sci-fi kind of company produced a perfect cat?"

I sensed the direction the conversation was cantering and that it was too late to close the barn door.

Before Grace could respond, Toogie continued, "If they can do that with a cat, why can't they make a perfect man?"

"Oh, that's precious," Grace giggled, holding both hands over her mouth.

The compliment didn't deter Toogie. She galloped on. "They could create a man who preferred romantic movies over football on television."

Grace mused, "He would be sensitive."

"I'd be happy if they could just make one that didn't pass gas!" Toogie hollered.

At this point, the two of them were off to the races.

"One who listens better," Grace offered.

"And looks into our eyes instead of at our chest when we're having a conversation," Toogie answered.

"More understanding."

"I'd settle for less hair in the ears."

At this point, they were both howling like hyenas.

"If the damn cat costs four thousand bucks, think what they could sell the man for," Toogie bellowed.

Grace wiped her eyes. "It should be on the cover of the Neiman Marcus Christmas catalog," she sputtered as they slapped their hands on the table.

"Are you getting all this down, Dalton?" Toogie barked.

"You two think you're funny, don't you?" I asked.

"Just a teeny bit," Grace giggled, holding her thumb and forefinger slightly apart.

"Oh, don't be a sourpuss," Toogie added. "You look like that face in the pickle jar."

Grace nodded.

"Then you two agree there is a face in the jar!" I shot back.

"Sort of a face," Grace said. "A Halloween kind of face, I'd say."

"I still think it looks like Elvis or maybe Mick Jagger," Toogie added.

"I feel vindicated," I replied, getting up from the table, "I think."

"So, are you going to write about the genetically improved man?" Toogie inquired.

"No way!"

"Why not?" Grace inquired.

"You two got my dander up," I answered.

"You think you're funny, don't you?" Grace queried.

"Just a teeny bit," I replied, walking toward the den.

Toogie called out, loudly smacking her lips, "You better write this story, or you'll never see your pickle again."

Grace squealed in response.

I could hear them talking and laughing all the way to the back porch. They were roleplaying a mock telephone call.

"Hello, Genetic Man Company. How may I help you?" Toogie growled.

"I'd like to custom-order a man," Grace chuckled.

"Would you like to hear about some of the options?"

"Well, I want one who always remembers to put down the toilet seat."

"That comes standard on our genetic men."

"May I get one that doesn't snore?"

"Sure, but that will run you extra."

"Fine, and how about not ogling when he passes a Victoria's Secret store?"

"That's a little tricky, but we can work on it."

"Well, do you have a perfect man?"

"You want a perfect one?"

"Yes, if it can be done."

"Ma'am, that's going to be priceless."

Toogie for President

M Y EYELIDS CLOSED AS THE afternoon news droned on... *Blah,
blah about which candidates were gaining and which were fading.
An endless flow of analyses, commentary, spin, and more blah,
blah, blah. One reporter offered a prediction... Dalton... Dalton...*

"Dalton, Dalton," my lovely wife, Grace, repeated emphatically. Snatched
from my slumber, I slurred, "Wh-what?"

"Come to the front door," she gushed. "You gotta see this."

"Wh-what?"

"It is such a surprise. Come quickly. That political blather can wait."

Finding my shoes and taking my usual two attempts to put each on
the correct foot (with the odds fifty-fifty, shouldn't it work on the first try
occasionally?), I trudged after Grace to the foyer. Standing there were Aunt
Toogie and her gentleman friend, Brevard, looking out the open front door
at a shiny, red convertible parked at the curb.

"New set of wheels?" I asked Brevard, quickly sizing up the situation.

"Yes, indeed," he smiled.

"When did you buy it?"

Brevard looked at Toogie, then Grace, before responding. "*Au contraire,* old boy. I didn't buy it."

"You leased it, huh?" I replied. "Smart move with the market being what it is these days."

"No, a thousand times no," Brevard answered. "It is not my car, dear boy."

"So…whose…is it, then?" I queried the group.

Grace grinned. "We'll give you one guess, dear."

I shrugged and looked quizzically at Grace, who tilted her head ever so slightly in Toogie's direction. My gaze went to the car and then to my shoes. Suddenly, I gasped.

"Toogie?" I exploded. "Toogie? Are you telling me it's Toogie's?"

"Should we give it to him?" Grace giggled.

Brevard snorted, "He didn't guess, he asked a question! Three to be precise."

"Yeah, but on *Jeopardy,*" Grace chuckled, "you answer with a question."

"He was close," Toogie chortled, "but the correct answer should have been 'Who is Toogie?'"

The three of them howled at their wit. Toogie chipped in, "I'll take 'new cars' for a thousand, Alex," which prompted more belly laughs. I refrained from making their assessment of the jocularity unanimous.

"Come in the kitchen," Grace finally suggested, dabbing her eyes. "I'll make us some hot tea."

A multitude of thoughts raced through my head… *Toogie should not be buying a new car…not one like this…at her age…. If Brevard put her up to this, I'll wring his gentrified neck….*

"Wh-what…in the world…motivated you to buy a new car?" I finally stammered.

"Well," Toogie replied, pulling her shoulders back. "Pass the sugar, will you please? Thanks. As I was about to say, after my hip surgery and recovery, I thought it was time for a change."

"That's it?" I replied. "A change?'

"Yep, change," Toogie smiled. "If not now, when?"

"What kind of change?"

"A fun change," Toogie declared triumphantly. "An energizing change!"

"I must say, you sound…," I mused, twirling the tea bag string around a spoon. "…sort of like those folks running for president. You know, with that *change* theme, and…"

Grace cut me off. "Now that you bring up the comparison, dear, I think Toogie would make a fine president!"

"Especially with that nifty new car in the inaugural parade," piped up Brevard, patting his palm on the table.

"Because it's only a two-seater," Toogie cackled, "Mr. Status Quo here will have to walk."

Soon, the trio was again mired in mirth. As the frivolities faded, I inquired, "If I may ask, Madam President, are you certain this is affordable?"

"Got a great deal," Toogie beamed. "Used my car-buying strategy."

I put down my cup.

"Well," Toogie explained as Grace poured more tea, "I did my homework first, determined the amount I wanted to spend, and then visited several dealerships. After test-driving a few models at two dealerships, I told each salesman that I had a check made out for a certain amount, but I just hadn't filled in to whom."

I leaned forward.

"Anyhoo," Toogie continued, "I told them if they wanted to have my check, I needed to have their best shot."

"Clever," I uttered, looking to Brevard. "And you…?"

"Don't look at me," he retorted. "I wasn't there. The first I knew about all of this was when Toogie picked me up today with her new car."

Turning back to Toogie, I continued, "So, you received the dealers' offers and then bought this?"

"Oh, good heavens, no," Toogie scoffed. "I walked away. Pass me the sugar again, will you? I played hard to get. Made 'em court me."

"Did they?"

"Sure did. One guy called three times. Each time I told them the price just seemed a wee bit high for an older lady on a fixed income like me, and perhaps I'd better look around a bit more."

"And…?" I prompted.

"They folded like a cheap suitcase," Toogie boasted. "Lowered their price every time they called. The last guy even gave me a gift certificate to a fine restaurant downtown and threw in the extended warranty."

"Extended warranty? At your—?" I wailed, stopping mid-sentence when Grace shot me a glance. I stirred my tea for a while and finally muttered, "Wow."

"Sounds like our candidate here is long on fiscal responsibility," Grace observed.

"Here, here, the Chancellorette of the Exchequer," Brevard boomed, slapping the table vigorously.

Toogie held up the thumb on each hand and grinned, stimulating yet another series of shrieks.

"Oh, my, this is fun," Grace tittered, and she rose to fetch some cookies. She returned with the teapot and an assortment of sweets.

"Here are a few things to put in your glove compartment," Grace also offered, depositing the goods on the table. "Some Purell and hand wipes— good to have when you fill your gas tank. Some tissues, ChapStick, and mints."

"Thanks," Toogie replied. "I will have to put my gun in there, too."

"Be careful with gum and your dentures," I remarked.

"Who said anything about gum?" Toogie barked. "I said gun! I need to put my handgun in the glove compartment."

I sat back in my chair, trying to fathom what I'd just heard. I turned to Grace and then erupted for the second time in a matter of minutes.

"Toogie? A gun? My sweet aunt? Packing heat? In the glove compartment?"

"I counted five questions that time," Brevard whispered.

Grace reached out and touched my arm.

"Oh, don't get your knickers in a knot," Toogie piped up. "I know how to use a firearm responsibly, and it's registered."

I started to say something but knocked over my cup.

Reaching for a towel, Grace announced, "I'll take care of it."

"Takes a steady hand," Toogie continued. "Your Uncle Harold showed me years ago. Plus, I'd say half the ladies in my needlepoint group own a gun."

I sat in stunned silence, absorbing a newfound image of my aunt as well as her needlepointing sidekicks.

Grace stood at the end of the table and began to intone in a stage voice, "My fellow Americans, I give you Aunt Toogie—the candidate of change, financial prudence, and a strong defense!"

"The queen of Homeland Security," Brevard bellowed, thumping the table once more.

Toogie held up her fists like a boxer at a weigh-in. A gale of guffaws followed from her fellow stooges.

I retreated to the den and turned on the television to drown their snickering. The TV chatter was as if I had never left... *The strategy of this candidate and that...who was leading in which polls...the projected scoreboard of various primaries...blah, blah, blah...*

About a half-hour later, Grace came in.

"What are you watching?" she inquired, sitting on the arm of my chair.

"Oh, just some political stuff," I replied. "Toogie and Brevard still here?"

"She's driving him home. Should be back soon."

After a pause, she asked, "So, what do you think?"

"About the new car or the race for the White House?"

"Either one."

"Hard to tell," I mused. "What do you think?"

"Well," Grace said softly, putting her head on my shoulder, "I think the new car is a wonderful change for her...and considering some of the presidential candidates, I believe we could do worse than Toogie."

"I see it a little differently," I replied. "I'm still not so sure about the car... but for president, I don't believe we could do better than Toogie."

Oh, Deer!

THE IDEA CAME TO ME as soon as the guys entered the fast-food restaurant just off Interstate 24 in western Kentucky. I sized them up immediately—four servicemen in camouflage fatigues probably on maneuvers on this, the Saturday following Thanksgiving. After placing an order for me and my lovely wife, Grace, I leaned forward and whispered to the young lady behind the counter, "Keep the tab open. I'll buy breakfast for these next four gentlemen and then settle up with you."

She smiled as I turned to the first soldier in line behind me.

"I'm buying breakfast for you and your buddies," I announced. "I appreciate what you guys do."

He gave me a wry smile and answered, "That's nice and all, mister, but I think you—"

"Already done," I interrupted and added, "It's my pleasure." Then I shook his hand, nodded at his companions, picked up our order, and headed to the table where Grace was seated.

"What were you saying to that man?" Grace asked as I delivered her coffee and breakfast sandwich.

"Tell you later," I smiled. "I gotta go back and pay."

The fourth soldier was receiving his carryout order as I approached the register. He turned and smiled at me.

"You really didn't have to do this, sir."

"Think nothing of it," I beamed in return, patting him on the shoulder. "Keep up the good work."

I paid for all the meals and returned to Grace's table.

"I bought breakfast for those young men," I declared proudly.

"That's very nice of you."

After a pause, during which I expected Grace to say more, I mumbled, "Military, you know."

"What about military?"

"They are in the army," I explained slowly. "Didn't you notice their uniforms? Probably special forces from Fort Campbell."

Grace set her coffee cup down and rolled her eyes, followed by a giggle that progressed into a full, shoulder-shaking laugh. As the guffaws began to subside, she wiped a tear from her eye and chuckled, "Oh, dear. Dalton, you are too much!"

"What?"

"Those aren't soldiers," she giggled. "They are deer hunters."

"But they are wearing camouflage pants and jackets."

"Yes, and they are also wearing orange vests with hunting licenses pinned on the back."

When I didn't reply, she leaned over, patted my hand, and added, "I'm sure they appreciate your kind and generous gesture. Who knows? This may even bring you good karma. At a minimum, you've provided them a grand story they can tell and retell for years to come."

While I would gladly buy breakfast for a member of our armed forces any day of the week, I was feeling particularly thankful this day. Grace and I were returning from a trip to St. Louis to visit with Matt and Maggie, our son and daughter-in-law, and their four children—Ellie, Nora, Luke, and Mary. These grandkids are in motion much of their waking hours. Keeping up with them would make a Whirling Dervish dizzy. Like children that age, they are unfiltered, sharing every joy and sorrow instantly and fully. Grace particularly relished seeing Mary walk (a new addition to her repertoire since our last visit), as well as their jumps and squeals when Santa found a way, thanks to a special delivery magical letter Grace helped Ellie pen, to drop off our Christmas gifts to them early (as we, sadly, will not be back before that day).

The importance of taking time to savor and be thankful for moments such as these was vividly reinforced on the trip to St. Louis. On a stretch of Interstate 40 between Asheville and Knoxville, our car was sideswiped by a tractor-trailer. Grace and I are fine; the vehicle took all the damage. The driver of the truck pulled his rig directly into our lane as we were passing him. Like the cliché, it happened in a flash. The truck plowed into the side of our car and fortunately then pulled back into his lane after the collision. Grace, who was driving, did a masterful job of keeping our fishtailing car from hitting the guardrail on our left or the truck on our right—Jimmie Johnson would have been proud. The car was still drivable and will be fixed, yet I am most thankful that Grace and I are around to treasure more holidays with family and friends.

"Hey, man, how are you and Grace?"

It was my insurance agent, Jerry, calling. His company had treated us promptly and effectively after the accident. After relaying some details, I assured him we were fine and now on our way home.

"When you get back, we need to take you and Grace down to my son's restaurant. My treat," he suggested. Jerry's son is the chef at a great place on upper King Street. Jerry boasted, "He's added a really delicious new menu item for the winter season."

"Sure," I responded, savoring the thought. "What is it?"

"Venison. He has it flown in fresh daily from western Kentucky."

CHRISTMAS

Christmas is a time of joy, hope, faith, and family.
We have written more stories with a Christmas setting
than are set at any other time of the year.

MANY HAPPY RETURNS

"DALTON, WE HAVE A PROBLEM," my lovely wife, Grace, announced sternly.

She had just concluded a telephone call where her end of the conversation consisted mainly of "uh-huhs," "yesses," a couple of "Oh, mys!" and ended with a "We'll take care of it right away."

Sensing this might be serious stuff, I set down my Sudoku puzzle.

"Your aunt," Grace began, creating a little familial distance between herself and what was about to follow, "instigated a food fight during breakfast."

Allowing a moment for the message to sink in, I finally asked, "At the rehab center?"

"No, at the Waldorf!" Grace scoffed. "Of course, at the rehabilitation center," she added, referring to the facility where Aunt Toogie has been convalescing since her recent knee replacement surgery.

"A food fight?" I smiled. "Kind of like Bluto."

"Like whom?" Grace inquired.

"Bluto. You know, in *Animal House*."

"Perhaps you mean the novella, *Animal Farm*, George Orwell's satirical allegory?"

"No, no! The movie. John Belushi plays the character, Bluto, who starts a food fight."

Grace folded her arms and fixed me with a stare. "This is a grave matter, and I suggest you take it seriously," she lectured. "You know very well this isn't the first time we've received such a warning from the management of the rehabilitation center," she continued, waving one arm in the direction of the phone. She was right. In fact, we had received several calls. The initial incident concerned Toogie playing gin rummy with her fellow patients. She had won all the desserts—nine pieces of coconut cake—and was earnestly resisting the nurses' efforts to return the sweets to the original owners. The next altercation involved Toogie's attempt to organize a synchronized walker drill team that the physical therapist labeled both foolish and dangerous. Now, a food fight.

I called the director of the rehab center. After a number of "uh-huhs" and "yesses," I wrapped up the discussion with an "I understand."

"Well, what did they say?" Grace asked.

One more strike, I explained, and Toogie was out. The rehab center had been firm, and frankly, fair. If Toogie created one more disturbance, she would be discharged to us or to another facility.

"Maybe we should move her back here," Grace mused.

"But the rehab center can monitor her progress and exercise program," I tried to interject.

Grace cut me off. "We can bring a physical therapist to the house. Plus, I've been thinking. Toogie should be with us, here at home, for Christmas."

"We'll see," I responded, trying a ploy I'd seen Grace perfect to deflect the direction of a conversation.

There was no outmaneuvering the master. "Nice try," she smiled. "But my mind is made up. This incident may be Toogie's way of orchestrating an early discharge. It's clearly a sign that she needs to move back with us as soon as possible."

That afternoon, I helped Grace tidy up Toogie's room. Clean linens. New soaps and toiletries. Fresh flowers. Current magazines. Her room looked as inviting as the Waldorf.

Carrying the vacuum back to the utility closet, I stopped and cocked my head toward a window. I detected the muffled rumble of an approaching motorcycle long before my eyes confirmed its arrival. Much like Mannheim Steamroller, Cousin Ronnie suddenly appears each December with no indication of when he will arrive, where he has been, or what he has been doing since his last visit. He rolled up to the curb as I opened the front door.

"It's Cousin Ronnie," I called over my shoulder to Grace, adding with a hiss, "Hide the good cabernet."

A second rider was seated behind Ronnie. Probably some new girlfriend of the month, I speculated.

"Hey, Dalton," he hollered, removing his helmet and helping his companion off the Harley. "Surprised to see me?"

Waving a hello, I whispered to Grace, who had joined me at the door, "Shocked, yes. Surprised, no."

That sentiment changed when Ronnie called out, "If you ain't surprised to see me, I'll bet you're sure surprised to see her."

Grace recognized Ronnie's passenger immediately and dashed down the front sidewalk. Buddy followed, wagging his tail. The next few seconds seemed to pass in slow-motion. Ronnie spewing his chaw of chewing tobacco into the curbside bushes, his companion removing her helmet and shaking her hair back, and Grace running toward her, arms outstretched, crying, "Toogie! Toogie! Toogie!"

"Oh, it is so good to have you home again," Grace giggled as she embraced Toogie. "How did you get…" she began to inquire, stopping in midsentence to look at Toogie, the Harley, and then at Cousin Ronnie."

Uh-oh, I thought to myself, taking a reflexive step backward.

"I brung her. She rides good," Ronnie replied. "Plus, I figured she ought to be with y'all for Christmas."

"You dear, dear man," Grace gushed, laying a bear hug on Ronnie. "And the people at the rehabilitation center were okay with her leaving?"

"Well," Ronnie explained, "we didn't exactly tell nobody we was leaving, or nothing," as he untied Toogie's walker from the rear of the bike.

"Never mind," Grace shot back, waving her hand. "Dalton will take care of everything. He knows the people there."

Grace took Toogie's arm and guided her up the sidewalk. "Come in, honey. We'll get you some hot tea and a comfortable place to rest."

"What I'd really like is a Maker's on the rocks," Toogie answered.

"Of course, darling," Grace cooed. "Dalton, run ahead and fix Toogie a nice drink."

Much later that evening, following a major league *mea culpa* with the rehab center and a big Maker's on the rocks for me, Grace and I prepared for bed.

"Looks like I need to get some Christmas gifts for Toogie and Ronnie," I observed.

Grace smiled. "Got it covered, dear. I have something for each of them."

"Did you know they were coming?"

"Not exactly, but you know Ronnie always seems to show up around holiday time."

"And Toogie?"

"I just had an inkling."

I sat up and bed and turned toward Grace. "Did you have something to do with this?"

"Not directly," Grace replied, patting my arm. "Unless you count wishing."

I laid my head back on the pillow, pondered her comment, and whispered, "I think wishing counts."

"Right answer," Grace whispered back, "and I wish you a Merry Christmas."

Dalton Drops Santa a Note

"Have you written to Santa Claus?" my lovely wife, Grace, asked.

I had just commented that I hoped to receive a new phone with a better camera for Christmas, what with our upcoming visit to see our son, Geoff; his wife, Suzanne; grandson, Charlie; and granddaughter, Ashleigh.

"Have you have been a nice boy this year?" she grinned.

"Sure," I replied, "but I haven't written to Santa in, well, let's see…over fifty years."

"You're never too old to start again," Grace replied. "Plus, it may improve your chances of getting that phone."

"You're kidding."

"I would never kid about Santa Claus," Grace proclaimed, pulling her shoulders back and giving me a serious gaze. Then she leaned forward just a little and added softly, "Age doesn't always determine whether or not one is a kid."

So, I found myself in the study, pen in hand, staring at a blank sheet of paper. How does one begin such a letter? Oh, I still believe, and all—just like the boy in the movie *The Polar Express*. It was just, how do you begin to write to someone you talk about every year and yet have neglected to correspond with for so long? It was definitely harder to write to St. Nick as a senior citizen than I recall it being at age seven.

I made a few feeble starts:

Santa: re: gifts, pls. c a word doc attached 2 an em I will send 2 u…

Santa: I was sorry to hear you were expelled from some schools in favor of winter solstice pageants. Don't pout. We had a guy in my school who was expelled (put a firecracker in the toilet), and he went on to make a gazillion in hi-tech…

I gave up and trudged downstairs.

"It's not working," I sighed. "I can't seem to find the right message."

"Perhaps you're looking at it from the wrong perspective," Grace offered. Before I could ask her to expand on the thought, the air was filled with high-pitched shouts of joy.

"We found it! We found it! Mimi, we found it!" they shouted. We followed the shrieks to the living room. Granddaughters Brooke and Kara, ages five and two, were jumping, both feet leaving the floor, and clapping their hands.

"We found it, Mimi. We found the pickle!"

"The pickle" is a Christmas ornament in the shape of, yes, a pickle. It comes from an old German custom. One line of Grace's roots traces back to Germany. A pickle ornament is placed somewhere on the Christmas tree, hidden from plain view. According to the tradition, the person who first finds the ornament receives an extra gift and a special blessing for the following year. Each Christmas, Grace hides the pickle ornament. It seems to have always been found by one of the children, and now by the children of those children. I mentioned to Grace that I had been looking for that ornament just the other day and hadn't spotted it.

"You need to get on your knees," she said.

"And pray?"

"That, too," Grace laughed. "But I mean to find the pickle. You need to see the tree from the perspective of the little ones. That's where I always put it."

"Now, girls," Grace declared, "I have one gift. Can you share it?"

"Can we give it to Nora?" inquired Brooke. Nora is her little cousin, born a year ago—just before Christmas.

"Yes, we want to give it to Nora," chimed in Kara.

Grace smiled. "How sweet of you. We can give this to her. Now, how would you two like to help frost and sample some cookies?" This was followed by a new round of squealing, jumping, and clapping.

I retreated to the den and picked up my pen.

Dear Santa:

I hope this letter finds you, the missus, and the team up north all well. We are well here—very well, in fact. Grace and I are blessed with a fabulous family, four wonderful children, their spouses, and ten delightful grandchildren.

We also have great friends and neighbors here on Daniel Island. Perhaps you may have heard of the local Rotary Club that raises money through a rubber-duck race to help others throughout the community and around the world. You and Mrs. Claus should really look at Daniel Island as a second home—escape the cold, and all.

We'll set out one of Grace's famous cranberry margaritas for you on Christmas Eve. We have only one wish. It is that you continue to bring happiness and love to children throughout the world. All kids are a joy and a delight. They are truly the light to our future. May it always shine brightly.

I'm sorry it has been so long since my previous letter. I promise to write again next year. No kidding.

Godspeed and safe travels,
Dalton Williams

THE GIFT

I T ARRIVED ON CHRISTMAS EVE. The fruitcake showed up with no return address as usual, on our doorstep. The exchange of this treasured token has been a tradition for years in my lovely wife, Grace's, family. Every Christmas, it appears at a family member's home. During visits at other times of the year, it can be tucked away in a linen closet or hidden behind a bookshelf for discovery later. The ritual remains the same: Don't reveal who has it now or where it is going next. Family folklore has it that this was started by Grace's mom, Pat, who received the fruitcake as a joke decades ago. It has been handed back and forth, like the "Old Maid" ever since. The gag has since taken on a life of its own—a cult-like status. Each Christmas, Grace and her sisters, Sally and Laura, exchange phone calls, asking, "Did you get it?" Of course, neither the sender nor the recipient fesses up.

When we opened the package and discovered that we were this year's legatees, I asked Grace, "How many miles would you guess this silly thing has traveled?"

"Quite a few, I'd say."

"The tin looks pretty banged up. Are you sure you want it under the tree?"

"Of course," replied Grace. "It's the custom."

That evening, after Grace finished putting bows on gift boxes and announced that she was going upstairs to bed, I remained in the living room to read a little. It seemed like a short while later when a voice said, "Around fifty thousand miles."

"Huh?"

"Fifty thousand miles, give or take a bit."

"Who said that?" I uttered.

"Down here." The voice seemed to be coming from the fruitcake tin under the tree.

"Grace," I called. "Come down here."

"She's asleep," the voice replied. "Anyway, this is between you and me."

"Are you talking to me?" I queried in the direction of the fruitcake.

"Yeah, and I didn't appreciate the remark about my tin being dented either."

"You *are* talking to me!" I exclaimed in astonishment.

"Merry Christmas, Dalton," cooed the crumpet after a pause. "It's good to see you again."

"You… You…" I couldn't complete the thought.

"It was fun to catch up on the family and see your granddaughters, Brooke, Kara, and Ellie tonight. I see why little ones are called toddlers. Then, one day, those toddling steps turn into a regular gait. It reminds me of the Christmas morning that your son, Geoff, toddled toward the decorated tree and stepped into a hot cup of coffee his Uncle David left on the floor. Christmas morning is no time to be in the emergency room."

"You were there?"

"Right under the tree. Saw the whole thing, just like now. By the way, are the kids doing well?"

"They're all fine. Grown up as you can see. Families of their own," I managed to respond, adding, "How are you?"

"Pretty well, thanks. Not too bad for a forty-five-year-old fruitcake with a banged-up tin, I'd say."

"I guess you've seen a lot in forty-five years," I remarked.

"Sure have! I've seen the addition of newborn faces to this family and noticed the chairs around the dining room table empty because those family members are no longer here. In fact, I miss Grandpa Bob very much—he was the only soul brave enough to have had a piece of me, so to speak. I've seen the children grow up and go off to college. I've seen times of great joy like the Christmas Eve that Matt proposed to Maggie right under that mistletoe over there. I heard his words and saw her happy tears as she said, "Yes." And I've seen times of sadness, too, like illness and Grace's cousin, Ed, losing contact with the family."

"So, who's your favorite family member?" I teased the torte.

"Everyone has been great and lots of fun to watch, but I'd have to say Grace's mom, Pat. She had an infectious laugh, loved a joke or prank, and she really delighted in the drama of who had the fruitcake. She loved passing me around. I really miss her. You all do, especially Grace and her sisters."

"You know, I've been held by over one hundred family members," the fruitcake added after a pause.

"Wow! I couldn't even name one hundred family members."

"That's okay, you have a lot going on. With me, the family is my full-time interest."

"Who had the most unique delivery?" I continued.

"I'd have to give that one to you, Dalton. Sending me from Santa Claus, Indiana. Nice touch."

"Where do you want to go next?"

"Glad you asked," answered the fruitcake. "I have had all year to ponder this, and I was thinking that it would be nice if you sent me to Grace's cousin, Ed. It might just thaw the ice a little. I am hard to resist, don't you think?"

I considered the suggestion but then changed the subject. "Sorry about the remark about your dented appearance."

"That's all right. Just like people, what is on the inside is more important than what is on the outside."

"Pretty profound for a nut cake," I responded. "Especially one that has been basting in rum."

"Hey, I'm the only one of us who weighs less than we did forty-five years ago," the fruitcake shot back.

"*Mea culpa*," I yelled, raising my arms in mock defense.

The motion shook me awake. The book was on the floor. The lights were still on. The room was quiet, too quiet. The fruitcake tin sat benignly under the tree.

"Were we just talking?" I asked.

No answer…must have been a dream…. Some dream, too. I rose and picked up the tin. Forty-five years, over a hundred people. This was no ordinary fruitcake. Nor was it an ordinary gift—especially tonight. This humble tin was a powerful connection of family across time. I buffed the top of the tin with my sleeve and put the fruitcake in the center of the gifts under the tree. I patted it goodnight and went upstairs to bed.

After the children and grandchildren opened presents on Christmas morning, Grace mentioned over coffee that she had had an unusual dream.

"Me, too." I echoed. "Very vivid. First, tell me about yours."

"Well," Grace explained, "I dreamed we mailed the fruitcake to my cousin Ed, and he even called to thank us. That got me to thinking, why don't we send it for his birthday?"

"Sounds like a good idea."

"What was your dream?" Grace asked.

"It was kind of bizarre."

"I thought you said it was vivid."

"Well, it was sort of, like, funny."

"Dalton Williams," Grace sighed, "I swear you are nutty as a fruitcake."

"I'll take that as a compliment," I declared.

"Anything else to say for yourself?"

"Merry Christmas, Grace."

A Secret Santa

"**W**ant to see the Christmas gift I purchased for Aunt Toogie?" I whispered to my lovely wife, Grace.

Grace peered into the box as I unwrapped the tissue paper. "It looks like a rock or fossil."

"It is. It's coal," I beamed. "A lump of coal. I found it at a novelty shop on Market Street downtown."

"That's not a very nice gift," Grace scoffed.

"Hold on, there," I replied. "Do you remember the gifts Toogie has given me in past years for Christmas, like the Chia Pet, the exploding golf balls, and the whoopie cushion? I'm just keeping the gag going."

"You better watch out," Grace cautioned. "Aunt Toogie might get you something nice this year."

"Fat chance. It's payback time, baby!"

Grace shrugged. "Dalton Williams, where is your Christmas spirit?"

The next day, I wrapped the present, tied it with a big red bow, and to add an element of intrigue to the surprise, addressed it: To: Toogie, From: Secret Santa. So Toogie wouldn't recognize my penmanship, I wrote the card left-handed. As Christmas neared, I checked each day to ensure the package was prominently visible beneath the Christmas tree. Toogie didn't mention or acknowledge it, but I'm sure she saw her gift. I couldn't wait to see the look on her face when she opened it.

After dinner on Christmas Eve, Toogie declared, "Who would like to open just one gift tonight?" I translated the female dialect: *I want to open a gift tonight.* So, I offered to pour a glass of eggnog while the ladies gathered near the fireplace next to the tree in the living room.

Toogie hollered, "Don't forget a healthy shot of Maker's in my eggnog."

As I arrived with the tray of drinks, I noticed Toogie placing a small gift near my chair.

"You go first, Dalton," she said with a smile.

I recognized this as the setup for this year's prank present. I winked at Grace to signal I knew what was coming. I opened the package and found a thick envelope. Opening it, I stared down in disbelief at a packet of tickets for the Masters. I was stunned and managed to only say, "Wow!" followed by a nervous laugh. Going to the Masters was one of my fondest wishes. Even attempting to fathom how she had managed to obtain such precious tickets was overwhelming.

Grace then opened her gift from Toogie. Grace gasped, "Are these your pearl earrings?"

Toogie acknowledged they had been her mother's and that she always wanted Grace to have them.

"The earrings will look so nice on you, and one day, you can have the joy of passing them on to someone else, perhaps to Jane."

Grace's eyes were moist as she and Toogie embraced. Finally, Toogie sat back and put her hands on her knees.

"I have enjoyed living with you since I gave up my house, and I can't thank you enough. You two are both so dear to me. So, I wanted you to have a family heirloom," she explained nodding to Grace. Turning toward me, she added, "And I wanted you to have something you have talked about so often." I took all this in, although the scene seemed to be passing in slow-motion. Then, it hit me—the lump of coal! How could I get it from under the tree?

With that, Toogie reached down and—*oh, no!*—picked up the box with the bituminous blunder.

"It says 'To: Toogie, From: Secret Santa.' I'll bet this is from you," Toogie declared, staring straight at me as she loosened the ribbon.

"It's not me," I stammered. "That isn't my handwriting."

"You probably wrote it left-handed," Toogie retorted without looking up.

Then she unwrapped and opened the box.

"Look at this," she uttered with a smile.

I arched my eyebrows and shot Grace a questioning glance.

"I believe I recently saw this in a magazine," Toogie said slowly, pulling a rectangular, chrome device from the box. She turned the new-fangled thing over and scrutinized it.

I stared at the unfamiliar object but couldn't speak.

Sensing my confusion, Toogie said, "This must be one of those picture frames that displays digital pictures. I think I can turn it on here."

As the screen lit up, Toogie sat back in her chair, hand to her chest.

"Oh, my," she said softly. "These are my old pictures! Oh, look—my wedding portrait. How did you do this?"

I didn't answer, nor did Grace. She only took Toogie's hand, and both of them dabbed their eyes and hugged again.

The next hour was spent scrolling through the pictures from Toogie's life: her childhood, school pictures, wedding, extended family members, and the various homes and cities in which she and Uncle Harold had lived. These memories rekindled stories of holidays past. I refilled glasses with the Maker's-eggnog concoction several times, moving to straight Maker's for me after the eggnog was depleted. Around midnight, Toogie said, "You kids need to get to some sleep. Santa's coming, you know." Then she held her arms around the picture frame and announced, "This is the most memorable Christmas present I have ever received. I am holding my entire life here in my hands."

After we were in bed, I turned to Grace and sheepishly said, "Thanks for what you did tonight. You really saved my butt."

"What?" Grace inquired, pulling off her glasses.

"Replacing the lump of coal with the picture frame."

"I had nothing to do with it," Grace declared. "I believe I saw the gift still had your 'Secret Santa' card on it."

"Well, if you didn't...?" I mused, the words trailing off.

"Who else?" Grace offered.

"You're not suggesting...?" I replied.

Grace put a finger to my lips to quiet me.

"Dalton Williams," she declared, "don't tell me you are too old to believe in Santa Claus."

Then she smiled and turned off the light.

My head spun from the events of the evening and the potent libation. I pondered how the picture frame came to be placed inside the present. Finally, I reached out, took Grace's hand, and whispered, "Merry Christmas, dear."

"Now, that's the spirit," Grace whispered back.

HAVE A TWEET CHRISTMAS

*W*ITH APOLOGIES TO GOSPEL WRITERS *St. Matthew and St. Luke, here is the Christmas story told, in 2019* Anno Domini *style, on Twitter in 140 or fewer characters.*

@CaesarAugustus
Whole Roman world go asap 2 own town 2 be enrolled. #CensusDecree

@Joseph
Going up fm Nazareth 2 Judea 2 Bethlehem. House of David. #Census. Couldn't come at worse time. Mary expecting child any day now. Still pondering how I'm not father but have faith. #Miracle

@Gabriel
#Miracle already explained. Remember dreams? The Lord is with U. #HighlyFavored!

@HolySpirit
RT@Gabriel

@VirginMary
Hope we make Bethlehem. Unto me according to Thy word really soon!
#HandmaidOfTheLord

@Joseph
Anyone know good, inexpensive place 2 stay N Bethlehem? Me & wife.
Donkey 2.

@InnkeeperBethlehem
@Joseph, All guest rooms booked. #Census. Have stable cheap.

@Joseph
@InnkeeperBethlehem, Copy that. Apple Pay?

@VirginMary
Time came for baby. Wrapped in swaddling clothes. #MangerNativity. A
Son, my first.

@God
Mine too! #Savior

@ShepardsNFields
Crazy night tending flocks. Angel appeared. Like, oh-so terrifying.

@AngelOfLord
@ShepardsNFields, B not afraid. Great news. Joy. #Messiah. A sign. Check
it out. #MangerNativity

@HeavenlyHost
Multitude of dittos! Glory 2 God. On earth peace. #Messiah

@ShepardsNFields
Visited #MangerNativity. OMG! Spread good word. #PeopleAmazed

@ShepardsNFields
#Messiah trending!

@MagiEast
Following bright star. King of the Jews?

@Herod
@MagiEast, Report back after finding child. Want 2 C babe 2. #SecretlyPlotting

@MagiEast
Worshiped newborn king F2F. Fab! Gold, frankincense, myrrh. #Jesus

@Herod
@MagiEast, Where R U? FOMO

@MagiEast
Warned in dream; definitely departing home different way. BFN

@Herod
Not helpful! ☹

@God
#Jesus My Son, love him. ☺ #WellPleased!

Santa's Workshop
North Pole

DALTON'S CHRISTMAS LETTER 2020

MY LOVELY WIFE, GRACE, ASKED that I write our annual Christmas letter to tell you a little about the many interesting things we did this year. Well, after our New Year's celebration with family from Houston, we drove to South Florida to visit our daughter Jane and her husband Eric. Grandsons Cole and Sam are growing up fast and are fully immersed in baseball. Cole's team won their state championship and qualified to play in a tournament at the Baseball Hall of Fame in Cooperstown next year. We then drove to Naples to see former neighbors. On the drive back to Charleston in February, we heard about the flu virus spreading from China and decided to pull the plug on a March trip to New Orleans.

From then on, it has been mostly ***COVID-19 Clusters Vitamin C Wuhan Elbow Bumps Lysol Spray Flatten the Curve Amazon Asymptomatic Stimulus Check National Emergency Shelter-in-Place Antibodies Clear Plastic Dividers One-Way Aisles Community Spread Forehead Thermometers Zoom Beard Stubble Self-Quarantine Clinical Trial Home***

Improvements Mail-in Ballots Phases 1, 2, 3 Audible Books Dr. Fauci Antigens Epidemic Travel Restrictions N95 Isolation Uber Eats We're Closed CDC Face Shield Positive Test Streaming Government Mandate Grub Hub Dr. Brix Scarves Boredom Virus Toilet Paper Walks Ventilator Screening Moderna Drive-Thru Testing Latex Gloves Hand Washing Lockdown Remdesivir Yadda Yadda Yadda Loss of Smell Comfort Food Outdoor Dining Social Distancing Hand Sanitizer Paper Products Shortages Layoffs Capacity Limits Declutter Carry-Out Chinese Flu Go To Meeting Spread Pfizer Telemedicine Jigsaw Puzzles Coronavirus Respirator Postponed! PPE Incubation Outbreak Drive-Thru Dining Essential Business Election Overload Hydroxychloroquine Cabin Fever Weddings Moved to 2021 Same Old Same Old Purell Gardening Wine More Wine Sweatpants Super-Spreader Canceled Trips Containment Masks False Positive Symptomatic Restaurant Closures Negative Test Weight Gain Home Hair Care Game Canceled Martial Law Quarantine Self-Isolation Clorox Wipes 2020 Sucks Contract Tracing Economic Shutdown WFH Baking Reading No Live Concerts Football Without Fans House-Cleaning Herd Immunity Schools Closed Netflix Droplets Pandemic Fever Home-School Spanish Flu WASH YOUR HANDS! Gym Closure MERS & SARS D3 Doses Unemployment Benefits Booze Don't Touch Your Face Transmission WHO Essential Workers FaceTime Immunocompromised Vaccine No Mask No Entry and Virtual Thanksgiving and Christmas.

That's been about it from here. The end of 2020 can't come soon enough. We are hopeful 2021 will be better—it has to be. Doesn't it? Grace and I look forward to getting together with you in person next year and wish you and your family a safe, healthy, happy, and prosperous New Year.

Epilogue

We edited and assembled this book in early 2021 as the nation and world entered the second year of the effects of the COVID 19 pandemic. We hope you and your family and friends have fared safely over this time. If you have experienced pain or loss, we offer our condolences. We pray for timely healing and a healthful future.

At the same time, we should all reflect on what we have been through together. Life, like our experiences writing stories over sixteen years, is as much about the journey as the destination.

With that thought, we leave you with one more story in this book.

THE JOURNEY

AFTER POURING A SECOND CUP of morning coffee, my lovely wife, Grace, asked, "What would you like to do once you are vaccinated?" When I didn't respond promptly, she added, "Did you hear me?"

I had heard her and, strangely, also the echo of my mother's voice asking old questions. *What would you like for Christmas?* and *What would you like to do this summer after school is out?* I recalled childhood days of wanting something yet also suffering through the reality that wanting it didn't make it come any sooner. It only made me want it more.

Suddenly an idea popped into my mind. "Go somewhere. Yeah, get in the car and drive somewhere," I replied.

"You can do that now," Grace answered, sitting down at the kitchen counter and opening the newspaper.

But I wasn't thinking of going to Mount Pleasant or even as close as, say, Georgetown. No, I wanted to go further. Over the state line. Make it plural. Over multiple state lines. Venture into at least Virginia, Tennessee,

Alabama, or Florida and perhaps beyond. Maybe way beyond. I'd drive to see children and grandchildren, but other destinations were fine, too. I just wanted to be moving toward someplace. I shared these thoughts with Grace. Without looking up from the paper, she offered, "Wouldn't it be easier to fly?" Air travel might be quicker, but it wasn't the experience I was yearning for.

Again, my thoughts drifted back to childhood. In the early 1950s, my family lived in Minneapolis, where my father was working on a doctorate degree at the University of Minnesota. Because he and my mother were born and raised in Birmingham, our annual summer vacation was a trip to Alabama to see their families.

While I never thought of our family as being poor, my folks did not have the financial wherewithal to fly or possibly even for overnight lodging along the way. So, they drove. Straight through. MapQuest says the trip today, substantially on interstate highways, is 1,079 miles. Our trips traversed federal highways that went through every town along the route, often were two-lane roads, and offered a maximum speed limit of fifty miles per hour. My folks would leave in the early morning, drive all day and through the night while I slept, and arrive the following morning. Looking at highway maps today, I believe they headed south from Minneapolis on Route 52 through Rochester, across the northeast corner of Iowa, and into Illinois a little west and south of Chicago. There, they picked up Route 51 that runs down the spine of Illinois, exiting the state at Cairo, and continued down the far western end of Kentucky. In northern Tennessee, they merged onto Route 45 and followed it south to Tupelo, Mississippi, where they then headed east to Birmingham on Route 78.

To this day, I can picture memories of the trip. Lunch, pimento cheese sandwiches my mother had made, along the side of the road in Iowa or northern Illinois. Gas wells, near Centralia, Illinois, that rocked up and down like seesaws. Playing games my father devised to pass the hours such as guessing the last digit on the license plate of the next car to pass on the two-lane road or to seek out as many different state license plates as we could spy. Being awakened from my sleep to see the lights of the big bridge at Cairo, where the Ohio and Mississippi rivers meet. Waking up the next morning near Tupelo to the heat, humidity, and red clay of the Deep South.

In Birmingham, I saw grandparents, aunts, and uncles and played with a collection of cousins. I went barefoot, ate fried okra and ambrosia, and once got a mohawk haircut, much to my mother's dismay. But my most vivid memories are of the trip to get there, not what we did, albeit all of it was pleasant once we arrived. I have no recollections of the trip back to Minnesota, although we traveled the same roads past the same sights. I guess that means the excitement of things to come trumped the experiences that eventually did occur.

Maybe that is the way things are today. We have been on a yearlong COVID journey. Vaccines are being administered, and yet there is still some distance to go. We will experience emotions from anticipation to angst, possibly endure more loss, pledge to be patient and safe, and probably fret and fuss a little on our way to the finish line. Like my parents' drive, it won't be easy, but we will get there. Years from now, the stories we tell will be mostly about the journey—masks and social distancing, so many activities canceled or postponed, PPE and paper product shortages, one-way aisles, losses and pains, temperature checks, virtual communications—and all that we did to get by, to get through.

Yet the vaccine destination, and what lies beyond, is the goal. When you arrive, do whatever is on the top of your wish list, be it a new car purchase or a mohawk haircut. As for me, I'm going on that car ride. I realize now that two of the paths I traveled in the 1950s, Routes 52 and 78, have their eastern terminus in Charleston. One might say I have already reached the end of my road. I like to look at it in the other direction—long, concrete ribbons reaching to somewhere I'd like to go see when all of this COVID stuff is in the rearview mirror.

ACKNOWLEDGMENTS

First and foremost, we thank Sue Detar, publisher of *The Daniel Island News*. She has been a great friend and counselor over the past sixteen years. The stories first appeared under the Dalton Williams *Drollery* banner in her newspaper, a truly great weekly publication. Weekly newspapers are a vital bastion of journalism in an international, 24/7 news cycle, social media world. Please support them. Sue Detar also provided wise and helpful advice on this book, having previously written and published *Don't Lose the Ball in the Lights*.

You can read past stories, including Dalton's annual predictions of the top news stories for the year yet to come, on the newspaper's website *thedanielislandnews.com*. Enter "Dalton Williams" in the search bar at the upper-right.

A huge thank you goes to Kathy Meis, Sean Kilkenny, Shilah LaCoe, and the team at Bublish, Inc. who turned our manuscript into a book and guided us throughout the publishing process. Bublish was recommended to us by Sue Detar and by friend and author Michael Ferrara, who used Bublish to publish his book, *Breezing*. Special thanks also goes to Mary Wessner Photography.

We have enjoyed being in a couples' book club with friends Jim and Gail Morrill, Tom and Pat Richards, and Bob and Carol Wood. They are great friends of Dalton and Grace.

Thank you to family, friends, and neighbors who have offered kind words about various stories over the years. In particular, early fans Faith White, Billie and Jerry Bacon (who encouraged this book), and the late Jim Hitchings. Also, Joe Boscoe, Ray Bolek, Bert and Tom Lammert, Steve Slifer, Chat Whitmore, and Father H. Gregory West.